D1541522

a wicked song

THE BRILLIANCE TRILOGY BOOK TWO

NEW YORK TIMES BESTSELLING AUTHOR

LISA RENEE JONES

ISBN-13: 979-8674495840

Copyright © 2020 Julie Patra Publishing/Lisa Renee Jones

All rights reserved. No part of this publication may be reproduced, distributed, or transmitted in any form or by any means, including photocopying, recording, or other electronic or mechanical methods, without the prior written permission of the publisher, except in the case of brief quotations embodied in critical reviews and certain other noncommercial uses permitted by copyright law.

To obtain permission to excerpt portions of the text, please contact the author at lisareneejones.com.

All characters in this book are fiction and figments of the author's imagination.

www.lisareneejones.com

Dear Reader,

Thank you so much for grabbing your copy of A WICKED SONG! I'm so excited to see what you think about the next book in Kace and Aria's story! If you haven't already, please be sure you've read A RECKLESS NOTE (book one), it does need to be read prior to this book, and prior to continuing this letter as I'm about to give a short recap of book one.

Aria Alard is really Aria Stradivari. She and her brother, Gio, are the last remaining family members of the Stradivari family, the family whose ancestor, Antonio Stradivari, created the infamous Stradivarius violins. Those violins are revered by artists worldwide, they now auction for millions of dollars and are coveted by those who have obtained ownership of the few that remain.

Aria and Gio's father went missing years ago, and their mother woke them in the night, and they fled to the states, to New York City, for safety. In New York, they started a new life, and hid, after their mother gave them the painful news that she believed their father was dead. For years, she taught them how to hide, and forbid them to be involved with music in any way, shape, or form. Years later, one fateful night their mother was killed in a mugging.

Aria and Gio stuck together. They bought a building, running a collectibles shop, where they now live and work, hunting for treasures for collectors. Aria lives by her mother's creed and keeps a low profile. Gio lives wild and free, bedding women, and taking risks.

When book one opened, readers learned that Gio has been missing for a few weeks and Aria is desperately worried. While hunting for clues to find him in his office, she finds a romantic, sexy letter from a woman named Sofia written to Gio. To Aria's anger and shock, the letter mentions a hunt to find the secret formula to create the Stradivarius instruments. Obviously, Gio has taken risk to a whole new level. There is also a mention of a violin going up for auction at the elite Riptide Auction House. Nervous about exposing herself, but seeing no other option, Aria heads to Riptide in hopes of finding clues that lead her to her brother. While her first contact, does not offer such results, she discovers there will be a VIP auction for the violin. She has to attend. Surely her brother, or maybe Sofia, will be there. This means earning an invitation from the ever-so-arrogant and pompous owner of Riptide, Mark Compton.

She does so by charging into the restaurant he's at and walking right up to his table. Mark is sitting with the famous artist Chris Merit, and the enigmatic, Kace August: a world-famous rock star violinist. Kace is a direct link to her past, to music, to her history, and a dangerous connection for her to make, but even in their first encounter, there is a spark destined to become a fire.

Through the slow burn of them getting to know one another, Aria is also trying to keep her business, Accent Collectibles, which she runs with Gio, afloat. In doing so, she attempts to bid on a rare wine for a client of hers, but is outbid by Alexander Voss. Someone both her client and Kace August have a tenuous history with, though she doesn't know much detail about either. Just that Kace and Ed don't want her between them and Alexander, or with Alexander at all.

Thanks to Mark Compton's wife, Crystal, Aria gets the invite to the VIP auction, and it turns out both she and Kace are set to big on the Stradivarius violin. As part of the auction, Aria is allowed an early look at the violin, and searches for the very distinct markings that would confirm it is a real and true Stradivarius, sadly, she finds this one is a fake, and tells Mark as such. He refutes her claims, but she tells Kace anyways, and he trusts her enough to not bid on the violin.

In a whirlwind of surrender and passion, Aria and Kace give in to their desires, and she ends up in Austin, TX with him for another of his charity concerts that he puts on with Chris Merit. Their time in Austin pulls them closer, and despite Aria's reservations due to Kace being so engrained in a world that is still a threat to her, she is finding herself falling for this man.

Kace eventually breaks Aria down and convinces her to reveal that her brother is missing. He wants to help and asks her to meet with his security team, Walker Security, to allow them to help find Gio. She begrudgingly agrees to meet with them. However, when they return to New York, and he allows her into his vault to inspect one of his Stradivarius violins, she cuts her hand and in her haste to find something to stop the bleeding she discovers profiles on her and her brother—with their real names attached and information on her family's history. Shellshocked and heartbroken that Kace has known who she was all along, and deceived her, Aria runs from Kace's place. And that's where we pick up, with Aria bloodied, shattered, and scared...

playlist

Back 2 Good by Matchbox Twenty
Pieces by Rob Thomas
Somewhere With You Kenny Chesney
Call Me When You're Sober by Evanescence
Say You Won't Let Go by James Arthur
Caprice No. 24 by Paganini
Can I Be Him by James Arthur
Pump Up the Jam by Technotronic
Purple Rain by Prince
Back in Black by AC/DC
Dark Waltz by Hayley Westenra

chapter one

I fly down the stairs of Kace's apartment building with one thing on my mind: *escaping*. Kace August played me with his wicked song of seduction and now I have to get away from him. And so, I flee, bleeding inside and out—my heart, my mind, my hand.

Quite literally, my hand is now dripping blood, adrenaline doing me no favors, and I have nothing to stop the flow. Halting a few flights down from Kace's floor, with many more to travel to the lobby, my attempt to inspect my injury is thwarted by the stream of red. There is just too much blood. Hands bleed a lot, I remind myself, a fact I learned years ago when Gio cut his finger. With blood now on the floor and no other option, I tug the end of my thankfully black T-shirt and wrap it around my palm where the wood stabbed me, trying to halt the flow.

Applying as much pressure as I can, I plod down the stairwell, and instead of thinking about my injury, my mind is on the documents I'd found in Kace's office. There had been photos, too, I now realize—photos of Gio, who was missing when I met Kace. In other words, they were taken before we met. I don't even want to go to the many jagged places that realization could take me. I want to scream. I don't know what to do aside from leave, regroup, and make plans that might include me on the run. Gio is missing and our identity has been discovered. The facts paint a grim picture.

Finally, finishing my trek down the stairs, I depart the stairwell into the lobby, and somehow, by some miracle, I walk calmly toward the door, exiting the sliding glass doors, only to come face to face with the doorman, Steven.

"Good afternoon, miss." His eyes land on my hand that is balled in my shirt, but as my gaze follows his, I find blood dripping from my exposed fingers.

He pales and his attention jerks to my face. "Oh my," he says. "What can I do to help? I'm here to serve."

"Thank you. I—ah—think the shock got the better of me. I left without a towel. Would you have a towel or bandage? And can I get a taxi please to get me to the hospital to stitch this up?"

"Right away." He shouts out commands to several employees and then refocuses on me. "Should I call Kace, or does he know?"

"Just the towel and taxi, please."

As if on cue, someone hands me a towel that I wrap around my hand while Steven whistles for a cab. "Thank you," I say again, becoming aware of the trembling of my body, though I'm not sure if that's about the cut to my hand or the deep wound Kace has sliced into my heart. The cab pulls to a stop just in front of me. I rush toward the car, and Steven is there before me, opening the rear door. "Thank you so much," I say, climbing inside.

Steven leans into the back with me and instructs the driver, "Get her to the ER." He then looks at me. "I'll call Kace and let him know where you're going." I open my mouth to argue, but he's already gone and shutting me inside.

I quickly lean forward and speak to the driver, reciting my home address before I settle back into my seat. I was never going to the ER, not when I know that Kace will show up. Why wouldn't he? I'm the key to a door he wants open. We were never about anything but my last name and the violin he loves. The formula to make that violin is worth so much money, I can't even fathom the number.

I glance at the white towel now around my hand, and so far, blood is not peeking though. I'm okay. The wound is closing. My eyes pinch shut and I press my good hand to my face and will myself not to cry. Not here. Not when I'm in this car. I'll melt down when I'm alone at home and then pull myself back together, and decide if home is even safe anymore. It's conceivable that Kace might be my enemy, but I remind myself, and sternly, that my heart isn't how I should make any future judgments about Kace August.

My phone starts to ring and I know it's him, I know it's Kace, and I let it ring. A second thought has me thinking of Gio, who I really need to hear from right now. I reach for my cell, struggling to remove it from my purse, and damn it, blood *is* seeping through the towel. I manage to snag my phone and glance at the screen. Sure enough, it's Kace. I hate how much I want to answer, how much I want to hear his voice. How much I want him to explain himself and make the lie good enough for me to pretend it's true. He *knew* who I was before we ever started dating and he didn't tell me. Who am I kidding? Every moment with him was *a lie*.

I hit decline and thirty seconds later, my cell starts to ring again. I hit decline again, but I'm not turning my phone off. Not when Gio could call. I know it's wishful thinking, of course. I know it's time I face that fact and really do something about his absence, but not today. Today, I cling to hope. Today, that hope includes me willing Gio to call me. I silence the ringer on my cell. In turn, my phone buzzes with a text message: *Steven just called and told me you cut yourself. I'm on my*

9

way to meet you at the hospital. Answer, baby. I'm worried about you.

I read that endearment with a twist of my gut and hear, "*Baby.*"

I'm not his baby or his fool anymore.

Unbidden, tears spill down my cheeks. I was falling in love with him. I was falling hard and as much as I've told myself "alone" worked for me, right now, alone feels pretty horrible. And I don't know what to do. Suddenly, I need to be both on the offensive and defensive. If Kace was after the formula for the Stradivarius—and obviously he was, or rather is—am I in danger? I think I might need to pack a bag and at least go to a hotel for a few nights while I think this through.

The cab halts and we're now idling in stand-still traffic. This doesn't work. I can't just sit here and bleed. I have to wrap my hand properly and decide if some sort of medical attention is mandatory. A few years back when Gio cut his hand on broken glass, he bled like a stuck pig, but he didn't need stitches. He was fine. I might be fine. I hope I'm fine. I yank my emergency cash from my purse, cash my mother taught me to keep at all times, and toss a twenty over the seat before opening the door. Once I'm on the street, the fact that I do not have a coat is bitingly clear. It's cold, like really cold, as it always seems to be at Halloween, which is now only days away. I scratch the idea of walking and hurry to the subway, ignoring all the stares at my bloody towel. The shock is wearing off and my brain is working, and so too, it seems, are my pain receptors. A throb is becoming real pain, but I have the mental fortitude to think of tetanus. I don't remember the last time I had a shot. I clearly have to go to the doctor.

Once my ride is over, and I'm street level again, it's a short but bitterly cold walk and then I'm at my place. I dig for my keys, but my one free hand is freezing. I finally catch them in my fingers but drop them. And my god, I'm losing my mind. I can just plug in the security code and open the door. Flustered, I kneel and gasp as a man kneels in front of me. I blink Alexander into view, his timing uncanny and uncomfortable.

"What are you doing here?" I sound snappy. I just can't help it.

"Apparently playing hero," he says, catching my arm and staring at the bloody towel. "What the hell happened to your hand?"

"I cut it on a piece of wood. I'm assuming I need to get stitches."

"I don't have to look at it to know, that yeah, based on the amount of blood, you need stitches. There's a minor emergency a few blocks over. Let's go there now."

"No, I—"

He pulls me to my feet, causing a dizzying rush that's momentarily blinding. "You're gushing blood," he insists. "I don't know why you're standing here right now when you need to get medical attention." He snakes his key from his pocket. "I'm in the delivery zone. I saw you walking and pulled over to catch you. Just come with me. I'll get you where you need to go."

"Alexander, no, I—"

"You need a doctor," he insists. "My help comes with no obligation, Aria. Contrary to anything Kace August has told you, I'm not that kind of an asshole."

"I don't have it in me right now for whatever war you're fighting with Kace."

His lips press together. *"Let me help you,"* he prods softly. He dangles his keys. "Let's go get you fixed up."

He says this help comes with no agenda, but we both know it does. I don't want to go with him, but my head spins and my towel is drenched. Logic and good sense must prevail—thus I say, "Yes. Thank you."

His broad shoulders beneath his ridiculously expensive suit relax slightly. "This way." He steps to the side to allow my progress forward, his hand settling at my back. I'm aware of his hand but not because I'm aware of him. It's the opposite. I'm aware of how little he affects me, and of how intensely Kace affects me. Our connection felt real but I'm not sure if that matters or tells me anything at all. I'm not sure anything will until later when I'm alone.

Alexander opens the passenger door, and I slide into his fancy Porsche, a beast, as Kace would call it. Actually, the car, and its description by Kace, is appropriate, considering Alexander is a bit of a beast himself. He's all force to Kace's sweet seduction, but that's the thing about seduction, it isn't always so sweet at all.

I'm struggling with my seat belt when Alexander settles into the driver's seat and comes to my aid, catching it and helping me seal it into place. Our hands touch and while there is nothing electric about the connection, I feel an awareness, his wholly male awareness. I yank my hand back and why do I feel like I'm betraying Kace? We are *not* a couple. Not anymore. I'm not sure anything between us was real, except my intense reactions to him. That was real. That was consuming.

My phone buzzes with a message and I ignore it. Alexander cranks the car. "Need to get that?"

I rest my head back on the leather cushion and shut my eyes. "No."

"How'd you cut your hand?" Alexander asks.

My lashes lift but I don't look at him. "A wooden drawer," I say, and my gaze shifts to the window. Only then do I realize that he's already pulled away from the curb. Actually, we're not even on my street anymore.

"That doesn't seem like a sharp object," he comments.

"A chunk of wood was sticking out," I say, my lashes lowering again. "Maybe there was steel or a nail, too. I just don't know."

"And you were alone with this wooden drawer?"

I jerk my head up and look at him. "Yes." That's all I offer and I feel no temptation to expand on my answer. I'm a practiced master of one-word replies. "Where is this minor emergency?" I ask, peeking out of the window.

"Right here," he says, pulling me to the door of a building with a big red cross on the front. "I told you it was close. You go in and get attention. I'll park and be right in."

"You don't need to come in, Alexander," I say quickly. "I appreciate the help, but I really am fine."

"I'd be a total asshole to leave you here alone. In fact, in the dictionary next to the word 'asshole' would be my name. I'm not leaving you alone. Now go before you lose any more blood. I'll be right there."

I could argue over him staying, but he's right, I'm growing concerned about how much blood is on the towel. I reach for my belt and I can't get it unhooked. He quickly comes to my aid once more, unlatching it before he orders, "Stay where you are." He shifts the car into park. "I'll come and get your door." He unhooks his own belt and opens his door. I reach for mine with my good hand and quickly shove it open.

I'm on my feet, the piercing cold weathering my cheeks by the time he reaches my side of the car, but my head spins and I sway. I reach for support and end up grabbing Alexander, but there is nothing romantic about this moment. "Oh God," I murmur, as my stomach rolls. "I feel sick."

"Because you've lost blood." He wraps his arm around me and I don't have the strength to push him away as he adds, "Come on. I'll get you inside."

"I'm fine. Your car. You need to—"

"*It's fine*," he says, and he's hauling me forward, the spice of his cologne permeating my nostrils, but it's pungent, it's too much. I think that's my problem with Alexander. He's too much. He's that beast, and yet he is being so kind that I wonder why I feel these things about him.

Double glass doors open and we head inside a typical doctor's office with white floors, vacant steel armed chairs, and a built-in reception desk. The fifty-something woman with spiky blonde hair behind the counter is focused on me and her eyes go wide.

"Oh my," she says, before she calls out, "Ellen!"

Ellen or I assume it's Ellen, rushes out to the lobby, and says, "Oh my," as well.

Ellen is wearing pink scrubs, her curling brown hair wild around her heart-shaped face. She's tiny but there's something fierce about her that I find appealing. The next five minutes are a whirlwind but the paperwork is discussed, and Ellen is the one with her arm around me now, and it's remarkably more comfortable despite both our petite sizes. "Do you want your guest to come back with you?" she asks.

"No," I say, twisting around to face Alexander. "I'll call you tomorrow. Thank you so much."

His jaw sets stubbornly. "I'll wait." He motions to the chairs. "I'll move my car and then I'll sit. I'll be right here."

My cellphone buzzes with a call, and of course, I know, without looking, that it's Kace—almost as if he's chosen this moment purposely to insinuate himself between me and Alexander. But then, that's not difficult when he's the reason I'm all but destroyed right now.

I turn away from Alexander, and it's not long before I'm sitting in a room with a doctor, a man I guess to be in his thirties, sporting a shaved head and a pleasant bedside manner. "You're lucky," he says after pulling a piece of wood from my hand and covering my hand with a bandage to apply pressure. "You were close to a nerve. The wood was allowing the bleed to continue. And you almost took the palm of your hand off. We're going to stitch you up, get you a tetanus shot and some pain meds, and get you home."

"Thank you," I say and it's all I can manage. I just want to go home. Now.

Half an hour later, I have stitches, a shot, a warning that my arm might hurt and/or feel heavy as a result of the shot, and two prescriptions. Thankfully there's a pharmacy in the clinic and Ellen heads off to have my meds filled for me.

While I wait, I check my text messages to find several from Kace. *I'm worried. Aria, answer. Please. See? I can use good manners, too. Baby. Please.*

I'd laugh but that's what he wants, to seduce me all over again with charm and his brand of perfection.

There's a knock on the door and the front desk attendant, who I now know to be Lynn, pokes her head into the room. "You have a visitor who wants to join you."

My brows furrow. "I have what?" Even as I ask the question, my heart starts to race and I don't give her time to answer. "Who?" I ask because it can't be him. How would he know where to find me?

But I know it is. I know even before she says, "He says his name is Kace August."

chapter two

Kace is here.

How can Kace be here?

But even as my mind asks that question, I know the answer. He's been having me followed since before we ever met. He's still having me followed.

Lynn clears her throat. "Should I bring Mr. August, or ah, Kace—he said to call him Kace—should I bring him back?"

"No," I say quickly. "I'll be out in a few minutes."

"Okay, but for the record, I'm not sure I've ever seen two such good-looking men in one place, and well, I'm not sure they can survive in the same room much longer."

My brows furrow. "Alexander's still here?" I ask because the truth is, I wasn't sure he'd have the wait in him.

"He is, and at the risk of being out of line, I might add, to the extreme displeasure of Kace." She winks and disappears, shutting the door behind her.

I press my good hand to my face. I don't know what to do. He probably doesn't even know that I've found those photos yet. Suddenly pain becomes anger. He doesn't know, but it doesn't matter. He doesn't get to use me and manipulate me any longer. I slide off the exam table and walk toward the door. Ellen enters at the same moment I'm about to exit, which successfully defuses my anger.

"You're all set," she says, indicating the bag in her hand. "You already took an antibiotic and a pain pill.

You should take another in four hours." She hands me the bag. "And remember, some people do get a heavy, achy feeling in their arm from the shot. That's why we put it in the same arm as your injury. That way only one side will be affected."

"Thank you, Ellen. You really are wonderful."

"I think you're the one who's wonderful, judging by the fan club you have in the lobby." She wiggles an eyebrow. "Hubba hubba." She backs up into the hallway to allow my exit.

Two men who want something from me do not equal a fan club, I think. I have never needed to be alone as much as I do right now. With my anger tamped down, I exit the room and hurry toward the lobby, but pause at the door, drawing a deep breath, steeling myself for all things Kace August. As if that has any chance of working.

I push open the door and enter the lobby.

Alexander is in a chair, his head back, eyes shut. Kace is literally at the center of the room, pacing, his back to me at present, a rock god in denim, biker boots, and his favorite tan leather jacket. He runs a hand through his longish dark hair, obviously frustrated, one might even think worried, and perhaps he is, just for the wrong reasons. As if they both sense my presence, Kace turns abruptly in my direction, and Alexander bolts to his feet. But it's Kace I'm focused on. Kace whose blue-eyed stare is locked on me. Kace who fills me up with so many emotions that they are now a waterfall, crashing to the floor beneath my feet.

He closes the space between me and him and I tell myself to back away, but my feet won't move. They have grown limbs and taken root right here in the tiled the floor.

He stops in front of me, and one of his talented hands is instantly cupping my face, the other branding my hip. His head lowers intimately, huddling us together, two people in a room with others, but somehow alone. "My God, woman," he murmurs, his voice gravelly. "I've been worried. So damn worried. What happened? How are you?"

He smells like man and musk, like fresh grass in the sunshine on a rainy day, like heaven in the midst of hell. He feels like the comfort of home and the fire of desire. For just a moment, I am lost in all of those things. I am lost in him.

"How did you find me?"

"I went to two hospitals, three minor emergencies, and your apartment first. I just didn't give up. What is going on with you?"

"You haven't been home, have you?"

"No. Why would I be there when you're here?" He glances down at my injured hand. "How bad is it?"

He always says the right things, does the right things, but everything right with him is wrong, I remind myself. I shove away from him and step back. "Go home, Kace. You'll figure out why I wasn't taking your calls when you get there."

"Did he do this to you?" Alexander demands, stepping inside the invisible circle that shunned the rest of the room just moments before.

Kace doesn't even look at him but warns, "Don't push me, Alexander."

"Why? You going to hurt me like you hurt her?"

I whirl on Alexander. "He didn't do this to me. Please don't start a fight with Kace." I turn back to Kace and add, "I know everything, Kace."

"And this everything you think you know, is that why you're with him?"

"He showed up at the apartment and I needed help."

"Which should have been me," he says.

"I *know*, Kace."

"Come with me, Aria," Alexander urges. "I'll take you home."

Kace steps closer to me, and this time, I step back at the same time. "Don't," I warn, pointing at him.

He lowers his voice. "Whatever you think you know," he says, "you don't. I promise you, baby. *Talk to me.* Let me explain."

I can feel him pulling me under and it's terrifying how easily I could drown in this man, quite literally. "We have *nothing* to talk about."

"And if you're wrong?" he challenges. "If you don't know what you think you know?"

"I do. I know what I know, Kace."

"And if there is even a small chance you don't?" he counters. "Is *he* how you really want to handle this? By inserting Alexander in the middle of us?"

I can't breathe for the emotion that has now balled in my chest. I should walk away. Why am I not just walking away?

"I'm crazy about you, Aria," he continues. "And we are *good* together. You know that. I know you know."

"He's a player," Alexander snaps. "Don't let him suck you in."

"You and me, baby," Kace says softly, his voice like lights dancing on a night ocean, the only thing that stops a spiral into darkness. "Don't just throw us away."

Us.

That's the word that gets me.

Us.

Don't just throw *us* away. I can't just throw us away. It's dangerous, I know, but I have to hear what he has to say. I *need* to hear what he has to say.

I turn to Alexander. "Thank you for helping me. I need to stay with Kace right now. I'll call you tomorrow. I do believe I owe you."

He cuts his gaze to Kace and then back to me. "Are you sure?"

"I am," I say. "But truly, thank you."

He hesitates, and then says, "I don't like leaving you."

"And you have been a gentleman, but I'm fine. I promise."

He makes a low growling sound and curses under his breath. "You have my number. Call me if you need me. Don't hesitate, no matter the time."

I nod. "Again, thank you."

His lips thin and instead of just leaving, he rotates to Kace. "I better not find out you did this."

Calm, cool Kace August isn't as calm and cool at all. He steps toward Alexander, and I rotate, placing myself in between them, dropping my medication bag, my one good hand flattening on Kace's chest. "No. Please. I'm begging you."

His jaw tics and I twist around to face Alexander. "Go. Now. Before this becomes something we all regret."

He scowls and glares at Kace.

"Alexander!" I snap.

"I'm going," he replies, holding up his hands. "I'm going." He turns on his heel and marches toward the door.

Kace grips my shoulders and he leans in, his lips brushing my neck. "Let's get you home."

Home.

21

That word guts me. I don't have a home right now. Nothing about anything in my life feels like home right now except Kace, and he's betrayed me. He scoops up my medication bag and wraps his arm around me, setting us in motion, his big body a shelter I would have cocooned inside just hours earlier. Now it frightens me how good he feels, how right he feels, how readily I want to trust him, and forget those photos.

The double glass doors open and we exit into a cold, harsh wind, but the cold is nothing to me right now. Not when I can feel myself suffocating in his perfection, and what feels like our bond. A bond that might not even be real.

Stepping onto the sidewalk, he motions left and we start walking. I shiver and Kace halts us, shrugging out of his jacket and wrapping it around me, the perfect gentleman that was stalking me before we met. He grips the lapels. "Better?"

"No. Nothing is better," I assure him. "I made Alexander go away, but I'm not going with you, Kace."

A man and a woman walk past us, and I try to twist away from him. I try and fail. The jacket is now my prison, leverage he uses to hold me in place, as he murmurs, "Don't do this."

"*You* did this," I bite out.

Before I know Kace's intent, he's backing me up. "What are you doing?"

By the time I finish the question, we're inside an alcove out of the wind, under a dim light, beside a doorway of some sort. "Trying not to end up in a tabloid tomorrow," he says. "They were following me today. Let's go to one of our apartments where it's warm and private."

"I don't care about the cold. I don't care if you freeze. I don't care if I freeze." I shrug out of the jacket and let it fall to the ground.

Kace grabs the jacket and pulls it back around me. "I care," he says. "I care if you're cold. I care about everything to do with you, Aria." His voice is soft velvet and a rough growl all at once.

Emotion wells in my chest. "I *know*, Kace. I keep telling you that I know. I *know* you know who I am. I found the file you have of me and my family. I saw the photos of Gio."

He doesn't even consider denial. His answer is quick, sure. "Aria Stradivari," he says. "Yes. I know who you are."

"You want the formula to make the violins."

"I want *you*."

"You knew who I was."

"Yes, but not for the reason you think. We met years ago, Aria. I recognized you when you showed up at the table to talk to Mark. I thought you remembered that meeting, but I soon found out that you didn't."

"*We met*? What are you talking about?"

"We were kids. You were eleven, by my present calculations, and I was seventeen. Meeting your father and touring your family factory was one of the biggest thrills of my young life."

My mind ticks back in time and yes, yes there is a vague memory of a good-looking boy who played the violin. "Why wouldn't you tell me sooner?"

"Two reasons. I knew your family had disappeared. I knew if you were alive there was a reason you were hiding and using another name. And we were young when we met. I wanted to be sure I was even correct. I had Walker do some digging."

My heart surges. "Digging is not good, Kace." My eyes go wide and I halt any reply. "No, wait. You had photos of Gio. Gio was gone when I met you."

"They're from your building's security footage. They're time and date stamped. I can prove it."

"Why hack my security system?"

"Gio was older when we met. I knew if I saw pictures of him, I'd confirm it really was both of you."

"In other words, you already knew he lived with me."

"Aria—"

"You let me believe everything I told you was fresh and new."

"It was. It was you telling me." His hands settle possessively at my waist. "Baby, I didn't want to scare you off. I damn sure didn't want you to run or disappear on me."

"You want the formula," I accuse.

"I want *you*," he repeats.

"I don't have the formula."

"I don't care about the damn formula, Aria." Exasperation touches his voice.

"How do I know that?"

A low, frustrated sound escapes his lips and he drops the medication bag, and spikes fingers into my hair, a low curse escaping his lips. His eyes meet mine, and the depth of the emotion he then spikes in me steals my breath. Before I can catch it again, he's breathing for me. His mouth slants over my mouth, his tongue licking a wicked, seductive note against my tongue. And despite my injured hand and my burdened heart, I melt the way I always melt for this man. I melt and I moan, and when he tears his mouth from mine, I am panting.

"*That* is how you know," he declares. "We are connected, you and me. We both feel it."

"All that says is that I want you and that I have the potential to be foolish because of that desire, but I won't live up to that potential, Kace."

"How do I know you aren't after my money?"

I blanch. "Because I'm not. You know I'm not."

"Can you prove it?"

"You *know* I'm not," I repeat.

His hands come down on my shoulders and he pulls back to look at me as he says, "I do know you, but that still requires me trusting you and I've had plenty of reasons in my life not to offer you that trust. Reasons you don't know. Many reasons, Aria. Many betrayals. But I give you my trust anyway. I'm not after the formula, but all I have to offer is my word. You have to decide if you trust me."

My hand settles on his chest, and his heart beats a rowdy song beneath my palm. "I'm very confused right now," I confess, and it's as honest as I have ever been with him or me. "And my head is spinning."

His hand covers my hand on his chest. "Then let me take care of you. Let me take you home."

There is a library filled with books the size of all the reasons I should say no, but even as I have that thought, he says, "Don't say no."

Words he's said to me every moment of indecision I've ever shared with him. And right or wrong, like every time before, I don't say no. I say, "Yes."

chapter three

Kace and I exit the alcove into the gust of wind and I swear my head spins with the mix of weather and drugs. I huddle into Kace's jacket, but it all but falls from my shoulders. Kace catches it and settles it back in place, sheltering me. He is the one in short sleeves, without a jacket, and yet he is quick to slide his arm around me, pulling me close, his big body holding the jacket in place and blocking the next cold gust. I snuggle in closer to him, and without reserve, I simply cannot muster, I cling to him with my free hand. The sun is a beam in my eyes, the light as illuminating as this day has proven to be.

Kace knows who I am.

He's the first person outside my family who knows who I am, who I *really* am. It's surreal, an odd feeling of liberation followed by fear.

We reach his Roadster and he clicks the locks, opening the passenger door, but doesn't just wait for me to climb into the car. He literally eases me into the seat and kneels down beside me. "You okay?"

There is tenderness in his question, and in the sea of emotions swimming in his blue eyes, the kind of tenderness I struggle to see as anything but real, honest. "That's a complicated question."

"I suppose it is right now," he agrees, smoothing my good hand down my leg. "Beyond us, your body, how do you feel?"

"Sitting is good," I say. "They gave me a pain pill. I think it's messing with me."

"We'll get you into bed and you can rest." He grabs the seatbelt and pulls it over me, his big, wonderful body pressing to mine as he latches it into place, but once complete, he doesn't move away. He hovers over me, his palm settling on my face. "I care, baby." His voice is a rumble of masculinity and emotion. "I *care*. Never doubt it." His lips brush mine, sending a shiver down my spine, and then he's gone, standing and shutting me inside his car. My world is spinning right now. I want to believe him when he says he wants only me, that he cares about me, not the formula to create a Stradivarius. I want to trust him, but I quickly remind myself that I need to tread cautiously. Kace has money, but what's the one thing a man who can have everything wants, but what he cannot have?

Kace joins me in the car, claiming the wheel while setting my bag of meds behind the seat. His scent is everywhere. On my skin. On my clothes. In the air. And his eyes are on me as he settles not into his seat, but facing me. I shift in his direction, meeting his stare, and only then does he ask, "Can I take you home with me, Aria?"

This is a loaded question. I know he knows it's loaded question. We both know it's a loaded question, that knowledge punching at the air between us.

If I go to his place, it feels to me that he's in total control, but if I invite him to mine, it feels as if I am offering him another piece of me. Right now, though, control feels important, my control. My home. Decision made, I say, "I need to be in my own space."

His lashes lower, the afternoon sunlight breaking across the hardening lines of his handsome face. "All right then," he says, his eyes meeting mine again, amber flecks in their depths. "We'll go to your place. Do you have everything you need in that bag they gave you?"

"They filled my meds for me," I say, a queasy feeling overtaking me. "And more than ever, I *really* don't think my body approves of what they gave me." I rotate and rest my head on the seat.

"Pain meds on an empty stomach are never good." He reaches over and strokes my hair. His touch is like silk on my frazzled nerves and I don't have it in me to fret over the fact that he also caused those frazzled nerves. My lashes lower, and I savor the warmth he's created in me, and ironically, considering the pain he's caused me, the only good things that I've felt in hours are because of him.

His lips brush my forehead and it's as if the hand of sleep reaches up and pulls me closer to it. Sinking into the heaviness of the moment, I am only remotely aware of Kace starting the engine, of the sway of the car.

For the next few minutes, I fight the drugs and conjure a memory of that day in the restaurant, when I'd hunted down Mark to beg for an invitation to the VIP event. Chris and Kace had both been with him. I sink back into the past:

Mark fixes his gray eyes on me. "What are you seeking?"

"A violin," I say, thankful to this Chris person for the pressure that seems to have made Mark ask for more information.

"Your buyer likes music, does he?"

The words spoken by the man to Mark's right draws my gaze and I blink into brilliant blue eyes framed by thick, longish dark hair and rugged, handsome features. I blanch with the knowledge of who this is. I'm standing across from the thirty-four-year-old rock star of violins. A man who uses his good looks, denim, leather, and arms tatted up with randomly colored musical notes to create an image. That, along with his re-mixed versions of hot new pop hits has done what many believe impossible—he's made the violin cool and sexy.

"You're," I swallow hard and force myself not to act star struck, which would certainly ensure I don't make it into the VIP room. I regroup and instead of saying Kace August, I say, "accurate."

His eyes, those famously blue eyes, narrow and his lips quirk slightly. Mark jumps in then and lifts a finger. "What song is playing right now?"

Ironically, there's a violin playing in the restaurant right now, and the question is a test, of course. Do I know enough to be worthy of this auction? To win his respect defies my mother's insistence that I deny my roots. This is not a work just anyone would know. But to fail could cost me the opportunity to find my brother. "'The Four Seasons,' Antonio Vivaldi."

Mark glances over at Kace. "Is she right?"

"She is absolutely accurate," he says, using my own word, which I do not believe is an accident. His eyes warm on my face, ripe with surprise, but there is more. He's pleased, I think. He likes that I know his world. I am drowning in this man's blue eyes, and before I'm too far under to recover, I jerk my gaze to Mark. "Can I at least get a private viewing of the violin?"

"Leave your card and show up to Friday night's event. Buy something. That's the best way to show intent."

Buy something, with all the money I do not have, I think, acid biting at my belly. I reach into my bag and pull out my card, setting it on the table in front of him.

I can feel Kace's eyes on my face, burning through me. That's when he shocks me and speaks to me in Italian: "Cambiano i suonatori, ma la musica è sempre quella."

It means, "the melody changes, but the song remains the same," but directly translated it's: "the players change, but the music is always the same."

I look at him and I know I shouldn't respond, I shouldn't connect myself to Italy with this man, but translation services are on my card. "No," I answer in English. "The musician, the player, makes all the difference, which is why he should have an instrument worthy of him." It's what my ancestor who created the Stradivarius violin believed. It's why he made the Stradivarius.

I glance back at Mark. "I'll be there Friday night."

And with that, I turn and start walking toward the exit.

My eyes open and I am aware now, if not then, that I'd not only confirmed my Italian heritage in that exchange, I'd also made it clear I understood the value of both player and instrument. The question becomes, was Kace confirming my identity in his own mind, or did he already know?

31

chapter four

The joy of Manhattan.

We end up in standstill traffic a block from my apartment. My lashes lower and I don't know how when the drive is short, but I must drift off to sleep. I wake to Kace leaning over me, unhooking my belt. "Wake up, baby. We need to get you inside."

I blink. "We're here?"

"Yes. We're here. No thanks to that traffic jam." He kneels back down beside me. "Where are your keys?"

"My keys?"

"To your apartment."

"My purse. Oh God, my purse. Where is my purse?" Not sure the last time I saw it, panic takes over and I reach for my hip, and thank God, it's actually there. "I thought I lost it." I try to open the zipper, but can't get my one hand to cooperate.

Kace closes his hand over mine, his touch warm, familiar, intimate. "Can I do it?" he asks.

"Yes," I whisper. "Please."

He kisses my hand and then quickly removes my keys before unhooking my seat belt. "Let's get you inside."

I shut my eyes against a wave of sickness. "Can I just stay here in your beautiful car?" I whisper.

"Your big, beautiful bed is a better idea." He catches my hands. "Let's get you there now." Before I can object, somehow he stands and takes me with him. He wraps his jacket around me and I wrap my arms around him, holding on, because well, I really want to hold onto him in all kinds of ways. "My bed is not big."

"Good," he says, his lips curving. "I'll take every advantage I can to hold you close."

"It's small, Kace. You're not small. Maybe we should go to your place?"

"I would like nothing more than to have you in my bed, Aria," he says. "*Tomorrow*." He drapes his arm around my shoulders and eases me out of the way to shut the door. "Right now, we're staying here."

I glance at the meter where he's parked the Roadster. "What about your car?"

"I'll feed the meter after I get you inside."

Right, I think. A two-hour meter, but then maybe he's not planning to stay. I recoil with the idea. Maybe I should want him to leave. I'm conflicted, confused. I just need to be in my bed, no matter its size. He sets us in motion toward my building, and when we reach the door, I key in my security code and glance up at him. "I am not in sound mind right now. You don't need the keys to get in the building."

He leans down and kisses me. "Hopefully you do need me." He doesn't give me time to reply. He opens my door and we enter the store, where rows of books and collectibles read like a library to a new visitor. "Where's your apartment?" Kace asks, shutting the door and resetting the alarm on his own.

I point toward the stairs. "But we actually *do* need the keys to get inside my apartment. And I need to sit a minute." I motion to a pair of cozy chairs in a small sitting area but never make it there. Kace scoops me up instead.

"What you need is your bed." The next thing I know, we're up the stairs at my door and he's not even breathing hard.

34

Kace doesn't even set me down to unlock the door. Somehow he manages to hold onto me and open the door. Only then do I realize how humble my world is compared to his. My bed isn't the only thing that's small. My entire apartment is a box. He starts forward, intent to move inside my apartment and I use my foot to halt us right in the doorframe.

"Set me down. I need down."

"On the bed," he argues.

"Now," I insist. "Here. I need down."

"Aria—"

"Kace."

His expression darkens, his lips pressing together, but he eases me oh so carefully toward the ground and once my feet are planted on the floor, my good hand plants on his chest. "You can't come in."

His hand covers my hand. "Don't do this. I am not your enemy. I'm—"

"This isn't about who I am or you knowing it and not telling me," I say. "I don't live like you, Kace. I can't—I just can't deal with how that makes me feel right now. I should have thought of this, but my brain doesn't want to work right now."

His expression softens and one of his hands cups my head while the other settles on my waist. He leans in close, and even in my diminished state, his scent is teasing me again. And how can I not? He smells like spice, the kind of spice a girl wants to press to her nose and just breathe in. "I care about you, not how you live." His lips caress mine, a feather-light touch that is so very tender. "Trust me. Trust us."

Those words are far-reaching beyond the moment, they are a star shooting across a dark sky, lighting a path he seduces me down, his path. And for now, it works. "What if I want your money?"

His lips curve, "What if you want my body?"

I laugh despite the screams of my own body. "Kace."

"Aria," he murmurs softly and before I know his intent, he's picked me up again, scooped me into those powerful arms, and walked to my upper-level bedroom, easing me onto the softness of my mattress.

He comes down with me, setting me on the edge of the bed, and easing my purse over my shoulder before setting it on the nightstand. He then leans over me, one hand on the far side of my body. "I'm going to get your medication from the car. Then I'm going to order us food. Are you thirsty?"

"No," I say softly. "You don't have to do this."

"No," he agrees, and in this moment, his famously intense eyes live up to their reputation, inviting me to drown in a sea of blue. "No, I do not," he adds softly, and then he kisses my nose, pushes off the bed, and heads down the stairs. I roll to my side and watch him disappear, sighing. Kace August is here in my apartment, and he knows who I am.

I'm suddenly drifting back in time again, and this time, I'm reliving the night he'd chased me down outside the bar:

I turn as Kace steps in front of me, his hand settling on the top of the door, successfully caging me between his big body and the car.

"I thought you'd come back by the table," he says.

"I didn't want to intrude."

"Alexander is intruding. You wouldn't have. And— about Alexander."

That statement is a stab of reality. He's not here for me. He's here because of some battle between the two of them. "What about him?"

"He's got an agenda."

I bristle, embarrassment heating my cheeks. I actually thought he came out here for me. And I don't understand this man or what game he's playing. "What about you, Kace? Do you have an agenda?"

His eyes darken, burn, heat. His gaze lowers to my mouth and lingers before it lifts. "Yes. I do." And before I know his intent, he's stepped into me, tangling fingers into my hair and leaning in close, his breath a warm fan on my lips and cheek. "This," he murmurs. "I've wanted to do this every damn second I've been with you."

Instantly I'm melting like chocolate under the hot sun for this man and doing it in the middle of a cold October wind. I sink into him, his hard body absorbing mine. And then he's kissing me, his tongue licking against my tongue, a delicious caress that tastes of passion and hunger. His hand slides up my back, molding me closer, possession in that touch that should scare me, but it doesn't. I'm lost in the intensity of my need for this man, a stranger I should resist, but I can't remember why. Why was I supposed to resist?

A horn honks, and Kace pulls back. "You are my only agenda," he says. "Don't forget that." And then he's setting me away from him, leaving me cold where I was hot only moments before. "Good night, Aria." He turns and walks away, leaving me panting and stunned.

I return to the present, and suddenly his vow that night has new meaning. He *knew* who I was. The question is: would he have told me sooner than later, or would he have waited for me to tell him? And really, at this point, does it really matter?

My lashes lower and I decide that no, it doesn't matter. What matters are his motives, and his agenda, which he claims is me, just me. But, is it?

And I've drifted into two memories in one night. Why these two memories?

chapter five

I blink awake to a throbbing pain in my hand, a dimly lit room and the ache of my hand and the leaden feel of my arm, no doubt from the tetanus shot. That's when I realize that I'm not only in my own bed but that Kace is right here with me, propped up on the headboard, watching television.

"Hey," he says, scooting down to lay next to me on his side, his hand settling possessively on my belly. "You're finally awake."

My brows furrow and I try to remember how I even got into bed. "Finally? What time is it?"

"Seven. You've been asleep for hours. I tried to get more pain meds down you about an hour ago, but you refused."

"I did?"

"You did. You just wanted to sleep. How are you?"

"I hurt and I need to pee," I confess. "And if that kind of frankness doesn't scare you off, I'm certain you either love me or you want the formula to make the violin." It's out before I can stop it, a product of pain, drugs, and grogginess. "And on that awkward note, I have to get up." I roll away from him, but just when I think he's going to allow my escape, he's already standing above me, offering me his hand. He's also shirtless. I'm instantly mesmerized by the musical notes on his naked belly. An easy fixation even if I hadn't just told the man he's in love with me or he's using me. So much so that I dare to reach out and press my hand to the taut hard muscle of his belly. He pulls

39

me to my feet, his free hand flattening on my lower back, and suddenly I am flush to his hard body.

"Careful, baby," he says. "You might start something you're not ready to finish."

I'm presently not sure if he means with my words or my hands. "What I said—"

The blue of his eyes fleck with amber. "What about it?"

"I wasn't suggesting—I just—"

His mouth brushes my mouth. "Have to pee," he teases, his perfect mouth curving. "I know." He strokes my hair. "Go pee. Jenny dropped by some soup, homemade bread, and cookies. I'll warm up the soup and bread so you can take some more medication."

My eyes go wide. "Wait. What? Jenny was here?"

"Relax, baby. I wouldn't let anyone into your home without your permission. I met her at the downstairs door. And her soup is incredible. I might have tested this batch out for you."

Emotion wells in my chest. No one has taken care of me in years, not even Gio. I mean, I know Gio would die for me, he would, but Gio is just—Gio. A player. A wild card. A man on a mission he never explained.

Spontaneously, I reach up and rest my fingers on Kace's jaw, searching his face for some sign of betrayal, some reason to send him away, but all I find is that bond I've shared with him. That magnetic pull between us dragging me deeper under his spell. He grabs my hand and kisses my knuckles. "Stop looking for what's not there and see me again."

"I just need—"

"I know. We'll talk. I'll explain. I promise. Right now, I'm going to get that food down you."

"Thank you, Kace."

"Her manners return," he teases, releasing me and heading down the stairs.

I inhale on the exchange, and God, I want this to be real, I want us to be real, but I'm scared. I turn away from the stairs, grab my purse, and head into the bathroom, the only other room on this level. Once I'm inside, I shut the door, pee, wash up, and then study myself in the mirror. I'm a mess. My hair is all over the place. My mascara looks like something out of a horror movie. My lips are bare. Meanwhile, my hand looks like it's ten times its normal size. The ER wrapped it with a ridiculous quantity of bandages.

Kneeling in front of my cabinet, I dig out some gauze I bought eons ago and set out to rewrap it.

Ten minutes later, I am thankful that the injury and leaden feeling is in my left hand, not my right. I've managed to re-wrap my left in a reasonable amount of bandage, my face is washed and bare, and that's all I have in me. I can't handle pain pills and I grab Advil from the cabinet, pop four, and use the glass by the sink to down them. That's when my gaze catches on my bare feet and pink painted toes. I didn't take off my shoes and socks. Kace did. On a subconscious level, I trust him so much that I didn't even notice. I have never trusted anyone but Gio. That means something. Doesn't it?

Exiting the bathroom, the scent of food teases my nostrils and rumbles my stomach. I quickly make my way to the stairs and pause as I watch Kace move about my kitchen, half-naked without his shirt, cooking for me. I'm not sure any woman could resist the appeal of this man in this moment or really any other. Considering the past twelve hours or so, it's pretty surreal.

I slip my feet into my pink fuzzy slippers I keep at the end of the bed, and then hurry down the steps, far more steady on my feet than I expected to be when I woke up. But then, the pain pill is now pretty much gone. Kace must sense my approach because his gaze lifts, his eyes lighting on my approach as if the sight of me warms him. I feel the sincerity of his reaction and with it, my sense that what we've shared is real, expands.

I join him at my small island and he sets a bowl of soup and a plate of bread in front of me.

"Just in time. It's hot and ready for you. And for the record, if you like it, you need to text Jenny. If you hate it, you need to text Jenny and still say you like it. It's her famous chicken dumpling soup."

I laugh and slip onto a barstool. "I'll text her with love in my heart and belly, I'm sure. You had me at dumplings. All things pasta and bread work for me."

"Which is why I know you'll love spaetzle. I still need to get you a good German meal." He sets two bottles of pills in front of me and then moves to sit on the stool next to me. "Your antibiotics and your pain meds. How did you hurt your hand? You haven't told me."

"The drawer in your vault. It had a piece of wood or maybe wood and a nail sticking out. Honestly, all I know is it hurt. It bled a lot. And here we are."

"Ouch damn, baby, I'm sorry. I feel like shit."

"I forgive you, but only because you wrangled me some cookies." I set the pain medication aside. "I just took four Advil. I have no desire to take another pain pill. All they do is knock me out."

"Sleep helps the body heal. And so does food." He steals a torn-off piece of the bread. "It's almost as good as her cookies." He takes a bite and then offers it to me.

I accept and the intimacy of the shared food is right there between us, thickening the air and ripening the awareness between us. I taste the warm bread and nod my approval. "It's wonderful."

"Good. I'm glad you like it. Jenny will be as well." He hands me my spoon. "Eat, baby. You'll feel better."

Despite his frequent use of the endearment, this time it does funny things to my belly. In defiance of what has happened these past few hours, there is a new intimacy between us that cannot be denied. I accept the spoon and begin to eat, finding the soup delicious. "Speaking of the perfect godparents—" My brows dip. "Actually, are Jerry and Jenny, your actual godparents?"

"Not officially, but that's what Jenny calls them."

"Well then, as I said: speaking of the perfect godparents, you had cookies, good food, and clearly love, from what I saw with you and Jenny."

"The love is mutual," he says. "And they are pretty perfect."

"You said they were good friends with your parents?"

"Jerry and my father went to school together. Jerry actually owned another bakery and had about fifty locations before he sold out. He doesn't have to work, but he kept this one location because he enjoys it. And why tell you that part of Jerry's life? Because if he wasn't that successful, my father wouldn't have had anything to do with him."

My spoon halts midair with the offer to slide under his wall, and glimpse a bit more of the real man he shelters beneath his rock star image. It's not exactly penance for the secrets he's kept from me, as that really isn't appropriate here, but rather a message I understand. He's telling me that he hasn't taken what he will not give. I set my spoon down. "Your father was really that cold?"

"He was," he confirms, and I don't miss the tic in his jaw, that tells a story. He's willingly toed this territory with me but the topic of his father is not a gentle one.

"Jenny is so sweet. I assumed Jerry would be a kind person, as well." In an effort to ease the intensity of the full force of my interest, I pick my spoon up again and scoop up a big, wonderful dumpling.

"He is. He absolutely is."

My brows furrow. "Then I'm confused. He and your father seem an odd pairing."

"It was all about money and convenience to my father. He invested in Jerry's bakeries. He controlled Jerry to some degree. And he turned him into a babysitter, which thankfully also created a bond between me and Jerry. And Jenny," he adds, "when she came into the picture."

"Babysitter? Why would they need a babysitter when you were always traveling?"

"I wasn't always on the road. I had windows, months at a time, when I was home. When my parents would travel during those months, they'd leave me with Jerry and Jenny."

I set my spoon down again. "Wait. So, when you were here, they would leave?"

"When business called, my father answered." He grabs another piece of bread. "And now you know why I have a sweet tooth. I was always around those damn cookies."

"We aren't so different. You lost your father, too."

There's a sharp spike to his energy but his answer is matter-of-fact. "I never had my father." In a swift change of topic, he asks, "What happened to your father, Aria?"

He's officially moved the discomfort from him to me. "I haven't told you?" It's not really intended to be a question.

"No. You haven't told me."

"Right well—he disappeared. My mother got us out of bed one night, packed us up and we came here."

"He just *disappeared*? And your mother left instead of looking for him? There's clearly more to the story."

"She told us she knew he was dead. She wouldn't talk about the details and believe me, I tried to get her to talk, *over and over* again. So did Gio."

"Could he be alive?"

"Gio and I have had moments when we've both leaned that direction, but we're always grounded back in reality by one certainty: if he were alive he would have found us. There's no way he would have stayed away."

"I can see that. He loved his family. I was young when I spent time with him but I felt that love. He was a good man." I can feel the emotion expanding in my chest and as if he reads my readiness for a change of topic, he eyes my bowl. "You ate it all."

He's right on that. Somehow I've managed to down it all while we've talked, while I dare think now that we've managed to grow closer in a time one would think we'd be farther away. "How could I not? It was delicious."

"How do you feel?"

"Much better."

"Your hand?"

"Hurts," I say, "but it's remarkably bearable."

"Then I have something to show you." He pushes to his feet and steps to my side, offering me his hand. That hand is always a question, one that I understand now more than ever. His hand is always about trust, him asking for it, and me giving it.

But he asks. He doesn't assume. He doesn't demand. The question is: *does he manipulate?* I'd say yes, he does. His decision to hold back his knowledge of my identity was, in fact, manipulation. I have reasons to doubt and fear Kace, I do. The problem is that I want to trust him. I have always wanted to trust him.

But trust is a two-way street and I believe Kace has offered me an olive branch; he's shown me trust tonight. It matters.

I press my hand to his hand and he pulls me to my feet, our legs aligned, his hard body pressed to mine. I feel delicate with this man and somehow strong but as I promised him, I will not allow feelings to control me. And so, I warn, "My trust is not unconditional, Kace. In fact, right now, it's fragile."

chapter six

Kace reacts to my declaration in that perfect way Kace reacts to everything. He doesn't push back. He doesn't throw words or anger at me. In fact, he doesn't use words at all. He simply cups my head and kisses me until I'm weak in the knees, and moaning with the delicious licks of his tongue. Just that easily he makes it clear where he stands, and that's with me. He catches my fingers with his fingers and guides me toward my living room.

More than a little curious about what he wants to show me in my own apartment, I follow quite willingly, and we sit down on the couch in front of an iPad. There is a bottle of wine and two glasses. "I wasn't sure if you'd be up to the wine, but you're off the pain meds, and I think it might be recommended."

Unease ripples through me. "What does that mean?"

"It means I'm going to take you on a walk down memory lane and I'm not sure how it will affect you." He fills my glass and then his. "It's nothing bad. I promise. Try the wine. It's another blend I favor."

"How did you get your wine to my apartment?"

He wiggles a brow. "Magic."

"You paid Steven to make it happen."

He grins, a charming grin. "I did." He motions to my glass. "Try it."

Because he has money and power, and I'm reminded of the men who visited my father before he disappeared. Men in suits and driving fancy cars.

Shoving aside the past, I'm now eager for the wine, and I sip from my glass, a sweet spice touching my tongue. "It's interesting. Good. Drier than the last bottle."

"It is. This is a French wine, which tends to be drier, at least to my palate."

"Did you buy it in France?" I ask, curious about his travels and wondering how he will adjust to life here, not on the road. I wonder actually if his life here will last.

"I did," he confirms. "I need to restock during my next visit. You could help me by going with me in December."

My mind is suddenly back in his vault, back in that moment when I found that file. When I found Gio's photos in the drawer. I set my glass down and stand up. He follows and links our hands. "Aria—"

"We can't just pretend you don't know who I am. We can't just pretend you didn't know before we ever started. We can't pretend that none of this happened."

"No," he agrees, his hands settling on my shoulders. "No, baby, we can't. We're not. That was never my intent. Sit back down and hear me out. Please."

"Well," I say. "Since you said please."

He laughs, a masculine rumble I feel all the way to my toes. "Yes, I did," he says. "I'm learning." He sobers. "I'm learning a lot about myself through you, baby."

"I don't understand what that means."

"I don't either, but you'll know when I do. Sit?"

I nod and sit down. He follows, maneuvering the wine out of the way to place the iPad in front of me. "Watch. Just watch."

I nod, nervous again. He immediately hits play on a video and I'm suddenly doing just as he instructed, and what I'm watching is a young Kace August, so very young—a teenager, I believe—play his violin. The song

48

is "Toccata and Fugue in D minor" by Johann Sebastian Bach, one of my favorites, a fast, complicated piece he masters in a way few can. This was one of his earlier versions that I remember well. The melody hums through me, his skills on full display. I hit pause. "My God, Kace. Even then you were brilliant. How old were you?"

"Seventeen. And anything I did right that day wasn't about me. This video isn't about me. Keep watching, baby." He hits play.

All the more curious now, my gaze shifts back to the video, and once again, I am lost in his performance, when suddenly the footage shifts and expands. I'm now staring at my father, standing in front of Kace, directing him with fierce sways of his hands. I gasp and cover my mouth, tears springing to my eyes. There's another shift of the camera and a little girl runs forward and wraps her arms around my father, successfully ending his dramatic direction. That little girl is me. Kace stops playing, laughing a youthful but robust laugh, and I run to him then and wrap my arms around him as well. That day explodes into my mind, crystal clear.

Kace told the truth. We had met before. I can't believe I don't remember, but he wasn't the star he is now and that was a traumatic year for me. All I remember is coming here, crying every night.

I punch the pause button and turn to him, my emotions ping-ponging all over the place. I'm shocked and relieved that he really did meet me in the past, but I'm angry that he didn't tell me, that I had to find out on my own. And there are other emotions, too, unnamed things that ball in my belly and chest, some of which may or may not even be about him.

Adrenaline surges through me and I stand up. He stands up. I step between him and the table and in front of him.

With my healthy hand and my body, I shove him back down and onto the couch. I follow, straddling him and almost fall on my hand, but he shackles my waist, catching me before I injure myself. His touch is electric, possessive, consuming. The heat between us is fiery, instant. *Powerful.* His blue eyes potent. "Crazy woman," he accuses softly. "You're going to hurt yourself."

"I'm more worried about you hurting me."

"No. Never. I would never—"

"You already hurt me. I trusted you."

"My judgment was poor but for good reason. I will never hurt you. I'll protect you. You're not alone anymore."

Not alone.

I repeat those words in my mind, but I can't accept that they are real. Not yet. "We met before, I get that, I believe that, but you *didn't* tell me."

"I told you. I knew you were hiding. I knew you'd be spooked. Baby, I didn't want you to run."

"Were you going to tell me?"

"Yes. Of course. When I was sure you trusted me."

"That feels like manipulation," I say, repeating what has already been in my mind.

"I can see how you might think that, but that was not my intent."

"I was eleven," I counter, not missing a beat. "There is no way you saw me at that restaurant with Mark and Chris and knew who I was."

"You were familiar." His hand slides under my hair and he pulls my mouth just above his as he whispers,

"*Cambiano i suonatori, ma la musica è sempre quella.*"

The same thing he'd said that night, "the melody changes, but the song remains the same," but directly translated, it's: "the players change, but the music is always the same."

I return to that moment with him and I reply the exact way I'd replied that night, "No," I answer in English. "The musician, the player, makes all the difference, which is why he should have an instrument worthy of him."

"And what inspired that reply?"

"It's what Antonio Stradivari believed," I say, repeating what I'd thought that day when I spoke the words. "It's why he made the Stradivarius."

"And that, Aria," Kace says, "is how I knew I was right about who you were. You not only understood Italian, you answered the way I'd expect your father to answer. You answered like a member of the Stradivari family. But it was also more, so damn much more. We just didn't know yet."

I pull back slightly to search his face. "What does that mean?"

"Six thousand miles and seventeen years later, Aria, and somehow we came back together. We are right where we're supposed to be. Right here. Right now. *Together.* And there is no place I would rather be than here, with you." His hand moves to my face, his thumb stroking my cheek, the gentle touch sending shivers down my spine. "I'm asking you to believe that," he says. "I'm asking you to trust me. I swear to you that I will never hurt you or your family."

A swell of emotions fills my chest. I have never in my entire life felt as connected to one person as I do to this man. My mother used to say, "Stay alert. Listen to your gut and think with your mind." And I am. I'm listening to my gut. I'm thinking with my mind. I press my lips to Kace's.

chapter seven

Kace moans with the flick of my tongue and cups the back of my head, deepening the kiss. In a shared breath, the divide between us of hours before is gone, and we sink into the kiss, into each other. The room fades, silent but for the sounds of need for one another, and the fingers of my free hand tangle in his hair, holding him to me.

His hand slides up my spine, strong and firm, and settles between my shoulder blades, his lips parting mine, his eyes meeting mine. A sense of exactly what he said, belonging here and now, together, swells between us, a flame that simmers and then ignites.

In this moment, the need to remove anything and everything between us overcomes me. I reach for the hem of my shirt but my injured hand and laden arm won't seem to cooperate. Kace catches the cloth with me.

"I'll do it," he offers, and when my hands fall away in silent approval, he gently eases my shirt over my head and my arm, tossing it away.

I'm left in a lacy black bra that he bought me and somehow that very idea feels all the more intimate. His hot gaze slides over the swell of my breasts beneath the lace before he folds me against him, his breath warm on my nipples.

He kisses me, just lips to lips, a soft caress, before he unhooks my bra, his hands sliding under the straps to slide it down my shoulders. My lashes lower with the heat radiating off his body into mine. I lean back and let the bra fall away, my nipples puckering in the cool air.

His hands caress my sides, and settle on my hips. When I open my eyes, he's watching me, not my naked body but my face. Slowly his gaze lowers, my breasts heavy, my sex clenched. And when his eyes meet mine again, he murmurs, "God, you're beautiful." He folds me into him, pressing my naked breasts to his naked chest, his lips brushing mine once more before he lowers me to the couch.

"We're going upstairs where we have more room and I know I won't hurt you."

"I'm okay right here."

"Until we hit your hand." He stands and takes me with him, reaching for my pants. "But we can leave these here. They bother me."

I laugh and a blink later, it seems I'm naked. Completely naked and he is not. This is not a first with Kace. In fact, it's a theme between us. With any other man, I'd feel vulnerable, but Kace is different. And this is not just about the bedroom games he plays. It's about control, something I've decided is important to Kace for reasons beyond dominance. I think it's about his father. About his life on the road that started so very young. I think it's about death and loss. Tonight, it's about our fight, about almost losing me.

He scoops me up and starts walking.

I curl into him, my hand on his thundering heart that tells his secret: he's not fully in control. There's power in this knowledge but I don't want power. He can have it. I just want him. And his thundering heart tells me what I've wanted to know: he's here, really here with me. He's *all* here with me. And I with him.

Kace climbs the stairs to my bedroom and lays me down on my back, leaning over me, his hands on either side of me. "Don't move," he orders softly.

He pushes off of me and stands up.

I move.

I lift up to my one good elbow, watching him reach for his pants. He pauses and fixes me in his stare. "You really are horrible at following orders."

"I prefer orders given while you're naked and up close and personal."

His lips quirk. "Is that right?" he asks, removing a condom from his pocket, and about ten seconds later, he's naked, his cock jutting out, hard and thickly veined. He is hard *all over*, a perfect masculine specimen by anyone's taste. And those tattoos, musical notes that dance a path all around his ripped abs and further down, get me every time.

He tears open the package holding the condom and my gaze jerks to his.

"Yes. And I'll, of course, be perfectly submissive when you're up close and personal."

He laughs, closing the space between us and when his knees hit the mattress, I ease onto my back. He's over me a moment later, his powerful legs shackling mine. "Here I am." The sweet weight of his body settles onto mine as he asks, "Now are you going to take orders?"

I wrap my arms around his neck. "What orders, Kace?"

He rolls us to our sides, the thick pulse of his erection between my thighs, while he has managed to ensure my injured hand is out of harm's way, and I know this is no accident. Kace does nothing by accident. I've learned that already about him.

"Not tonight," he says. "No orders tonight. No games tonight." He strokes a hand through my hair and tilts my face to his. "But if I could order you to trust me, I would, but then it wouldn't matter as much if it was a demand, now would it?"

"No," I whisper. "No, I suppose it wouldn't."

"You can trust me, Aria," he vows.

He wants me to say that I do. I want to say I do, but my life isn't that simple. We have proven we are not that simple.

"I want to believe that," I say instead because it's true. I have never wanted to trust anyone the way I want to trust Kace.

He breathes out and presses his forehead to mine. "I *hate* that you don't know you can."

I pull back and look at him. "We're naked in bed together Kace. We aren't in a bad place. I just—my life has been about—"

"Fear."

"Yes," I say, and it matters to me that he understands. "Fear."

"I need you to know that I understand, probably more than you think I do."

My mind goes back to the words he'd spoken outside the ER: *I do know you, but that still requires me trusting you and I've had plenty of reasons in my life not to offer you that trust. Reasons you don't know. Many reasons, Aria. Many betrayals. But I give you my trust anyway.*

I don't know what his betrayals might be, but I know they splinter painfully and bleed into the center of the darkness that I've always sensed in him. Suddenly I don't want this to be all about me trusting him. I want it to be about him trusting me. "You can trust me, too. I know you said that you do, but I just want you to know that you can."

A sharp emotion flickers in his eyes but before I can even begin to name it, his mouth lowers to mine, his breath a warm fan on my lips. "I'll be gentle. I don't want to hurt you."

For just a moment, I'm not sure if he's talking about my hand or my heart and I never get the chance to find out. His mouth closes down over my mouth. His tongue licks past my teeth and one hand flattens between my shoulder blades, molding me close. His kiss is velvety warm and liquid sweet. His taste is both demanding and somehow gentle. His hands are magical, and I swear I can feel the glide of his fingers down my spine in every part of me. My nipples tingle, my sex clenches and as if he knows this is the perfect moment, he presses inside me, hard and thick. I moan with the feel of him, arching against the shock and pleasure.

He swallows the moan with his kiss, and I can feel the intensity in him, the arousal, the need, and it affects me. I am burning alive for this man. The heat between us is searing, and with my good hand buried between us, my injured arm is all I have to hold onto him and it's not enough. Kace seems to know, though. He cups my backside and drives into me, rocketing sensations through me. I pant and arch into him. His hand is on my breast, fingers teasing my nipples, and when he nips at my lip and tugs on my nipple at the same time, my back arches. He thrusts into me, tangles fingers into my hair and kisses me. We are in a wild frenzy that becomes soft, sultry, erotic, tender even. It no longer feels like sex. It feels like something much deeper, something I have never known. It's in that place, with this amazing man, that we both tumble into release, and each other.

When it's over, we don't speak, but that tenderness between us doesn't fade. We end up naked under the blankets, the lights out and our warm bodies pressed close.

And in the darkness, that fear we discussed is a shooting star that streaks into the distance and fades away. Lying here in Kace's arms, it too has faded. It's gone, at least for one night.

chapter eight

I wake to my arm frozen on top of the mattress. It—won't—move. "Oh God," I whisper and roll to my back, with no sensation in my limb at all. "Oh God!"

Kace is instantly leaning over me, one hand on each side of my body, his body over mine. "What is it? Pain?"

"I can't move my arm. That stupid shot they gave me did something to my arm. It's bad, Kace. I can't move it."

"What shot?"

"Tetanus," I say, trying to move my arm again and failing. "It won't move. It won't move!"

"Maybe it's just asleep."

I shake my head. "I don't think so. It feels dead."

He dares to laugh. Asshole. "It's not dead," he assures me, rubbing my arm for a few seconds. Suddenly some feeling returns.

"Okay, maybe it's not dead," I concede. "I think I was laying on it, but please keep rubbing it because I have never experienced this level of dead arm."

"I got it and you," he promises, his lips curve at the edges. "I have experienced this, especially after a long show."

I start moving my arm around. "Oh thank God. It's still not right from that shot but it's alive. And," I add, "this is a very sexy way to wake up with me, right?"

His gaze does a hot sweep of my naked body and then back up at me. "It's pretty sexy, baby. And you even gave me an excuse to put my hands all over you. Not that I need one." He shifts to settle between my legs, his hands on my hips, his lips pressing to my belly. "How about I give you something other than your arm to think about?"

Already my arm is forgotten and my heart is racing. "I'm pretty sure you've already succeeded," I dare to confess.

His eyes light and his mouth, such a delicious mouth, curves. "I'm just getting started," he promises and his thumb strokes the sensitive skin just inside my hip bones, sending a rush of goosebumps all over my skin. Another caress and my sex clenches, my hips arching into the touch. Kace responds by leaning in, his longish dark hair tickling my belly as his tongue flicks into my belly button.

I gasp with the wet, warm sensation and that's when a strange beeping sound pulses in the air. I blink in confusion while Kace groans and buries his face in my belly. "That," he says, tilting those perfect blue eyes my way, "is my alarm. I have a meeting across town." He glances at his watch and grimaces. "Way too soon, considering I have to go home and change." He leans in and kisses my belly again and then to my shock, slides lower, and the next thing I know, his deliciously skilled tongue, licks my clit. Just one sizzling lick.

"That's to give you something to think about today," he declares, the erotic heat in his eyes almost as scorching as his tongue.

"That's just evil," I accuse, but there is a stab of broader disappointment overtaking the heat he's so easily stirred in my body. He's leaving. For someone who never wanted to see him again, I really don't want him to leave.

He kisses my belly. "Just making sure you miss me."

"Again," I say, my legs pressing to his sides, holding him in place. "Evil."

He winks and scrapes his teeth on my knee before salving the sting with his tongue. A touch I feel in my sex, exactly where he needs to be right now. "I promise to make it up to you." He shifts out of the grip of my legs and rolls off of me, my body silently groaning in protest, but it's too late to pull him back. He's now sitting up on the edge of the bed to grab his phone on the nightstand.

I scoot up the mattress and holding the sheet to my chest, sit up and lean against the headboard. Kace is already standing, walking in all his naked hotness to my side of the bed, where he grabs his pants. "Our donor for the violins for the California event is meeting me at the attorney's office to sign the documents today," he explains. "I'm taking possession and Mark is securing them in his vault." He pulls on his boxer briefs and then his pants.

Understanding washes over me. He's leaving for a good reason and with that knowledge comes relief, driving home how much his departure really bothered me. "Those are expensive violins. One man is donating all of them?"

"A different donor for the ones in California than New York but yes, the donations are generous as hell. I still have to sign the papers on these particular instruments and he's leaving the country in the morning." He walks to the other side of the bed again, grabs his T-shirt from a blue cushy chair, and pulls it over his head. I, in turn, indulge myself by watching all his muscles flex before he's covered up and pulling on his socks and boots. "He's a bit of a cranky bird, too, or I'd make him wait." He closes the space between me and before I know his intent, he's caught my arm, pulled me out from under the sheet, and up into his arms. I am now naked and once again, he is not, one of his hands cupping my bare backside, the other resting on my shoulder. "I'll have to be gone a big chunk of the day, but I'll be back as soon as I can. That is if you don't lock me out after I leave."

My good hand flattens on his chest. "You *know* I'm not going to do that. Why would you even say such a thing?"

His lips press together, consternation in the firm line that tells me he's quite serious. "You could start doubting me as soon as I leave."

My fingers wrap in his T-shirt, my chin tilting up, my eyes meeting his. "No."

He stares down at me, his lashes half-veiled, the lines of his handsome face pulled hard. "Are you sure about that?" he challenges.

"Yes. Very. I am very sure about that."

"Then stay with me tonight. Or hell, I'll stay with you again. I don't care where we stay."

That location being a control thing is back in play, but after his remark about being locked out, and all the intimate secrets of his life he's shared, I decide he needs it more than me. And I want to know more about his world. "I'd love to stay with you."

I can feel the tension slide from his body and his hand settles on the side of my head, a dominant and yet somehow tender gesture. "I have to take the donor to lunch which wasn't my initial plan. Between this and our unexpected challenges, I put the meeting with Walker on hold until I knew you'd still agree to the meeting. We'll reschedule it right away and find your brother. Yes?"

"Yes. Please."

"I'll handle it. It could be late afternoon when I get done. I'll come back and get you."

"That's perfect. I have some work to do anyway."

He squeezes my backside. "I really do *not* want to leave you right now."

His voice is low, rough, affected. My body is aching, breasts heavy. "I don't want you to leave, but I know why you have to."

"You do." He strokes my hair and then catches my fingers in his. "I want to see your hand before I leave." He's already leading me into my tiny bathroom, where he grabs my robe from behind the door and holds it out for me.

"If you stand there naked much longer, I'm not leaving."

A smile on my lips, I quickly slide into the robe and then turn to face him. He quickly ties the sash at my waist. "Let me see your hand."

"You need to go."

"I need to know you're okay."

"It doesn't even hurt all that badly this morning."

He backs me up and sets me on the toilet, going down on a knee beside me. There's a shower at his elbow now. It's a tiny space and he's a big man. He's also a rich man in my very humble space but if he notices, he doesn't show it at all. He reaches for my bandage. I pull my hand back. "You have to go. And I don't want to unwrap it yet. I'm fine."

His hands settle on my knees. "You're sure?"

"Positive."

He studies me, his blue eyes probing, something ticking in the air around him.

"What?" I ask, suddenly nervous about what he wants to say and has not.

"In defiance of a highly public life, I am a private person. The things I shared with you, the things I share with you in the future are for your ears only."

"Are you serious, Kace? I'm Aria Stradivari. I'm not going to burn you. And you have insurance. I know how badly you could burn me."

"You see," he says, "that is just one more of the reasons I didn't want to tell you I knew who you were. I don't want your loyalty because I hold something over your head. I will never use that against you. Ever."

I can feel the blood drain from my face. He's been betrayed. He's told me that. He's now showed me as well. "And now," I say, going where these realizations lead me, "because I said that, because I know you know who I am, you think I'm only loyal because of that." I don't give him time to reply. I cover his hands with mine. "It's not true. That isn't who I am. You sharing all you shared with me, matters to me, it matters deeply. I would never betray your trust."

He strokes my hair. "I believe you. And I'm glad that it does. This isn't about you proving yourself to me. Not at all. I just need you to understand why I made the decision I made and that it was not out of malice."

"I know that. We've talked about this, Kace."

"I come with the baggage that is my past, Aria. That past is a part of me even if I don't want it to be. It guides my decisions."

"Like not telling me you knew who I was."

"Yes. Among other things. Some of that past you won't like. In fact, I'm certain you'll want to run away."

"And if I don't?"

"I'm not ready to find out now."

"I don't even need to know."

He cuts his stare and then fixes me back in his turbulence gaze. "If only it were that simple, but we're together now. And we both know that's not the foundation for a relationship." His cellphone rings and a muscle in his jaw tics as he grabs it from his pocket.

"Mark," he tells me before he leans back on his haunches and answers. "Morning, sunshine," he greets.

I smile at this greeting as Mark is so far from sunshine, it's not even funny.

"Yes. Yes. Probably about eleven. Right." He disconnects and slides his phone in his pocket. "He's the biggest control freak you will ever know. No matter how many times I tell him the plan, he confirms the plan at least two more times."

"*He's* a control freak?" I challenge.

His lips quirk. "You think I'm a control freak?"

"I know you are."

"Baby, what we do in bed and what we do out, are two different things. That's about escape, trust, and pleasure. Outside of that, I'll protect you. I'll do that with no apologies, and most likely overbearing stubbornness, but outside of those things, no. I hope like hell that's not how I'm coming off."

"I'm only teasing you, and you can have control in bed," I say, "most of the time."

"Is that right?"

"It is," I assure him.

"I'd test you on that if I didn't have to go. One more thing." He pauses. "Alexander."

"He showed up," I say quickly. "I didn't call him. I wouldn't play those kinds of games, Kace."

"I know that, Aria. He's a problem."

"What happened between you two?"

"That," he says, "is a story I will tell you, just not now. I have to go. But I will. Just know this. I would not warn you if I didn't have a damn good reason." He kisses my injured hand. "And be careful. Don't overdo it today. I'll be back as soon as I can. Text me or call me if you need anything at all. I *will* answer." He starts to stand, and I catch his hand, smiling as I do.

"Before you walk out of the door." I run my fingers through his hair, "your hair is wild right now."

His eyes twinkle with mischief. "Good. Then everyone will know that you keep running your fingers through it." He kisses my knuckles. "See you soon, baby." He pushes to his feet, and without a look in the mirror, he exits the bathroom.

Now I'm alone again, but there is a difference between being alone and *being alone*. I am no longer *alone*. I'd consider that a positive except for one thing. I haven't talked to Kace about the dangers of being a Stradivari. Or being close to one.

chapter nine

With the thought of danger comes the thought of Gio. I haven't checked my phone in forever. Hopping to my feet, I speed out of the bathroom and into the bedroom, where I find my phone is lying on the nightstand. I snatch it up to discover it's connected to the charger. I don't remember doing that, which means Kace did it for me. Only, I don't remember him doing it either. The blank spot bothers me but then, I remind myself, I was drugged. Of course, I don't remember.

Dismissing the issue as nothing, I perch on the edge of the bed, check my call log, and discover a missed call from an unknown caller. I don't get many unknown callers, except of course the one at Kace's event, and I check my messages to find there is, in fact, a message. I hit the playback button but there's nothing but static recorded. Brows furrowed, I'm bothered by the call which is probably nothing, much like me not remembering my phone on the charger.

I'd like to believe the caller was Gio, but Gio doesn't accept defeat. He'd call back the minute he got my voicemail, well, unless of course, he couldn't call back and he thought the message went through. Still, it feels "off" for lack of a better word. I check the time of the garbled message. It was at three in the morning. That's not a client. That's not a telemarketer. I change my mind—it *had* to have been Gio.

Or Sofia which is more disconcerting than a missed call from Gio. What, is she's trying to tell me something is wrong with him? Or worse, that he's dead?

Pushing to my feet, I start to pace, confused now, unsure what to think. I dial Gio and the call, once again, lands in voicemail. Is he in trouble? My gut says yes and that's actually good news. If he's in trouble, he's not dead—not yet, at least. Sureness firms inside me. We're bonded Gio and I. I would know if he was dead. That was him who tried to call me.

Comforted by this certainty, but more determined than ever to find him, to get him the help I have to assume he needs, I head to the bathroom. First things first, I set out to inspect the injury I don't have time for. The wound is nicely stitched, though quite large and throbbing. Thankfully I'm allowed to get it wet, so I force myself to ignore the ugliness of it that is starting to freak me out, and head to the shower.

Once I'm under the water, my mind starts racing. Kace offered to help me hunt for Gio, but a) I don't want to take his money and b) is that even a safe option? In response to those questions, my mind starts ticking off more questions: am I putting Kace in danger just by being close to him? Despite Kace's good intentions, could his people at Walker Security potentially be after a big payoff I might represent?

The water runs cold and I am chilled when I grab a towel. I am also without an answer to one of those questions. With some struggles, thanks to my injured hand and laden arm, I dress in black slacks, a red silk blouse, and my new black heels. I've decided I need to just have an honest conversation with Kace about me, my family, and the danger we present. In the meantime, the business attire is for a reason. I will not let him pay my way to find my brother—okay I might let him help, but I will pay him back. Time is too critical where Gio's safety is concerned for me not to allow him to help, no matter how much that kills me.

A few minutes later, I'm in the kitchen with a pot of coffee brewing when I spy the box on the counter with the Jerry's Bakery logo. I open the lid and find a dozen or more delicious-looking iced cookies. I'm immediately reminded of my promise to text Jenny, but Kace didn't give me her number. I shoot him a text instead: *Can I get Jenny's number to text her?*

While I wait for his reply, I fill a coffee cup, pour in white mocha creamer, and dare to make my breakfast the breakfast of champions: a pink iced sugar cookie. I've almost finished it off, promising myself I will not indulge in another when Kace replies to my text with nothing but a phone number. I frown with the cold reply and inhale on a pinch in my chest.

"I will not read into this," I promise myself. "I will not read into this." I stare at the message again and repeat, "I will not read into this."

Almost as if he heard me, my cell phone rings with Kace on the caller ID. Nervous energy thrums through me as I answer and say, "Hey."

"Hey, baby. Sorry to be slow to reply. I was in the shower. Traffic was hell. It took me forever to get home."

"Are you going to make your meeting on time?"

"Not even close. I had to call the donor, who is thankfully fighting with his 'bitch of an ex-wife,' his description not mine, and was running late as well."

"Well then," I say. "That's something, I guess."

He laughs that low, rough, wonderful laugh of his that is both masculine and musical, as crazy as that might sound to someone else. "Yes, it is."

"Is she a bitch?"

"I haven't met her and thank God for it. I don't need to be in the middle of that fly trap." He changes the subject. "Before I forget, I missed a call from Jenny, but she left me a message to check on you. I haven't had time to call her back, so the minute you text her, expect her to call you instead. You okay with that?"

"Of course," I say, "Why wouldn't I be? I loved her when I met her, and I owe her a thank you."

"Good. Just making sure. I won't call her back right now then. Can you tell her that I'm headed to my meeting now?"

"Yes, of course," I say again, the idea that I'm passing messages to his family speaking of just how real this thing with me and Kace has become. "I'll text her right after we hang up," I add.

"Perfect." He hesitates. "And, Aria?"

My heart flutters with the expectation that pause has obviously, but intentionally, created. "Yes, Kace?"

"Save me a cookie."

I laugh. "I don't make any promises. There are only a dozen or less now, actually."

He laughs, too, and we say a short goodbye. I sip my coffee, the warmth of the liquid, and that intimate exchange with Kace, warming me. I've never in my life been a real couple with anyone, but that has changed. We're together, me and Kace. We're not just together, he's a light in the suffocating darkness of years on the run.

I steal a bite of another cookie and then text Jenny: *Kace is headed into a meeting. This is Aria. I'm eating cookies for breakfast. I'm on the mend and need the gym for sure! Thank you for the wonderful soup, bread, and cookies.* Message sent, I glance at the clock that now reads nine AM. Eager to get to work, I exit my apartment and head downstairs, but I make it to the last step and freeze with a shiver of unease. A second later, my nostrils flare with a sweet scent, something floral, almost like perfume. I ease further into the hallway leading to mine and Gio's offices. "Hello?" I call out.

The creak of wood, of an old building settling, is the only reply. I inhale and the scent is lighter now. Maybe it's not even real. Maybe it's my imagination? A bit tentatively, I walk to my office door and peek inside, to find it peaceful. Turning toward Gio's office, the thundering of my pulse is instant, and for no good reason. I actually tiptoe in that direction, glance around the entryway, and then with sharp disappointment, discover that he's not here.

I knew he wasn't here, I chide myself. Like he'd just show up after all this time, and get to work, without saying a word to me.

Shifting back into the hallway, I inhale, and the smell is gone, which has me really doubting myself and this silly unease. Regardless, I need to put my mind at rest. I hurry forward, facing my fears and rushing through the rows of books and collectibles in the store, to find it all clear. Just to be safe, I check the front door and find it locked. Kace even figured out how to re-arm the security system when he left. Clearly, I'm losing my mind. I turn and scan the store. No one is here. Still, I walk behind the front desk with the intent of checking the security feed. I've just keyed the computer to life when my cellphone rings with Jenny's number.

I settle onto a stool and answer her call. "Morning, Jenny."

"How are you, Aria?" she asks, her voice warm with an offer of friendship and support.

"I'm much better, thanks to you and Kace. I'm convinced the soup, bread, and cookies took away my pain."

"I'm sure it wasn't Kace's kisses," she teases.

My cheeks burn with the unexpected brazen remark from his godmother, of all people. "The delicious dumplings," I say. "Absolutely it was the dumplings.'"

She laughs a sweet laugh. "I'm sure it was. How did you cut your hand?"

"A piece of wood in a drawer at Kace's place."

"He had wood sticking out? That boy. What was he thinking?"

"Don't be too hard on him. It's in his vault so it's not like many people go in there."

"Wait. What? He let you in his vault?" She doesn't give me time to reply. "Well, now that answers any questions I have about how serious you two are."

Serious? I think. Are we serious? "We're dating," I say. "We're not getting married." It's out before I can stop it. Married? Good grief, where did that come from?

"Yet," she says, and while my mouth hangs open at her fast reply, she adds, "Kace hasn't dated in a very long time. I'm eager to get to know the woman who brought him back around. You two need to come by and have dinner. When can you fit us in?"

He hasn't dated in a long time. I'm having a hard time getting past those words, but manage a reply of, "I'm quite sure seeing you and Jerry is never 'fitting you in.' He loves you two. That is obvious."

"As we do him, but you didn't answer the question about when you can see us. I'll just decide for you. I'm pushy like that, but I promise to pay for your forgiveness in cookies. Sunday brunch. We have a favorite spot. Kace knows it. Tell him I insist. Eleven o'clock."

"As long as you're paying in cookies," I laugh. "I'll tell him."

"Fabulous. And if you want more soup, I can drop it by late afternoon. I'd love to check out your collectibles."

"You are welcome here any time and I'd enjoy visiting, but I'm headed to Kace's place later today."

"An excellent reason to turn me down. Feel better, honey."

After a brief goodbye, we disconnect and I wonder about that comment she'd made, about me bringing Kace back around. Back around from what? His parents' death? That was years ago though, and it just doesn't seem right. He wasn't close to them, but our conversation from this morning comes back to me. *Some of that past you won't like. In fact, I'm certain you'll want to run away,* he'd said.

I wonder if that comment has anything to do with why he hasn't dated. I wonder so many things about Kace August.

Forcing my attention back to the security system, and the issues at hand, I haven't had time to even hit a computer key when the *actual* security system buzzes and I jolt as the front door opens.

chapter ten

Pushing off my stool, no weapon readily available, I turn to the front door, holding my breath. To my utter shock and relief, Nancy, who is supposed to be on vacation, enters the storefront, her long brown hair wind-blown, her pale cheeks pinched pink from the wind, and two cups of coffee in her hands. "Morning," she greets. "I brought you coffee."

I pant out another breath of relief, inspecting her perfectly prepped make-up that says she's here to work. "I thought you were on vacation?"

"Okay, that was like two weeks ago, Aria. You're scaring me right now. Obviously with Gio gone, you're overwhelmed and it's a good thing I'm here."

I gave her the time off to keep her safe, and clearly not enough, I think, before I say, "I just thought I gave you more time off. Were you here earlier this morning?"

"Yes," she says, joining me behind the counter, and handing me my coffee. "I came by about half an hour ago to check the messages and decided to go and grab a coffee."

I'd be comforted by this announcement except she's standing close to me now, and she smells like roses. It's a delicate, subtle smell, not the same sharp, sweet smell that had greeted me earlier. I accept the cup. "White mocha," she declares as I do, and her eyes go wide. "Oh my God. What happened to your hand?"

"It's a long story," I say, "but I'm fine. You need to go home."

"Not with your hand all bandaged up. No. Absolutely not. Now," she says, pulling up a stool. "Tell me the story. How'd you get hurt?"

I know Nancy. Once her jaw is set hard, there's no getting her to budge. She's not leaving and if Gio's alive, and I believe he is, I could also use her help generating revenue anyway. I concede and offer her the short version of my mishap. "I cut it on a piece of wood that might have had a nail in it." I change the subject. "Was the security system on when you arrived?"

"Yes," she says. "Why?"

"I just wasn't sure I put it on." I indicated my hand. "I wasn't exactly myself." As expected, this leads to more questions about my hand, but it avoids topics of safety and security, as I'd hoped. We chit-chat for a few minutes and I get her started calling around to hunt down bottles of wine before I head back upstairs to grab my MacBook that I'd forgotten up there. Once inside my apartment, I pause and inhale, looking for that sweet scent I'd smelled downstairs, but find nothing.

Returning back downstairs, I find no hint of that smell and once I'm in my office behind my desk, I can't seem to dismiss it as my imagination. I pull up the security feed and start tabbing through it. To my surprise, there's a random three minutes blacked out at seven AM, which could be when Kace left but that feels too early, though I never checked the time. Seven just doesn't feel right, though, and why would Kace blackout the feed? Confused and concerned, I tab further into the feed and find Kace leaving at nearly eight. Maybe the blackout was a power outage. This building is old.

Nancy buzzes me with a client call I take, followed by another, but I never stop tabbing through the feed.

I've just finished a promising call with a lead on high-dollar wine when the feed catches my eye again. I straighten, a chill running down my spine. There's another dead spot in the security feed, for three minutes again, but the timestamp is what sets me on edge. I grab my cell and check the time of the missed call. Three-eleven. I then check the time of the dead spot on the security feed. Three-eighteen.

A chill runs down my spine. Was someone here when that call was made? I swallow hard, thinking of the perfume I'd smelled. Could it have been Sofia?

chapter eleven

Two hours later, those missing spots on the camera footage still taunt me, even with my work in full gear. I've located a treasure for a client, a set of antique clocks she's been pining for, and while it's only a five-thousand-dollar commission, it's a start. Unfortunately, the wine hunting is going slower than I'd hoped. I've found small jewels here or there, but nothing that will appeal to buyers like Ed and Alexander. I need a prize bottle to attract those kinds of high caliber collectors, and to ensure a pricey commission. And this is important to me now not just for the singular urgent need for a big commission. It also seems logical and smart to approach Ed about a retainer to replace the one Alexander offered me and that's my plan. A deal with Alexander is not a good idea and as panicked as I am in some ways, I'm not a rash decision kind of person. The problem is, Gio is not me. He would make a rash decision. He's seen the carrot and bitten it before he realized it had its own teeth.

About noon, Nancy sets a takeout container and plasticware in front of me. "Surprise. I ordered you lunch. I opted for your favorite mac n' cheese from Cindy's Diner, since it requires only one hand to eat."

"You're an angel."

She grins. "I know."

I open the plastic around my spoon. "When are you leaving?"

"So much love it's killing me." She pats on her chest above her heart. "And I'm leaving at the usual time,"

79

she says primly. "Two o'clock." She doesn't wait for me to argue. She disappears into the hallway and I sigh. She's stubborn and I love her. I wish I could do more for her, but right now, keeping her safe is my number one goal.

I open the lid to my mac n' cheese which looks like nothing but cheesy wonderful goodness and a million calories. But what the heck. I've eaten a cookie for breakfast. Why not pasta for lunch? It's not like I'm rolling around naked with the hottest man I've ever known and want to look good or anything like that. Okay, I am, and I do want to look good, but whoever said skinny tasted better than food was lying. Kace has a gym. I'll use it, but I'm not skipping my meal.

I'm three bites in when my phone buzzes with a text where it lies on the desk next to me. I do some maneuvering with my injured hand, manage to punch the appropriate buttons, and find a message from Kace waiting for me. There are two photos of two violins with a message that reads: *Charles Francois (pere) violin 1840 and a Lorenzo Carcassi violin 1743. What does it say that I wish you were here to see them with me?*

I'm filled up in the best of ways with those words and set my fork down to reply. After only a moment of hesitation, I dare to type exactly what I feel: *I wish I was there, too. I can't wait to hear you play them. And those violins, while amazing, are not Stradivariuses. They will be worth more once you play them. But then, so is any violin, in my opinion.*

Refusing to worry about a reply I don't expect, not in the middle of his meeting, I set my phone down and take another bite of my pasta. I'm just about to make that two more bites when another message dings. I hit the button and bring another message from Kace into view, another photo, but this one has me gasping and sitting up straighter. This one is a photo of an extremely rare Stradivarius violin.

I don't even think about what I'm doing. I dial Kace. He answers on the first ring. "Why did I know you'd call before I could call you?"

"Is that the 1685 Le Marquis Doria?" I sound breathless but I can't help it. I know this violin. My father and I talked about this violin right before he disappeared.

"Long lost and pined for," he confirms. "Yes, and color me impressed you knew that from one photo."

"It's a certain design in the wood," I say quickly. "Is it right there with you? My God, Kace."

"It isn't. My donor said the photo was sent to him with a promise it would soon be auctioned off. Starting bid of ten million."

I think of the formula, of our belief that it's hidden inside one of the long-lost instruments. Could it be this instrument? Did my father talk about this one for a reason beyond admiration? A hint of unease overtakes me at the timing of its appearance but I focus on one thing: a mission I need to fulfill.

"Can we see it?"

"I knew you'd want to. I want to. I'm working on it, baby. I promise."

"Kace," I hesitate, but only a moment. "There are reasons—there's—" My throat goes dry. "If I could see it, just see it, I would be so very grateful."

"I know how important each of the Stradivarius instruments are to you. I'll make it happen, but I have to go. I should be done in a couple of hours, maybe sooner. You okay?"

"Yes. Good. I'm good. I'm—so many things right now after that photo, actually. I can't wait to hear about everything."

"And I can't wait to tell you. Holy hell, I'll say it again. What are you doing to me, woman?" He doesn't give me time to reply. "See you soon, baby." He disconnects and I shove away my food. Kace, the violin, Gio—it's a mix of wonderful and scary that I can hardly manage to process. Could the Marquis really be on the grid again? And if so, why now?

My cellphone rings and I grab it to find Crystal's number on the caller ID. I take a deep breath and shove aside thoughts of the violin to offer a friendly greeting. "Hey, Crystal."

"Oh my God," she gushes. "I just heard about your hand from Kace. How are you?"

My takeaway from her question is twofold: her concern and the fact that Kace has been talking about me. I swear the man's seducing me when he's not even here.

"I'm better," I reply. "Thank you for checking on me. Kace took good care of me last night."

"Kace as a mother hen," she muses. "Who'd have thunk it?"

I laugh. "And don't forget the part where I said he was a very good mother hen, at that."

"I knew he had it in him. And you brought it out in him. I can't wait to hear the story of all of this. In fact, I was going to call and ask you to lunch tomorrow, but if you're not up to it, I understand."

"Of course, I am. I'm working today. I'm fine."

"Excellent. I have a lead on some wines, and I convinced Mark that you and I could work out a commission. That way we bypass Alexander, who is going to outbid you."

I'm stunned by her offer. "You did that for me?"

"I did it for both of us."

"You lose money if he doesn't outbid me."

"Maybe," she concedes, "but there is value to new, expanded partnerships and friendships. And I might have another motive."

"Motive?" I query.

"I still want you to consider working through Riptide. Don't say no. We'll start with some side deals. And friendship. Noon tomorrow? Can we meet here?"

"Noon tomorrow," I confirm. "And yes. We can meet there. And you are the nicest pushy person I've ever known."

"Mark would agree." She laughs. "It's a necessary skill as his wife for all kinds of reasons."

We say a short goodbye, and when we disconnect, I consider her push for me to work through Riptide. Perhaps the money she hints at might make it worth considering. Nancy could run the store, or not if I decide it's not safe. I just don't know. Maybe I could take her with me to Riptide. All I know for sure is that I have to think about funding our future here. We've gotten by rather than thrived for far too long. Besides, I'd like to fund the hunt for Gio, without taking Kace's money. Kace matters to me, perhaps too much, too soon. Some might say he came into my life at a vulnerable, even convenient time. But just as easily, some might say, I let that happen because I need him.

And that might just be true. At least, the part where I need him. Kace is becoming necessary, and that has nothing to do with anything but him and me. Us. I hope. Because I've decided to trust him.

chapter twelve

I finish my lunch with Kace on my mind. And thinking of him reminds me to call my gynecologist. By the time I'm sipping my after-meal coffee, the nurse at my doctor's office is on the phone, and after a few questions, and a hold for her to talk to the doctor, they agree to call me in my first-ever prescription for birth control pills. In a short time, Kace has changed my life in all kinds of big and small ways. And I am changing— a bird with her wings clipped who's flying for the first time ever. I can feel it happening, and it's not about Kace. It's about me. I was suffocating in captivity. I can't do it anymore.

Gio couldn't either.

And I don't know where that leads him or where it leads me, but I know it's too late to look back.

With that thought, I look forward. I get back to work, determined to make the money to survive and thrive, to hunt for him, to hunt for our destiny and our future, *with him*. I should never have allowed the divide between us to form. As my mother always said, we are better together than apart. I think of that carrot Gio is chasing and somehow that collides with the promise of viewing the violin Kace has just discovered with his donor. It's the only violin on the table.

And now I'm the one with a carrot.

I reach in my purse and pull out the business card Kace's agent, Nix, gave us or really he gave it to Kace. Kace gave it to me. On the back is a handwritten name and number: *Donelle Bianchini*. A man with a

Stradivarius violin to sell. A chance to find our family secret in that violin. A chance to make a fortune by selling it after I inspect it. His name is Italian, and this bothers me but if this is shady, it might also lead to my brother.

I grab my phone and punch in the number. He answers on the first ring. "Ciao," he answers, hello in Italian.

"Ciao," I reply and I shift to Italian. "This is Aria Alard from Accent Collectibles. I understand you have a Stradivarius for sale."

"And you heard this from who?"

I brazenly drop Nix's name. "Which violin is it?"

"The Fetzer, a brilliant instrument created in 1695."

"You have the Fetzer? It's long been missing. May I ask how you came upon it?"

"It's been a long-hidden jewel in our family."

"And you're parting with it now, why?"

"My daughter died last year. I have no one left to pass it down to. It needs a proper home. This isn't about money to me though I expect to be paid well."

"What would you like to get for it?"

"This is a rare find. I believe at auction it could go higher than fifteen million. I might go less if I feel the buyer will love it the way my family has."

"I have the perfect buyer."

"Would I know this buyer?"

"Kace August."

"*The* Kace August?"

"Yes."

"My God. Have you heard him play 'Caprice No. 24' by Paganini on a Stradivarius?"

"I have. And he's brilliant."

"The most brilliant violinist who ever lived. To have him even play my violin—I would die a happy man."

"When can we see it?"

"I'm in Italy. Can you come here?"

Alarm bells ring in my head. "When will you be in the states? Or will you?"

"I'm far too old for that trip, I'm afraid."

"I'll see what I can arrange. Do you have photos you could send me to show Kace?"

"Of course. Send me your email and I'll have my attorney forward them."

We chat a few more minutes and disconnect. I sit there a moment, pondering the conversation. He wants us to go to Italy. It feels all too convenient. But the Fetzer is a prize, a long-lost prize that I believe he undervalues. I consider calling Kace, but I know he's with his donor. Instead, I wait for the photos but not without a glance at my ring and the pull of my homeland.

It's nearly two when Nancy pokes her head in my door. "I'm headed out, but there's a really big, hot man at the front for you."

My first thought is Kace, but then she adds, "He's also kind of scary. He has a scar down his face and he calls himself—"

"Savage," I say, fairly certain he must be here to pick me up and take me to Kace's place. "I know him. He's a friend."

Her eyes go wide and she steps into the doorway. "Wait. What? Are you dating *him*?"

"No," I laugh. "Check his finger. He's married. I'm not dating him."

"He's a *friend*? Do people have friends like that man? Do women?"

"Yes, Nancy, they do."

"I guess," she replies.

"You're being silly," I chide.

"Is it safe to leave you here with him?"

"Very," I say, and there is only a tiny whisper of worry in my mind. *I don't know him well but Kace does*, I remind myself. I push to my feet and round my desk. "I'll walk you out."

We exit my office together and walk toward the front. Savage is by the front door, leaning on the wall, casual in jeans and a T-shirt that accent bulging biceps and thighs. "He's very big," she whispers conspiratorially.

"Sometimes God makes 'em that way," I laugh.

"Actually, not often," she says. "Too bad he's married."

Savage straightens upon our approach to a good six three-ish, by my estimate. "Aria," he greets. "How's it popping?"

"She's not popcorn," Nancy says. "Who says popping?"

Savage eyes her. "Mary Poppins for one."

"That's the corniest joke I've ever heard," Nancy says.

Savage gives her a deadpan stare. "Who's joking?"

I laugh, remembering his big personality to match his big everything else. I also now know why Nancy is single. "I'm popping just fine," I say. "What's up Savage?"

Nancy grimaces. "You sure you're okay?" she asks me, glancing between me and Savage.

"I promise not to kill her," Savage says dryly. "At least, not until I fatten her up for dinner."

Her eyes go wide. "Kill her? Dinner? Who says something like that?"

"Someone who likes his dinner fatter," Savage says.

I laugh. "Nancy, stop. He's teasing you. He's with Walker Security. He protects people."

"And sometimes kills people," Savage adds. "It's part of the job."

"Savage!" I chide. "Stop. She's a worry-wart. *Go home*, Nancy."

Nancy looks like she might argue and Savage adds, "I'll kill anyone that tries to hurt her." He holds up three fingers. "Boy scout's honor."

Nancy finally heads for the door, mumbling, "He was never a boy scout," under her breath. She opens the door to exit, but pauses, "I'll call you when I get home, Aria," she calls out, as if that tells Savage she'll know if I'm dead so he better not kill me. She disappears outside and shuts the door.

I laugh, pointing at Savage. "You're mean and bad."

"Only on Wednesdays."

"It's Tuesday."

"Well then, it's the wrong kind of hump day." He reaches into his bag and pulls out a folder, motioning to a wooden table. "Kace wants you to see something. Let's sit."

My brows furrow. "See something?"

"Yeah. Something. Let's sit." He walks to the wooden table between a couple display shelves and sits.

"Why can't Kace show me this 'something'?" I ask, claiming the spot across from him.

He proceeds to set photos of Gio in front of me. My heart skips a beat, and previous question forgotten, I reach for them. "What are these?"

"The photos you saw in Kace's apartment. We pulled them from your security footage because Gio's driver's license photo is horrible."

"He doesn't have a driver's license."

He slides another photo in front of me. And it's Gio's driver's license. Apparently, my brother's been living La Vida Loca a lot longer than I knew.

"Obviously, I was wrong." I glance up at Savage. "So you hacked my security feed? That's extreme."

"Kace was insistent he wanted a photo of present-day Gio and he expressed some concern that you might be in trouble."

"What kind of trouble?"

"He said that would be a topic for a later date. He had one goal for us. He wanted to see present-day Gio. He was nowhere to be found, which meant going back in time digitally. Which we did." He points to the date and timestamp. "The photos are dated before you met Kace. We were not following Gio. And yes, we have the skills to doctor the date stamp, but the feed is still on your security backup to compare."

I glance at the stamp and then him, focusing for now on what is most obvious. Kace wants my trust. He's trying to prove he deserves it and that matters. "He didn't have to send you here, but thank you for coming."

He studies me a moment, his jaw set hard. "That was the last time Gio was seen here at your building."

I dread the answer but ask anyway. "Do you know where he's at?"

"No," he says giving me the answer I did not want, "but," he adds, "if anyone can find him, we can."

Now *I* study *him* for a few beats, trying to read an impossible-to-read man. "What do you know?" It's a generic question but all I dare.

"Very little. We knew he wasn't around, but we simply bypassed that problem and got the job done. We weren't aware he was missing because we weren't looking for him, but rather his photo. Therefore, we haven't had the chance to dig deeper. At least not until we were informed you wanted to meet to discuss finding him. And Kace wants your approval for us to move forward with that process."

The chimes on the door sound and with the entrance to his back, Savage rotates to eye the visitor. I have a clear view myself as Alexander, in another of his expensive blue suits, steps inside, halting at the front desk. He must sense our attention, because his gaze shifts, flicks over Savage and settles heavily on me. "Just came by to check on you and chat a minute. Is it a bad time?"

"I'll leave," Savage says, pushing to his feet, and when I follow, he leans in closer, his voice low, for my ears only. "Choose your loyalty and do it quickly," he warns, making it clear he knows how Kace feels about me and Alexander. I think Savage knows a whole lot more about a whole lot of things than I know right now. "Kace already has," he adds, straightening. "If you want to continue this conversation, Kace tentatively set up breakfast tomorrow for us to do so with or without him. Let me know." On that note, he heads for the door, but instead of leaving, he halts in front of Alexander and says, "Alexander," making it clear he also knows Alexander. "Always looking so damn spiffy. Mr. Tall Dark and Pimping, my man."

Alexander smirks. "Funny seeing you here, Savage."

"No," he says sharply. "It's not funny at all. She's not yours. Don't forget that." That's all he says before he sidesteps Alexander and heads for the door.

I'm already at the front desk, and quickly call out, "Savage."

He flicks me a look over his shoulder. "Yes?"

"I *have* chosen."

He eyes Alexander's back and then me. "We'll see." He exits the building, leaving me with the certainty that he's about to call Kace and tell him I have company. And I just have to pray Kace really does trust me more than Savage does.

My attention slides to Alexander, to find his dark eyes watching me. "Savage doing security work for you?"

"Something like that," I say, quickly walking around the desk, and placing a barrier between us. "Thanks for all you did yesterday."

He steps to the opposite side of the counter, his stare probing. "How are you?"

"Remarkably well. I think the tetanus shot weighing down my arm has been the worst part of the day."

"They suck," he says, sounding surprisingly human. "I'm surprised you're working."

"Life goes on and I'm really fine. But really truly, thank you for yesterday."

His eyes take on a predatory gleam. "You owe me a bottle of wine. One we drink together."

And not so suddenly, I think, this is awkward. That's all there is to it. "How about one on your wish list?" I counter.

"You found one of my bottles?"

"I'm working on it."

His eyes probe. "Does this mean you're going to cash my check?"

My spine straightens. "No. I'm not going to be exclusive with you, Alexander."

His jaw tenses. "Kace doesn't want you to work with me."

"Kace doesn't make my decisions."

"He's rich and famous. He makes a lot of decisions for a lot of people."

My defenses bristle. "He's not like that."

"Isn't he? The man has a side you don't know."

"Don't we all?" I challenge.

"He has secrets. Things you need to know before you get hurt. Why do you think he wants you to stay away from me? I know those secrets. Let's go get that bottle of wine and I'll open your eyes."

"No," I say and not just because of the talk I had with Kace this morning. Because of my life and who I am. And just plain respect. "I'm a person who respects privacy, Alexander. And a person's right to expose whatever they want exposed themselves. Kace will tell me what he wants me to know."

"Aria, we are friends and I want to protect you."

"Alexander, I want to be friends, but please respect my boundaries. I owe you a bottle of wine for your help. I'm going to surprise you with a special find. Wait and see."

"Kace—"

"Stop," I say. "Stop or we aren't going to work together at all."

He inhales a breath and lets it out. "Fine. I'd better leave."

"Okay." That's all I say. Just okay.

He turns and heads for the door, opening it, but when he would leave, he glances back at me and says, "Ask him about Maggie. You'll want to know."

He exits and anger stabs at me. I now know the name. I can't un-know it and he knew that. I'm around the desk and at the door in a flash. I yank open the door and call out, "Alexander."

He's already in front of me. He never left. "I thought that would get your attention."

"I told you that I didn't want to know your version of Kace's secrets. They're *his* stories to tell. Yet what do you do? You still blurt out some name that you obviously think will lead me to bad places with Kace. Really, Alexander?"

"Aria—"

"Don't say another word. You showed me your character. I told you not to tell me anything."

"I'm just trying to protect you."

"Go, Alexander. We're done."

"You're clearly angry,"

"I'm furious."

"I'll call you—"

"Don't. And I'm tearing up your check."

He turns and walks away. And that is when Kace steps in front of me.

chapter thirteen

Kace stands there at the door of my store, looking imperfectly perfect, his dark hair mussed by the chilly wind. My gaze traces the hard lines of his face, reading the anger there that I'm not sure is for me or Alexander, or perhaps both. And God, he's just so Kace August, so ruggedly handsome and deliciously male in black jeans, a black leather jacket, and boots, his blue eyes fixed on me, his handsome face like stone. He isn't moving or speaking. He is unreadable and my heart is thundering in my chest.

"How much did you hear?" I manage finally.

"Enough," he says, and as if my words have shifted his mood, or perhaps the very ground beneath his feet, he steps toward me.

I back up to allow him to enter and he's right there with me, catching my waist, pulling me to him before we ever make it inside the building. "Enough," he repeats, his hand coming down on the back of my head, his mouth closing down on mine, a slice of sensual tongue stealing my breath. I moan with the unexpected, bittersweet invasion, sinking oh so willingly into the kiss, my arms wrapping his hard, warm body beneath his jacket, the scent of him—all earthy and masculine—as consuming as the feel of his hard body next to mine.

He walks me backward, kicks the door shut, and turns me to press me against it, his powerful thighs encasing mine. "Are we alone?"

"Yes," I whisper and he locks the door.

Suddenly, I need to make sure his version of "enough" really is enough. "Kace," I whisper, and when his fingers tangle in my hair, I say, "I didn't—"

"I know, baby," is all he says before his mouth closes down on mine again, and words no longer matter. How can they? His hands are all over my body now, caressing a path over my waist, over my breasts. I arch into the touch and I use my free hand to absorb the hard lines of his chest. He reacts, nipping my bottom lip, and cupping my backside, molding me firmly against him, the thick ridge of his erection pressed to my belly. "Why are you wearing pants?" he murmurs. "They're too damn hard to get off."

"It's cold outside."

"I'll keep you warm." He squeezes my backside and leans in to kiss me again when the door unlocks and starts to open behind me.

My heart races and Kace shoves against the door, holding it shut. "What the hell?"

That's when we hear. "Aria! Aria, are you okay?"

"That's Nancy," I say quickly. "She works here. She was here and left. She must have forgotten something."

"Nancy has very bad timing," he says, leaning in and kissing my neck, his breath a warm tease as he whispers, "I should be inside you right now."

My sex clenches and I press closer to him, tilting my chin up, offering him my mouth. His lips lower, so close to mine that I can almost taste him when he murmurs, "I missed you today. I don't remember ever saying that to another woman."

I am both shocked and pleased by his confession. "I missed you, too."

"Aria!" Nancy calls out. "Aria, I'm calling the police."

Kace pulls back sharply. "Calling the police?"

"Savage was here. He scared her."

His dark brows furrow. "How did Savage scare her?"

"He's an intimating guy, Kace, and she cares about me."

"Aria!" she calls out again and my cellphone starts ringing.

"That will be her," I say without ever reaching into my pocket to grab it.

He groans, lifts me off of the door, and opens it. Nancy rushes in the door and gives Kace a once over, her eyes going wide. "You're not Savage."

"No," Kace agrees. "I am not."

She shuts the door and her gaze slides between me and Kace. "He's," she says, and looks at him, "you're Kace August." Her attention returns to me. "He's Kace August."

"And I didn't know you were into violins, Nancy," I say.

"I wasn't until I started researching Stradivarius violins for one of Gio's clients and making a log of everyone who is known to own one." She eyes Kace. "That's when I found you on YouTube."

I blink, and after about ten stunned seconds, anger surfaces, barely contained. I officially wish Gio was here so I could scream at him. Or hit him. I'd hit him for sure. That's a sister's prerogative. He wasn't avoiding trouble. He was asking for it and I'm afraid he found it. I'm afraid we've all found it.

"And he," Nancy continues, pointing at Kace, "has not one but three Stradivarius violins. Do you know how expensive and elite they are? Who has three Stradivariuses?"

"An elite violinist who can do them justice," I say. "For instance," I motion to Kace, "Kace August."

"Yes well, I figured that out when I googled him and started listening to his music." She eyes Kace. "You made me love the violin."

Kace gives her a little bow. "Happy to hear that I brought you to the dark side."

She laughs, her cheeks flushed. "The dark side. That's funny. Please tell me we're helping you find another prize violin. I'm ready. I have my list."

Kace wraps his arm around me and pulls me close. "I have my prize."

Nancy's eyes go wide all over again. "Oh. I—" She motions between us. "You two are—and actually, Kace you have lipstick on your face." She eyes me and smiles. "You do, too."

Kace laughs and rubs his face. I don't laugh or wipe my face. I'm focused on that tidbit of news she just delivered. "When exactly did Gio have you researching violins?"

"A few weeks before he took off."

"Do you still have that list?"

"I do," she confirms. "On my MacBook, which is at home. I can email it to you."

"Yes. Please. Who was the client Gio had you working for?"

Her brows furrow. "Thinking—Sylvia. Or Stella. Or hmmm—"

"Sofia?" I supply.

Recognition lights her face. "Yes! That was her."

"Have you met her?" I ask, praying we're about to find Sofia, right here, under our noses.

"Not in person," she says. "I talked to her on the phone a few times."

"When?" I press.

"A few weeks ago, I guess," Nancy says, her brows furrowing. "Why?"

"On the store phone or your cell?" Kace asks before I can answer.

"The store phone." Her eyes land heavily on me. "Aria, what's going on?"

"Do you have her contact information?" I ask.

"No," she says. "She called in for Gio. Why?"

She called in for Gio and did so on the store phone, I think. To me, that says that she didn't have his cellphone. Their relationship started as business, be it legit or some sort of trap for Gio, is yet to be determined. "Can you tell when she called based on the dates you worked on the documents?" I ask, snapping me back to the conversation.

"I should be able to tell," she confirms, "but it was only maybe two times. She called Gio on his cellphone after that. Aria, *what* is going on?"

I can't keep avoiding her so I don't. "Gio got personal with Sofia."

She snorts. "Why does that not surprise me?"

"And," I add, "he's off running around the country with her and I need to reach him for about ten different reasons." I don't give her time to dig for more. "Send me the reports and estimate the timelines you talked to Sofia. I need to check the phone records."

She nods. "Is Gio okay?"

"Only until I get my hands on him," I assure her.

This draws her laughter. "Right. I bet. You two are always squabbling." She seems to relax and motions to the desk. "I'm back because I forgot my purse, by the way. Don't ask me how. I never do that. It's like I had to come back to look in on you and my subconscious did it, but clearly, I was wrong. You're pretty darn good from what I can see. Anyway, I'm going to grab it and head home. The neighbor has my son but she has a houseful of kids on her hands with her own. She needs me to hurry back home." And so, she does hurry. She hurries behind the counter. I follow to stand on the opposite side, across from her.

"I'm going to be traveling with Kace so I'll be away more than here. And," I add, "I'm in talks to form a new partnership that will be great for the store. For now, I need you to work from home."

Before I can blink, she's on this side of the counter, standing in front of me, lowering her voice. "What's wrong?"

"Nothing is wrong. Everything I just said is good."

She presses. "What partnership?"

"With a large auction house. And it could very possibly represent real, much needed, growth for us."

"Oh. Okay. I—guess. I hope." She frowns. "Are you sure everything is okay?"

I hate lies, but this one is about keeping her safe. "Absolutely. Now, hurry home. And get me that report."

"I will." She rotates but instead of heading for the door, she pauses directly in front of Kace. "You musicians break hearts. Break hers and I'll break you, well, if Gio doesn't beat me to it."

"Nancy!" I chide, shocked at her behavior but maybe I shouldn't be. She cracks a whip on Gio when he's here. "Kace I'm sorry."

Kace laughs and flicks me an amused look. "It's okay, baby." He returns his attention to Nancy. "I promise you, I would never hurt, Aria. If anyone is going to end up with a broken heart, it's me."

"Really? You're that into her?"

"Are you serious, Nancy?" I demand.

"I am, in fact, that into her," Kace replies.

I facepalm and recover to find her still staring at him. I'm about to just end this myself when she says,

"Your version of 'Bittersweet Symphony' is *so damn good*." And on that note, she steps around him and walks to the door. The minute she exits the store, Kace crosses to the door and locks it behind her.

The minute he turns to me, I say, "I'm so sorry about that."

"No need to apologize, baby," he says, joining me at the counter, where we both lean an elbow on the counter. "Friends are supposed to be protective of each other. But I didn't miss the obvious. You're worried about her."

"Yes. I need her out of the middle of this. That auction house stuff was real, though. Crystal wants me to do some work with her. And I might. I'll listen to her ideas."

"Crystal told me she was plotting to get you involved over there," he says. "How do you really feel about that?"

"I don't yet, and sorry, I'm jumping subjects right now. My mind is on Gio. We know Sofia must have talked to him on his cellphone, but I can't find his cellphone records. Or rather, I can't get to them. I don't even know his carrier."

"Walker can get to all of that information and quickly," he promises. "Which speaking of, how did you feel about the meeting with them, after talking to Savage one-on-one?"

"About that. You didn't have to send him here to prove you were telling the truth. I believed you, Kace."

"It was about more than that, but yes. I wanted you to know I told you the truth. I want you to know when I tell you something, it's the truth. How did it go?"

"I'm afraid to trust them. I'm afraid to not trust them. I'm afraid of pulling you into this and putting you in harm's way."

His hands settle on my waist, and he steps closer. "If you're there, I'm going to be with you."

My hand flattens on his chest. "You don't understand. They will come for me. I don't know who *they* are, but they will come. My mother always knew they would come. Maybe Sofia, maybe she was the beginning. Maybe she came for Gio."

"We don't know that. Let's not assume. We know how they met. That helps, but we have to trust Walker to help. I trust them. And when I talked to Savage this morning I told him I want only him and his boss Blake in on the first meeting. We need them to know just how tight we need to keep this circle. Okay?"

"Yes. Yes, okay." But I'm not okay. My mind is racing, a bad feeling in my gut. "She—Sofia—came to us looking for a Stradivarius. That wasn't an accident. And he didn't tell me. Of course, he knows I wouldn't approve. Our mother preached distance from all things music, let alone a violin. I would have freaked on him, but surely he knew that was weird, her coming her for a violin. And I—"

He leans in and kisses me, his hand sliding under my hair to my neck. "You're talking a million miles an hour. Deep breath, baby."

My hands go to his waist, the warmth of his body a comfort I have never known before he whisked into my life, riding the wind of a new season, I both welcome and fear. "I'm trying. He's my brother. I have to find him."

"And we will," he says. "*We will.*" He catches my hand. "Let's head to my place, open a bottle of wine, eat cookies, and decide what comes next."

"That sounds so simple and perfect," I say.

"It is, baby. It can be. We just have to make it simple."

I don't argue because I want it to be possible too damn much.

We head to my apartment for me to pack up, but Sofia lingers on my mind, the words which she'd written to Gio whispering in my head: *Come see me. I won't keep secrets any longer. I'm done with secrets.*

chapter fourteen

Kace plops down on my bed with a box of cookies, a rather surreal moment for me. This crazy talented, sexy, perfect man is not only in my bed, but very much in my life. "Finally something good to eat," he says, taking a bite of an extra-large sugar cookie.

I lean on the doorframe of the bathroom, practically right in front of him, in the tiny room. "Didn't you go to some fancy lunch with your donor?"

"Fancy translated to vegan," he says. "There was tofu. There was *lots* of tofu." He inhales the cookie and reaches for another. "Disgusting."

I laugh and walk into the bathroom, removing an overnight bag from a small closet. "Some people love tofu," I say because my room is so close that my stepping into the bathroom does nothing to douse our conversation.

"Do you?"

"No," I reply, shoving hairspray in the bag. "I'm Italian. I live for pasta."

"How about more tacos?" he counters. "You liked those, right?"

"Loved them," I assure him.

"You up for tacos tonight?"

"That sounds great," I say, feeling another surreal moment. When have I ever planned dinner with anyone?

"Tomorrow night I'll take you to a German spot I love," he says.

I laugh, packing my eye shadow palette. "You're determined to feed me spaetzle."

"You'll love it," he promises. "Not as much as these damn cookies I can't stop eating, but you'll love it."

The cookies remind me of Jenny and I walk to the doorway to watch him finish off what's left of one. "I talked to Jenny."

"She told me." He seals the box. "She really wants to come and see your store."

"I invited her to come by at any time. She wanted to come by tonight, but I was afraid you'd show up before she did and we'd be gone. Kace, she—well, she invited us to brunch Sunday and I wasn't sure what to say."

He stands and that's all it takes. One step and he's right there with me, his hand on the doorjamb by my head, his big body radiating heat. "Yes," he says. "The answer should be yes."

"They're your family and I'm—"

His fingers brush my cheek. "We're together, Aria. We do things together. And just in case you need me to even more direct—" His hand slides around my hip and splays on my lower back. "I want you to go with me. And they want to get to know you." His hand falls away. "Unless you don't want to go—"

"Don't you even say that." I capture his hand and press it right back on my hip and hold it there. "I do. We're new and I'm not used to this whole relationship thing."

"Get used to it. I'm not going anywhere." He leans in and brushes his lips over mine, his tongue doing a slow, silky slide across mine before he murmurs, "Capisci?"

I smile at the Italian word that in this case means *do you understand*. "I do. And you taste like cookies."

"I'd rather taste like you."

My cheeks flush and now *he* smiles. "Why did I know you'd blush? I think I need to give you a little warning, Aria Stradivari."

His words promise that warning will be hot and naughty and I happily take the bait. "Warn me?"

"I'm going to say and do such dirty things to you that you won't be able to blush any longer."

A low burn simmers in my belly. "If I let you," I taunt.

His lips, those brutal, sexy lips that I know will do many of those dirty things, curve. "Challenge accepted." He strokes my cheek and then turns me in the opposite direction. "Hurry." He smacks my backside just hard enough for me to feel the erotic sting. "We need tacos, stat."

With a curve of my own lips, I hurry forward, unable to deny the clench of my sex and nipples at that palm on my backside. I barely know myself with this man. I *am* a control freak, and yet the dominant, dirty side of this man, arouses me. I'm not sure what to do with that.

"Pack for the weekend," Kace calls out.

I abandon my bag and appear in the doorway. "The weekend? It's Tuesday."

"Exactly. Almost Friday. You might as well just stay the weekend."

I laugh. "It's *not* almost Friday."

"Close enough."

"I worry about being away from the store that long."

"Walker will have your place under surveillance the minute you give them a thumbs-up. Tonight if you want. But we'll stay here if you prefer."

"No," I say quickly, far easier than even I expect. "You need to have access to your violins to practice. And I like listening to you play."

107

Surprise flickers in his eyes and fades into warmth. "Then go pack, baby. I'll call Walker and make sure they have eyes on your place tonight."

"Thank you, Kace."

He winks and reaches for his phone. Mine buzzes with a text where I've set it on the bathroom counter. Thinking of the Fetzer, I rush and grab it, and I'm not disappointed at what I find. The text is from Donelle's attorney and refers me to my email for photos. I rush back into the bedroom. "Kace."

He's on the phone. "Hold that thought," he tells whoever is on the line. "What's up, baby?"

"I called about that violin. It's the Fetzer."

"Holy hell." He speaks into the phone. "I'll call you back." He disconnects. "Are you sure?"

"They sent me photos." I pull up my email and sit down on the bed, Kace is right there by me when I open the email and we both are instantly in awe. "Oh my God," I murmur. "It's beautiful."

"Where is it?" Kace asks.

"That's the catch. He's old. He can't travel. He's in Italy. And I was suspicious but now that I've seen the photos, you can't miss out on this."

"*I* can't miss out on this?"

"He wants you to have it. He's the last of his namesake. He wants it to go to someone who deserves it and when I said your name he was in heaven. You need this violin for you."

"Baby, I told you this was for you to make money."

"It belongs with you."

He studies me a moment, his expression unreadable. "Then I'll pay you the finder's fee."

"I'm not taking a finder's fees for a violin you found yourself. Not happening. Were you able to get a viewing of the Le Marquis Doria?"

"He'll be back Thanksgiving week. We can see it then."

There's a pinch in my chest at the idea of Gio still not being home by Thanksgiving, but I shove aside the thought and focus on the violins. "I'm excited to see them both. And on that note, I need to go pack." I stand up and Kace is right there with me, twining fingers in my hair, his lips near mine. "You really aren't about the money."

"You thought I was?"

"No, but I'm used to being disappointed and you are never a disappointment, Aria Stradivari." His mouth comes down on mine and the kiss that follows is dark and sultry in all the right ways. I'm breathless when our lips part and he turns me toward the bathroom. "Go pack, baby. I have plans for you tonight."

chapter fifteen

I'm standing in my walk-in closet that I'd insisted on when Gio and I built this apartment, fretting over my limited clothing choices when Kace appears in the doorway. "Don't forget you have clothes at my place," he says. "If you need something more—"

"I don't," I say firmly. "Thank you, though."

"Aria—"

"I'm with you, Kace, not your wallet. We, in fact, just had that conversation." I shut my suitcase and zip it up. "Besides. I was just trying to make sure I have everything covered that I might need. I have a business lunch with Crystal tomorrow, by the way."

"Mark and I need to talk through some things anyway. Why don't I see if we can make it a foursome?"

"I think no. Mark makes me uptight, for a lack of a better word."

"And he likes it that way, but if you're going to work with Riptide, you need to nip that in the bud."

"Good point," I concede. "I really do and I love Crystal. Surely he can't be with her and be the asshole he seems to be."

"Mark's complicated. I'll let you define what that means. I'll call him. And I talked to Savage. He can ramp up the surveillance here at your place. I'd like to tell him about that, the security feed, and the calls now. Let them see what they can find out."

I abandon my suitcase and fold my arms in front of me. "What *do* they actually know about me?" My hands go to my hips. Obviously, I have a little nervous energy. "I just want to know before I meet them."

"They don't know who you are, Aria. I didn't tell them. I kept my request limited and in a narrow scope."

"You had a lot of details about my family in that file I found." I try not to sound accusing. I trust Kace. I do. In my gut, I trust this man in ways I never thought I'd trust anyone, but I'm also afraid of that trust.

He steps toward me and sets my suitcase aside, his hand settling warmly, dare I say even possessively, at my hip. "I promise you, Aria. I was careful. I gave Walker a limited, specific task."

In earnest, I search his face, and I believe him. Still, I worry that he's opened the door to trouble, and that's not about fear. It's about birthright. "You understand that I have—"

"I do, baby. You don't need to explain yourself. At all. Ever. But I want you to think about something my father said to me years ago. It's a quote by Dan Montano. 'Every morning in Africa, a gazelle wakes up. It knows it must run faster than the fastest lion or it will be killed. Every morning a lion wakes up. It knows it must outrun the slowest gazelle or it will starve to death. It doesn't matter whether you are a lion or a gazelle: when the sun comes up, you'd better be running.'"

"All my life I've been the gazelle trying to outrun the invisible lion, Kace."

"And you think that's control?"

"It's the only way I had *any* control."

"Because that's what your mother taught you. My father was always the lion. And he made damn sure I knew you can only run so long before the lion catches you unless you catch him first. I don't disagree with Gio. Control is a façade when you're the hunted. We need to find a way to take control, really take control. Be the lion, not the gazelle."

"And while I don't disagree, there isn't just one lion, Kace. The people who would want that formula, even just to sell it, are endless."

"Agreed. But there has to be a way to ensure you're not the path to their payoff. We'll find Gio and then we'll find a way but we need help. We need Walker."

He's right. I know he's right. His idea represents a mammoth feat, but then so does running for the rest of our lives. And I'm no fool. I do need help. He's offering me help and someone he trusts is a blessing compared to a stranger I might have called on my own. I grab a small empty bag from the shelf. "I need to go to his office on the way out. There might be something there that will help Walker find Gio."

He smiles and grabs my suitcase. "Lead the way."

I point at him. "I'm not promising that I'm telling them who I am."

"You will. They'll win you over." And with that, he backs out of the closet, leaving me to think about those words. I don't have to think hard. I want him to be right.

chapter sixteen

Kace and I head downstairs and my path is straight to Gio's office and his desk. Kace props himself in the doorframe, watching me as I scoop up all the papers on top of Gio's desk and slide them into the shoulder bag I'd grabbed from the closet. Next, I open the drawer to my right where I'd found the evidence that he'd been diving deep into a hunt for all things Stradivarius. There's nothing here that feels helpful and Lord knows I've looked, and looked some more. Well, except for one thing. There is one discovery that feels important: I lift his desk calendar and remove the letter from Sofia.

I slide the letter into the bag, stand up, and turn, pausing as my gaze catches on the painting on the wall behind his desk: a famous church in Italy, but it's not the actual painting that has my attention now. It's the way it's tilted right.

Kace steps to my side, eyeing it with me. "What are we looking at, besides a tilted painting of an Italian church in your hometown of Cremona?"

My look is, no doubt, incredulous. "You know that church?"

"Of course. Cremona is home to your ancestor, the great Antonio Stradivari. I know everything about that city." He motions to the painting. "That's the Cremona Cathedral, baby. I visited it when I was there to visit your family. It's dedicated to the Assumption of the Blessed Virgin Mary. It's also the seat of the Bishop of Cremona. If I'd suspected who you are, that would have told me."

"Of course, you would. I warned him not to put it up. I told him mom was going to roll over in her grave, but he didn't listen. He claimed he needed something to connect him with home."

"In his defense, few people would know the church like I do by sight. The violin is my life and that visit to Cremona was memorable in ways it would not be to someone else."

I frown and settle my hands on my hips. "The painting is tilted. It wasn't tilted."

He eyes it and then me. "You think someone was in here and knocked into it?"

"Yes. I mean, it could have been Nancy, but why touch the painting?" I study it where it hangs over a credenza. "Actually, how would anyone even knock into it at all?"

"Maybe they moved the credenza?" he asks. "Is there anything worth inspecting inside?"

"He barely uses it," I say. "There was nothing worth seeing inside. I'm sure of it. And the safe is a full foot from the painting. It also has nothing to help us inside."

I glance over at him. "But there are a couple of dark spots on my security feed, as if someone turned it off. I know that could be a tech issue, but the timelines are weird."

He arches a dark brow. "Meaning?"

"Last night after we came in and this morning before you left."

"You think someone could have been here while we were in asleep?"

"It's a creepy thought, but yes. When I came downstairs this morning, I smelled perfume. It wasn't Nancy's."

"You're sure?"

"Yes," I say, without an inch of hesitation. "There was perfume in the air. I didn't imagine it. It was a sharp floral scent that lingered but the very fact that I could smell it means the person had been here recently. Clearly, my security system was no help."

"Which can be hacked but I'm wondering if Gio sent this Sofia person to get something for him."

"Or she knew the code and snuck in herself. I mean why would Gio send her and not come himself?"

"Maybe he's not in the city."

"That would mean he's outright avoiding me. And the blips on the camera were oddly timed."

"Walker can check nearby camera feeds. You need to tell them everything. Make a list in advance."

"I've also had a couple of weird hang-up calls. One before your first show I attended. Another last night around three AM. I never get hang-up calls."

His brows furrow. "Do you think it was Gio?"

"Why call and hang up? And the first call was different than the second. It seemed like someone was there, on the line for a few seconds. I actually thought maybe it was Sofia, but the minute I said her name, the caller hung up."

"And the second call?"

"Voicemail of just static before it went dead."

"You need to be with me at my place and Walker needs to be actively involved until we find Gio." His brows dip and he lifts his chin toward the painting. "Is there a safe behind it?"

"Not that I know of but apparently there's a lot that was going on with Gio that I didn't know about."

"Let's find out," he suggests. "If you don't mind me taking it off the wall."

"No, of course not. Please do."

I scoot back and lean on the desk while Kace lifts the side of the painting and rotates to face me. "I don't have to take it down. There's nothing there, but the hook is slightly pulled out of the wall. The painting's too heavy for the frame. That's probably why it tilted."

I grip the edge of the desk and nod, a stab of disappointment inside me. For a moment, just a moment, I'd thought we were onto something. I'd thought we were closer to finding Gio.

But I was wrong.

I'm back to Kace's comment moments before. "You said that if you already suspected that I was Aria Stradivari and you saw this painting, you'd have known you were right."

"Absolutely. And Aria and Gio aren't common names. Your mother should have changed your names."

"I asked her about that when I was old enough to understand the implications."

He leans on the desk next to me. "And?"

"She said she hit some roadblocks changing our names and didn't know how to get around them."

"I imagine she didn't know who to trust."

"Considering she trusted no one, I'd agree. She used her middle name. She had her birth certificate and no one she trusted to help her change her name in any other way. She never got a driver's license."

"Which is easy to get away with in New York City."

"Exactly. That's what she said. That's one of the reasons she chose New York for us to live. She's from Texas. She said New York was far from Texas and an easy place to get lost in, but unfortunately not an easier place to be poor."

"One of the most expensive cities in the country."

"Her plan seemed to work, though," I point out. "We came here when I was eleven. I'm twenty-eight. No one found us. Until Gio crawled out of the hole. Sofia approached him, not the other way around. You got that from the Nancy interaction, right?"

"Or maybe Gio went hunting and found her. He lured her to him and then away from you."

"And that means what?"

"She thinks she's the lion and he's the gazelle and it might just be the opposite."

This assessment brings me hope that Gio is alive and it also has me silently vowing to never, ever be the gazelle again.

chapter seventeen

Once we're cozy and warm inside Kace's fancy car, he glances at the clock. "It's almost six now. How about I order the food so it can be waiting for us?"

"My stomach approves. I'm actually starving." My phone buzzes with a text and I pull it from my coat pocket to glance at the screen. "I almost forgot. We need to detour to the pharmacy first. They just sent me a message to tell me my prescription is ready." I motion to the upcoming street. "Turn right here, please. The Duane Reade pharmacy I go to is a block up."

"Pharmacy?" he asks, casting me a worried look.

"Yes," I say primly, trying not to smile. "My doctor approved me starting on the pill."

"Really?" His eyes light like a kid in a candy store about to indulge.

"Yes. *But*," I quickly warn, "I have to be on it for seven days before we're safe to go without a condom."

He maneuvers the car onto the street I'd indicated and grimaces. "It's going to be a long seven days."

"It's one week. Only seven days of practice." I motion to the pharmacy. "Just drop me at the door. I'll run in and out."

He cuts to the curb in an emergency lane to let me get out, and I don't blame him. Parking sucks in New York City. "Are we talking about seven days of me practicing with my violin or you?" he asks.

My lips curve. "Both actually," I say, reaching for the door.

He catches my arm and pulls me backward, his hand catching my head as he leans over me, his mouth quickly next to my mouth. "Seven days of practice requires you to stay with me all seven days," he informs me before kissing me soundly on the lips.

I twist around to face him. "Are there cookies in this for me?"

"Every day if you want them. I'll call Walker and update them on everything while you're inside."

"Maybe you should promise them cookies, too?"

He laughs and a car honks. "Have to go," I say, opening the door and darting out of the vehicle, smiling as I do. Kace makes me smile. He makes me laugh. He makes me happy. And I don't remember happiness ever being a priority in my life.

I've just entered the pharmacy when my cellphone buzzes with a text. I grab it from my purse and eye a message from Nancy. *Oh my God, he's gorgeous and famous. And I need to know everything. I'd call you, but I know you're with him. Please have pity on me and call me soon.*

I smile yet again, with Kace at the core of that smile. She's right. He *is* gorgeous and famous, but Kace August is so much more. Damaged. Complicated. Sweet. Demanding. Too many things to discuss right now with Kace waiting for me. And honestly, I'm not sure I'm ready to discuss me and Kace at all. And so, I reply to Nancy with one word: *Tomorrow,* that at least buys me time before I head toward the pharmacy window.

A few minutes later, I'm talking to the pharmacist about how to dose my medication he's filled when the hair on the back of my neck bristles. My gaze lifts and cuts right, where I find a tall, broad-shouldered man, staring at me, part of his face hidden by a display. I stare at him. He stares at me. Now the hair on my arms is bristling, too, and my heart is racing.

Reigning in the fight or flight reaction threatening to take control, I warn myself not to overreact.

This could be one of Savage's men, I reason, but that's not what my gut tells me. Kace has only just given them a partial go ahead. He is *not* one of Savage's men. I know he's not.

He cuts away from me, out of sight, and my heart leaps. What if that man knows where my brother is? I have to go after him. I mean no, I don't dare approach him, that's not safe, but can I, from a safe distance, snap a photo of him or a license plate or something, anything that I can give to Savage to find my brother? I have to try. With my drugs in hand, I excuse myself from the pharmacist, cutting toward the man.

I hurry in the direction the man traveled, hoping I can catch him or see where he went. Or just get a better view. Darting around a corner I'm now at the endcap that covers several aisles, but the man is nowhere to be found, and considering he was quite tall, he's either ducked down or just gone. Maybe this was all my imagination anyway. Maybe Gio's disappearance and my deep-rooted need to control all that's around me, no doubt inherited from my mother, has me looking to take it to places where there is nothing to be found.

I rotate and run smack into a hard body, gasping with the impact and jolting away from the connection, only to be pulled into Kace's arms. "Easy, baby. I didn't mean to become a brick wall that all but knocked you over, but I saw you barreling down the aisle and was worried."

"I just—I thought you were waiting in the car?"

"The paparazzi are still on the hunt. They must have followed us from your place. We need to get out of here before you end up as their target."

A small degree of relief washes over me. That man wasn't about me or Gio. He was hunting gossip about Kace, which is a whole other problem for later.

"There was a man staring at me, but the minute he knew I knew he was there, he took off. I was concerned he might be somehow connected to Gio disappearing, so I tried to catch him and get a photo and see where he went, but he vanished."

Something I can't quite name flickers in his eyes. "You thought he was watching you and you tried to confront him?"

"Yes. No. No, I'm not that stupid. I wouldn't confront him."

His jaw clenches, his lashes lowering two beats before he steps closer, the very action protective. "It's your life I'm worried about. What if he would have been luring you somewhere to grab you?"

"I was in the store."

"Until you weren't, Aria. Gio is missing." His jaw sets hard. "I shouldn't have let you come in alone."

I frown. "Since when do paparazzi kidnap people, Kace?"

"We don't know he was paparazzi."

"You think he was here for me, not you?"

"I don't know and neither do you. Do you have what you came for?"

"Yes." I hold up the package. "I'm set."

"Then let's get out of here because they'll find us." I don't know if he means the press or someone else and he doesn't give me time to ask. He takes the bag and sets us in motion, but not toward the front door. We're heading to the rear of the building.

"Where are we going?" I ask.

"Ditching the press. I dropped my car at a hotel a block down and paid them to park it. Walker is picking it up and giving us a ride home." He cuts us down a hallway leading to the bathroom and directly to an exit, which leads us to an alleyway where an SUV is waiting.

Kace opens the door and helps me inside, before following, sealing us inside. He speaks to the driver who sets us moving. "I can't believe you just pulled that off in a blink of an eye."

"Experience and I was ready for them. I pay Walker to be on standby, especially now. The charity events got some press and I knew that would put me on the radar again. And I knew you wouldn't want to be in the press." His eyes meet mine and I know he sees the concern in mine when he adds, "The attention will fade."

And then return, I think, and I don't doubt that he thinks so as well, because it's true. We've *both* been hiding from the problem his career and my birthright represent. We are like two sides of a coin. One side is the two of us together soaring as beautiful and high as an eagle, with wings spread in the lift of a perfect wind. On the other side, we are the same eagle crashing into a turbulent storm riddled with unexpected blasts of hail. We can no longer pretend those two sides are only one.

We have to talk about this. We have to consider the risk to him and me alike, and we have to do it tonight. He knows it. I know it.

chapter eighteen

With what feels like a question of our future together in the air between me and Kace, I rotate and sink lower into my seat. The problematic mix of his career and my past is a topic we've avoided for a reason. It could be the end of us and we both know it. And perhaps selfishly, I don't want to let go of Kace. Minutes pass and awkwardly—when we are never awkward together—neither of us touches the other. I want him to touch me. I want to touch him, but there is an invisible wall between us. Perhaps that wall has always been there, but we had climbed it, scaled right over, and jumped right into all things me and him.

A good ten minutes pass, with traffic just one more obstacle to overcome in these turbulent few days.

Tension pulses in the air, or maybe it's more like a ticking clock with a heavy, exaggerated arm. A million thoughts charge through my mind, many of them warnings my mother spoke to me over and over, about not just protecting myself but others around me. She would not approve of Kace August. She'd like him. She'd admire his talent. But she would not approve of a man that is a poster child for the world I'm never supposed to visit again. She'd claim he represents danger to me and me danger to him.

But I give a mental push to her assumed arguments.

I was eleven when I left Italy. The odds of someone recognizing me like Kace did are next to zero. Even if they dig around, my history is long and established right here in New York City. And Gio didn't accidentally find trouble. He went looking for it. In fact, after years of hiding, I think he welcomed it.

I don't *want* to walk away from Kace.

Almost as if I've spoken this desire out loud, Kace reaches for me and scoots over, aligning our legs. His touch sizzles through me, electric, and somehow soothing. That's the thing about Kace August. He, like his music, manages to be so many things at once. We don't immediately look at each other, but there is a magnetic pull between us. In unison, we turn to each other and the minute our eyes meet, we lean into the connection. His fingers tangle into my hair while mine twist around his T-shirt and our mouths collide in a scorching, deep kiss. A kiss that consumes. A kiss that both demands and gives in the same breath. We only come up for air, and reluctantly, when the vehicle halts. Kace strokes my damp lip, glancing over my shoulder to the window.

"We're here," he murmurs, his hand sliding down my hair the way he always does, tender and possessive at the same time.

He leans forward and speaks to the driver, his voice muffled before he shifts his attention back to me. "He called ahead. The door is clear. No press."

The driver flips the locks on the doors and exits the vehicle. He must signal the building staff because my door is opened by the doorman, a chilly air piercing the warm heat of the vehicle. I slide across the seat, and exit the backseat with Kace on my heels, his hand settling possessively at my back.

Steven, dressed in his blue official jacket, welcomes us. "There she is," he greets warmly, the lines by his eyes and gray at his temples, aging him older than I'd remembered. Fifty-something, I think today. "Please tell me you are on the mend," he adds.

"I am," I say. "Thank you for your help. I was a mess, I know. I barely remember what I said or did."

"You're better now," he says. "That's what matters."

Kace slides his arm over my shoulder. "Thank you, Steven."

Steven gives a tiny nod. "No thanks needed."

Kace guides me into the building and to the lobby, but instead of heading to the elevator, he detours to the security desk and the tall, red-haired man in the same blue jacket Steven wore behind it. I expect Kace to discuss the press and the security risk. Instead, he says, "Mitch, this is Aria Alard. I need to add her to my approved entry list."

My gaze jerks to his, and while there might be surprise in my action, it quickly transforms into understanding. He's still looking at Mitch, not me, but I know what he's telling me. We're not over. He's telling me we are not over.

"What do you need from her?" he presses Mitch.

I glance at Mitch, and inside his probing stare, I decide I'm not the only one surprised by this request. He recovers a perfectly stoic expression to flavor his tone as he greets me. "Good evening and welcome, Ms. Alard. Can I get a copy of your ID please?"

My heart thumps against my breastbone, and when I look at Kace, I find a question in those intelligent deep blue eyes: *what will I do?*

For him, I sense, this is about a commitment. Him giving it. Him asking for it. But for me it's not that simple, not that commitment is ever simple. I avoid showing off my ID for obvious reasons. But it seems that somewhere between the day Gio disappeared and now, I've decided owning my identity is far more powerful than praying it's good enough. And then there is Kace, whose name and presence, as cheesy as Gio would say it sounds, has become a healing song filling my empty heart. I reach in my purse, find my ID, and then offer it to Mitch. He gives it little attention, simply copying it at the mini machine right next to him. That copy stirs a hint of unease, but not enough to have me yanking it away from the man.

"You're all set," Mitch announces. "Just show your ID if there's someone here other than me."

"Thank you, Mitch," I say, and when Kace slides an arm around me, setting us in motion toward the elevator, all my unease slides away.

Once we're at the elevator banks it's not long before we're alone inside, on our way to his floor. Kace leans on the wall and folds me close, our legs pressed intimately together, and when I meet his stare there's a charge between us that steals my breath—but there is also a world of unspoken words between us.

The car halts, and he's holding my hand now, leading me toward his apartment, his private fortress, his kingdom, and he's sent me a strong message tonight. I'm no longer an outsider.

As if driving home that point, we arrive at his door and he places me in front of him beside the security panel, leaning in to kiss my neck, before he whispers the code into my ear. It's as good as being offered a key. "Punch it in, baby, so I know you remember it."

He's daring me into his world, asking me to step wider, longer, further. All things I would never have done in the past. All things no other man could tempt me to do. And yet he does. And I answer.

I punch in the code and when the panel beeps its approval Kace opens the door to allow my entry. With a rush of adrenaline and nerves, I step forward, aware of him behind me. I shrug out of my coat, hanging it and my purse on a coatrack, my actions meant to reinforce a message I believe I've already delivered: *I'm here. I'm staying.* Nothing that happened with the press or Alexander, or anyone else for that matter, has changed that. The door shuts and I turn to find Kace watching me, removing his jacket, and his eyes have darkened with something akin to a predatory gleam. My body responds, tingling with awareness while my mouth goes dry with the stretch of his T-shirt across his broad chest. Once his jacket is on the coatrack, we end up standing there, staring at each other. Almost as if all those unspoken words are too complicated but the pull between us is not.

There is a current in the air, crackling all around us, to the point that there must be sparks. My God, I can feel this man in every part of my body when he has not even touched me yet. My experience is limited, it's true, but no man ever came close to affecting me the way Kace does.

He moves first, one long stride, and I swear my sex clenches. That's the power of this man. I blink and I'm against the wall, his powerful legs shackling mine, his hand sliding into my hair, tilting my eyes to his. "We are not over. The damn paparazzi does not end us. You will not walk away over this."

"I don't want to walk away," I say, my fingers tangling in the hem of his T-shirt.

"You don't want to, or you aren't going to?"

"What I want is not always what I get."

"You are exactly where you belong. Say it."

"I'm a Stradivari and with that comes risks."

"Say it, Aria. You belong here."

"I'm where I *want* to be."

"Damn it, woman," he murmurs, his mouth crashing down over mine, his tongue a wicked slice of demand, his hand on my back, molding me closer. And just that easily, I am lost in the ache of my burn for this man. He believes he can protect me, but I remind myself that I must protect him. He says he won't lie to me, but he admits he has secrets. I'm conflicted with Kace over my anger, but unsure how to move forward, but oh so certain that I am a whisper from drowning in my need for him.

His hand slides over my backside, and he scoops me into him, the hard line of his body absorbing mine, the harder ridge of his erection pressed to my belly. And then, unbidden the image of that man in the pharmacy drags me back to hell and I shove on Kace's chest. "Kace, what if—"

"What if what, baby?"

His breathing is ragged, his breath a velvety promise of another kiss. "Something goes wrong?"

"What if everything goes right?"

"That's not who we are."

His hand caresses a path down my arm, a gentle tease of a touch that sends a shiver through my body until his hand covers my injured hand. "How's your hand?"

"Better. Why?"

"Just making sure I don't hurt you, baby, because it's time to be here, and present." He catches the hem of my blouse and drags it over my head, tossing it away. "And I plan to do whatever it takes to make that happen."

chapter nineteen

Kace's hand splays widely between my shoulder blades, molding me close, my breasts against the hard wall of his chest. "We're here," he says, "we're alone. Let the rest go. Let it all go."

My fingers curl on his shoulders, the heat of his body rushing over me. "I'm trying. I'm just—"

His hand cups my head and he kisses me, a slow slide of tongue seducing me while his fingers deftly unhook the clasp at my back. "Right now," he says, "we're exactly where we're supposed to be. You and me, together. Believe that."

"What if I drag you to hell, Kace?"

"More like you dragged me out of hell, baby," he says. "And I thought I was there to stay."

"What if I'm the devil in all the details?"

"Then hell hath no fury like a man chasing a woman."

"You aren't chasing me."

He leans in and kisses my neck, his breath a sweet, warm tease as he whispers, "Run and find out, baby." He drags my bra down, and then his fingers are on my nipples, arousal warming my skin and pooling heat low in my belly.

My fingers curl on his arm and I pant out a soft breath.

He shackles my hips, his powerful legs back to caging mine, his gaze doing a hot sweep over my naked breasts, his fingers gently, oh so gently, teasing one of my nipples. I suck in a breath, drawing in air, heat spreading low, a fan across my belly.

"What are you thinking?" he asks.

"You know what I'm thinking about."

"Tell me," he orders, working the zipper to my pants.

"You."

His hand slides over my face, down my side, over my hip, settling there, a flex to his fingers. *"What are you thinking about, Aria?"* he repeats, and it's not a question. I quiver inside at the erotic command, surprisingly enticed by this game he's playing, we're playing, and it *is* a game.

"You," I say. "Nothing but you."

Amber heat flecks in his deep blue stare and he nuzzles my neck before his lips travel a delicious path to my ear. "Where do you want my mouth?"

My sex clenches and heat floods my body at the bold question. "Kace—" I whisper and I'm not sure if his name is a question or a plea.

"That's not an answer," he says, and I am quickly pinned in his smoldering stare. *"Where* do you want my mouth?"

My belly trembles. "My mouth."

He leans in close, his lips near my lips, his breath a warm tease, that next taste of him just out of reach. "Just your mouth? *Only* your mouth?"

"No."

"Where else?" he presses.

My fingers curl on his belly. "Can I just be surprised?"

"You want to be surprised?"

"Yes."

His fingers twine in my hair, a rough erotic tug, that draws my eyes to his. "Then I have your permission to put my mouth anywhere I want to?"

"Is this a trick question?"

"Do I *have permission*, Aria?"

"Yes," I breathe out, impatiently now. I'm eager. I'm burning alive. "Yes you can put your mouth wherever you like, just do it. Do it now."

"What about my hands?"

"Yes. What are you *doing*, Kace?"

"Giving you something to think about." He releases my hair and his hands caress over my shoulders, teasing a path over my fingers. His hands fall away, and I crave their return. He's doesn't immediately give me what I want. He lets me burn. I reach for him. He presses my hands to the wall. "Wait," he orders.

"Wait for what?"

"Until I tell you to touch me."

"Don't you want me to touch you?"

"Do you want me to touch you?"

'Yes."

"Then wait." He releases my hands and presses them to the wall, his legs lifting from my legs. "What are you thinking?"

My lashes lower with the fury of my body's need. "That this game is dangerous."

His slides a finger under my chin, willing me to look at him. "Why is it dangerous?"

"Because I want to hurt you for teasing me."

His lips twitch. "Is that right?"

"Do you doubt me?"

"I don't doubt you one little bit."

His finger slides over my lip. "Better?"

"No."

His hands wrap my waist. "Better now?"

"Not yet," I say, breathless now.

He lowers his heads and licks my nipple. I gasp and when he suckles it, I arch my back and my fingers dive into this thick, lush locks. He heads lifts, his eyes burning amber, and when I think he might deny me his touch he doesn't. His hands slide under my waistline, caressing my pants down, my panties with them, and with remarkable ease on his part, I am naked and he's on a knee in front of me. His hands grip my hips, his lips press to my belly. I moan with the intensity of my reaction, with the anticipation of where his mouth might go next.

His eyes lift and find mine, and when I shiver, he gives me what I burn for. His tongue does a wicked slide over my clit but when I reach for him again, he suddenly stands up, pressing my hands to the wall. "I told you not to touch until I said so, and you agreed. There's a price for that. Always."

"I don't remember agreeing."

"No?"

"No."

"What are you thinking about now?"

I am not the me of the past right now. I have no shame, no inhibitions, but I do have wants. I do have needs. "About all the places you aren't kissing me."

"What else?"

"I'm naked and you're not."

"And who has control, Aria?"

"You do."

His hand is on my face, forcing my gaze to his, fingers closing around my hair. "No. *You* are in control."

"I'm naked, you're not," I repeat. "*You* are in control."

"No, baby. I'm not. You let me undress you. Did you not?"

"Yes."

"Did you want me to undress you?"

"Yes."

"I won't do anything you don't want me to do. No one gets to say what happens to you, but you, Aria. *Ever*. Me included. I need you to remember that. That's how you win. That's how you get our life back."

"If only it were that easy."

"It *is* that easy. I want to spank you. Can I?"

I blanch. "You—you want—" My mouth goes dry. "—to spank me?"

"Yes. I want to spank you. And if you say yes, when you are waiting for my palm on your pretty little ass, I promise you that you won't be thinking about violins and danger. You'll be wet and hot and ready, filled with anticipation. And then the pleasure comes wicked hot and fast. It's pleasure, baby. Only pleasure."

My fingers twist in his shirt. "I don't know."

"I know." His grip in my hair tightens ever so slightly. "What are you thinking about?"

"What you just said."

"Which is what?"

My thighs are slick, my nipples so swollen they ache. "You spanking me."

"What do you want, Aria?" Kace presses.

My backside tingles with the idea of his hand. "I seem to want you, in all kinds of ways I didn't think possible."

I'm over his shoulder before I know what's happened, and he's walking, while his palm rests possessively on my backside. Blood rushes to my head and my cheek beneath that hand of his. *Is he actually going to spank me?*

My answer comes when we enter his bedroom, and he lays me down on his bed, removes his T-shirt, and then and comes down on top of me. "One day," he says, "*I will* spank you."

"If I let you."

His really sexy mouth quirks. "Yes. If you let me." His voice lowers, roughens up. "Just not now."

I'm not sure if it's relief or disappointment I feel, but my reaction is forgotten quickly as he adds, "Now," his lips brush mine, "I'm going to make love to you, Aria."

The words pulse in the air.

Make. Love.

Not fuck.

Not have sex.

Make love.

I don't want to read into his meaning, and yet, there is no denying the many levels or the response he's stirred in me. Nor is there any denying the yearning inside me that I can't quite name. His lips find my neck and my fingers slide into the soft, dark strands of his hair, a shiver running down my spine. My feelings for this man are dangerously close to love, and I know it. I'm falling in love with Kace. Perhaps I have been since the day our eyes met in that restaurant. His lips caress over my jawline, my lips, down my neck and he inches lower, spreading my thighs, cupping my breasts. He lowers his head, his hair brushing my collar bone, his lips, tongue, and teeth teasing one nipple and then the next. And when he suckles, I moan and arch into those sweet pulls.

He's back then, kissing me, claiming my mouth only to deny me another taste, as he moves lower again. His hands are on my hips, his lips pressed to my belly, tongue doing a little tease that I feel in every part of me.

"Don't go away," Kace murmurs, but he does. He pushes off the bed, and I have to catch my breath from the loss of his body on my body. I sit up and he's already slid out of his pants and underwear, his cock thickly veined and jutted forward, a condom package in his hand.

My mouth goes dry at the sight of him, tall, broad, tattooed, muscled, powerful. This man is as much a work of art as his music. He tears open the package and I scoot toward him, taking it from his hand. "I'll do it," I say.

He stares down at me, his eyes heavy-lidded, a pulse of desire in the air between us. My hand wraps the hard length of his cock, and I watch pleasure slide across his handsome face. Leaning in, I lick the tip of him and then swirl all around. He groans and pulls back. "As much as I want your mouth all over me baby, not that. Not tonight." He snatches the condom from my hand and rolls it over himself.

The minute it's in place, he's taking me down on the bed again, the sweet weight of his body back on top of mine. He perches on an elbow, one hand on my face. My hand finds his jaw, the rasp of his whiskers beneath my fingers.

He leans in closer, our breaths mingling, a tease of a kiss yet to happen. The air thickens around us and I can't explain what passes between us in those next few seconds, but it's as if we speak a million words and say nothing. What I find in the depth of that silence is the truth I cannot run from. I'm connected to this man. I'm connected in a deep, powerful way, in a way that I never believed possible.

I crave him, every part of me craves him, but still, he does not kiss me. His hand slides over my body, under my backside, and his cock nestles thickly between my thighs.

His big body perched on his elbows, he presses inside me, stretching me, filling me. A deep thrust buries him to the hilt, and I moan with the feel of him, with the sensations lighting my nerve endings on fire.

"God, woman," he murmurs, and his voice is a low timbre, tight, a tremble in its depths.

And then finally, *finally*, he kisses me. His lips meet mine, his tongue stroking long, the taste of him all spice and man, etched with demand. He begins to move, a slow dance and sway, and when his lips part mine, he's watching me, his expression drawn tight with desire, and something else I cannot name, something that's like a sweet floral blossom, tender and sweet.

In contrast, he thrusts hard, his hand squeezing my backside, the mood shifting between us. His lips find my nipple, teeth scraping roughly. My next moan is swallowed by his kiss, and then we're bucking with each other, desperate to the point we might as well climb under each other's skin. I'm right there, almost over the edge, and I grab his hair, and not gently. He scrapes my neck with his teeth and I pant out, "Kace," so very close to tumbling over the edge.

A low, raw, hungry growl rumbles from his perfect chest, and his hand slides over my hair, tilting my head back, delivering my mouth to his. "You are mine, Aria. Say it."

I'm lost in the claiming of my body and the demand of his, lost in the moment, in the man. "Yes," I say. "Yes."

He lifts my hips, thrusts into me, once, again, driving, thrusting. The world fades, the room disappears. I could be floating in the air, and all I would know is his body pressed to my body. He doesn't stop and thank God for it. The power of him consumes me. He owns me and I should care, but I don't. Nor can I hold back any longer. My body spasms around him, sex clenching his cock.

He moans, the muscles of his shoulders and back tensing, and then he's shuddering, with his release. We spiral together and then sink into the mattress and each other. Kace rolls to his side and takes me with him. Our limbs are tangled together, our bodies warm and sated. He didn't spank me but did so much more. He made me see a part of me I'd never seen, a part with needs and wants, beyond survival.

The part of me that is still to my core Aria Stradivari, my father's daughter. And Gio was right. My father would never hide, nor would he approve of me hiding.

chapter twenty

Kace and I share his clothes.

We're now sitting on his bed, me in his T-shirt, him in his pants, while we eat tacos and talk about his upcoming charity events. I've just stuffed a taco in my mouth when Kace suddenly says, "You do have a perfectly sweet, spankable backside."

I all but choke as I try to swallow and Kace hands me the large drink we're sharing. I recover to Kace's mischief-filled stare.

"You did that on purpose. Why would you say something like that while I'm stuffing my face?"

He holds up his hands. "In my defense, I didn't mean to catch you mid-bite. Off guard, yes, mid-bite, no."

"Why off guard at all?"

"The same reason I got you naked in the hallway. I took your focus off the wrong things. In this case, being embarrassed."

I hand him the drink. "That was unfair play."

He sets the cup down. "Not intentionally, but since we're talking about a spanking."

My lips part. "Are we?"

"We are," he assures me.

"Which was your point."

"Actually, not my point at all." He doesn't expand on that thought but moves on. "I know you said you have never—"

"I haven't." I sound prim and proper because I am mostly vanilla and prim and proper. He's my only other flavor. I cut my stare before we both drown in my inexperience.

He reaches over and gently strokes hair behind my ear, a barely suppressed shiver sliding down my spine. "You hate the idea?" he asks.

I dare to meet his stare, and while I can't read his expression, I read his anticipation. I could retreat. I could play coy. I could dodge and weave but this is Kace I'm with. One of the many things that draws me to him is how raw and real everything feels with him when so little else does in my life. And I believe we get what we give. And so I dare to step outside the confines of my comfort zone. "No," I say, giving him my version of raw and real. "No, I don't hate the idea and I really don't understand that about myself."

"I'll take that as a compliment."

"A compliment?"

"That's right," he says. "It requires trust for someone who's a total control freak to even consider something that places you in a submissive role even for a few minutes."

My lips press together. "You think I'm a control freak?"

Laughter rumbles from that perfect chest of his. "Is that a real question?"

I smirk, but concede quickly. "Okay, I am."

"You *are,* and a chance to hand it over, in a safe place, for just a small escape, is underrated. Think about it. Just talking about me spanking you has you hyper-focused right here in this conversation."

He's right, of course. It did. It does. It is. "What do you get from a spanking?"

"Once you give me the control, I have the control. We are then sharing it by choice, a ball we've volleyed. But getting to why I brought this up, which wasn't about a spanking at all. I used the spanking earlier to shift your attention away from your fear. This is not something I have to have. It's not something you have to turn into a fear between us. Fear is our enemy. It's not about control. And control isn't hiding. It's not running from me or this world I live inside, Aria. It's your world, too."

As he does often it seems, he's managed to slide right into my mind and home in on what matters. I shut the lid on my takeout container and shove it away. Kace does the same with his. "I've been thinking."

"And?"

"Well, for one thing, I know that my mother meant well in every action she took. My father disappeared. She believed he was dead. She believed all eyes looking for the formula would turn on her, and endanger us."

"You don't think that's true?"

"Maybe. Probably. But didn't running send the message that she had something to run from?"

"I believe that might be true, but it doesn't sound like she had the resources to face the threat and defeat it. You do. You have me."

"We talked about this and I can't rely on—"

He arches a brow and challenges. "Me?"

"You know this isn't about you."

"Isn't it?" he challenges. "Trust isn't a group activity. I'm not going anywhere."

Easily, perhaps too easily, I'm reminded of how many people once were with me and now are gone. "Everyone says that until they do."

"One day," he promises, "you'll know I'm not everyone else." He presses his hands to his knees. "Now. How about I play some violin and you critique me?"

Just that easily, he snaps me out of the past, and settles me firmly right here in this room with him. "There's nothing to critique."

"There's always something to critique. Your father told me that, by the way."

And now I'm back in the past. "What else did he tell you?"

"That you would one day teach *me* a few lessons about the violin."

I blink in surprise. "He said that?"

"He did. Obviously, you wanted to play."

"I did," I admit. "but that was then and this is now. I listen to you play and I don't feel any urge to play at all. I feel the urge to relish in the beautiful man and the music the violin creates. In some ways, I feel like I'm discovering myself again, through you."

His hand slides under my hair to rest warmly on my neck and he presses his forehead to mine. "I still think you can teach me a few things. You already have."

"I doubt that."

"Then you would be wrong, Aria Stradivari." He stands up and offers me his hand. Oh how quickly times have changed because I don't even hesitate. Any question he could ask me with that action is a sure "yes."

A few minutes later at my request, he's playing Tchaikovsky's "Concerto No. 1" beautifully and I'm thinking about more than his music. I'd expected a man who is dominant, who wants to spank me, to tell me to trust him. Instead, he's showed me the depth of his character that is not all about power, control, and success, certainly not about a world that revolves around himself. He's stunned me by telling me to do what no one else has, and what I have never done in my life: *trust myself.*

chapter twenty-one

Hours later, Kace pulls me into his bed and his arms.

I settle into the hard lines of his body, and I don't remember a time in my life before this when a day drifted into a sense of belonging and peace. I don't even remember falling asleep. There is just a blink of twilight that wakes me up. Now, I'm on my side, with Kace wrapped around me from behind. A smile touches my lips and I close my eyes, but somehow the impending meeting with Walker Security pierces my mind. I will it away, and while slumber begins to seduce me, so does a memory. I'm suddenly back in time, back to the months before Gio disappeared, at least this time—

My coffee steams in a cup next to me, while the soft leather of my favorite brown chair in the store hugs me. A book sits in my lap, guiding me through the ins and outs of the most expensive comic books in the world, for a client meeting. A client I'm trying to win and to do so, I need to impress them with my knowledge and convince him that I'm the one to help him complete his massive comic collection. That means understanding a value which can be quite pricy. A Superman "Action Comics" #1 sold for three-point-two million dollars. I've decided I like Superman much more than Batman, and not because of the three-point-two million dollars. Batman's bad attitude and disappearing act remind me of my brother. He's been gone for three days. He's not taking my calls and while sure he's played the Invisible Man a few times in the past, he's never cut off communication in the process. I can't help but worry but then, it's probably a new woman. There's always a new woman. Or maybe there are several or a mix of old and new. A player's gonna play and all that stuff.

I sip my coffee and part of me thinks he's smarter than me. He avoids commitment by the necessity of our family name, but at least he does so in a way that doesn't leave him alone and cold in bed. I, on the other hand, am always alone and cold, no matter the heat of summer. In fact, I think I should buy a new mattress. It's my only companion. It should be a top-notch one. I glance at my watch, almost eleven. I was up at five AM to prepare for a breakfast meeting and that cold, lonely bed is calling me. I've just set my cup back down when the locks on the security system buzz. I straighten, certain this is Gio finally coming home. Either that or I'm about to be robbed by someone who knows the security code. I set the book down and the door opens, but no one enters.

"What the fuck are you doing here?" I hear Gio demand, his tone low, and gruff. This isn't a moment of jest at all. The door shuts again with him on the other side. I stand up waiting for it to open, not sure who he could possibly be talking to. A client? Someone he outbid on a collectible? A friend that isn't such a good friend that I don't know? Seconds tick into minutes, and I begin to worry, which morphs into pacing. I'm just about to head for the door and go outside to check on him when Gio walks in, his dark hair windblown, cheeks pinched with the mix of August heat and I suspect anger. He's in black jeans and a black jacket, neither of which I recognize.

"Who was that?" I ask.

"Who was what?" he counters, playing dumb, and I don't miss the thick shadow on his jaw that tells me he hasn't shaved since he left.

I fold my arms in front of me. "I heard you snap at someone."

"Someone who is no one you want to know," he says, immediately changing the subject. "Why are hovering in the lobby at this time of night?"

"Why are you incapable of answering your phone or text messages?"

"I lost my phone. I ordered a new one that should be in here in the morning."

"You didn't think about finding a way to contact me?" I challenge. "I was worried."

"I wanted to surprise you." He closes the space between me and him, halting in front of me, the sticky-sweet scent of perfume clinging to him and the air around him.

"You smell like you dropped your phone in someone's bedroom."

His lips quirk. "You would do well to do the same. It might make you relax at least marginally." He reaches in his pocket, to produce an envelope he hands me. I glance down to gape at a wad of cash and then back up at him. "What is this?"

"I wasn't just off fucking around. I made a large sale for the business. And on that note, I'm going to bed." He leans down and kisses my temple. "Night, sis." He steps around me and I thumb through the cash.

Rotating I call out, "What did you sell? There's at least fifty thousand in cash here."

He pauses at the railing and turns to look at me. "Seventy-five. It was a high-priced piece of art. The client wanted the deal off the books."

"Was the art stolen?"

"What the fuck, Aria? You know me. Do you think I'd steal something?"

"I know you wouldn't steal, but did someone else?"

"I didn't ask why the client wanted to deal in cash, but we're depositing the money and claiming it on our store ledgers. I'll log the deal on the books in the morning."

"That's not an answer."

"It is an answer. Be happy. That's a sweet payday we needed. I have a good feeling about the future." He heads up the stairs.

I stare after him, nervous about all of this—his disappearing act, the cash, and his behavior in general, but still, he's home. He's safe. And I love Gio, which is why I call out, "I'm happy because you're home."

He leans over the railing and gives me one of his big ol' Gio charming grins. "Me, too, sis. Me, too." He winks and disappears from sight.

I stare after him again.

Art.

That description stands out to me.

Our father used to call a magnificent instrument "art."

Please, Gio, whatever you're up to, and I know you're up to something, be careful.

I blink awake and sit up to the sound of Kace's violin coloring the morning hour with his beautiful musical notes. His music is art. His skill is art. His composition this morning of Paganini's "Caprice No. 24," is a brilliant work of art. It's also one the most difficult pieces to play in existence and he owns it. And for that reason alone, any other time I'd revel in this breathtaking way to wake up, but not now. I'm still too in the past, too in my memory of some kind of art Gio sold for seventy-five thousand dollars. He never told me what he sold. I pushed and he dodged. My lashes lower and I slide back into that memory. He smelled like perfume. The same perfume I'd smelled in the store the other night.

I throw off the blanket, and hurry into the bathroom, zipping through a short morning routine of necessities which include brushing my teeth and face. Not much more. I'm still in Kace's T-shirt when I hurry back to the bedroom and find my suitcase that Kace brought up for me last night, pull out my slippers, and then grab the bag I'd packed in Gio's office. Sitting on a loveseat next to the patio doors, I open the bag, pull out the letter from Sofia I'd found in Gio's desk, and read it again. Something about Sofia's words nags at me and I can't quite name why. Kace's violin goes silent and with the letter in hand, I hurry to the door, rushing down the stairs.

I find Kace's violin, but not Kace.

Certain he's in the kitchen, I pad up the stairs, and sure enough, Kace is there, fully dressed in black jeans and a black T-shirt, with his back to me while he pours coffee. Closing the space between us, he turns as I reach the island across from him.

"Morning, gorgeous," he greets, his blue eyes warm, while my cheeks are warmer with the compliment. "I'd say I hope I didn't wake you," he adds, walking to the fridge and opening it, "but we have Savage and Blake here in an hour, plus our lunch with Mark and Crystal."

My eyes go wide. "An hour? What time is it?"

"Nine. They arrive at ten." He returns and pours creamer in the cup and then hands it to me. "You were knocked out though, so I let you sleep." He rounds the island and pulls out two stools for us. "That's an Italian bean coffee," he says, indicating the mug as we both sit down, angling toward each other. "You were young when you left, but I thought it might give you a little taste of home."

My heart swells with his thoughtfulness and he watches me expectantly. I set the letter down and sip the warm, wonderful brew. "It's perfect. I don't remember it from home, but now this taste will always make me think of Italy."

We're close, our knees touching, his hands settling possessively, warmly on my leg and I can almost feel our bond growing. "One day," he says, "when all of this is over, I'll take you home, baby."

As if my heart wasn't full enough this morning with this man, he now has it overflowing. "I'd like that very much."

"Good. It's a date then, and I have a good feeling about where this meeting takes us today."

"About the meeting," I say. "I remembered something that may be important, Kace."

"Something good I hope?" he asks.

"No. It doesn't feel good. Not at all. Remember I said that there was a perfume smell in the store when the security system had those hiccups?"

"I do," he confirms.

"Well, a few months before Gio disappeared, he came home after being gone for three days. He handed me an envelope of cash, a lot of cash." From there, I recap the entire memory, the person he confronted outside. The reference to "art." The missing phone. "But here's the thing," I say, wrapping up. "He smelled like perfume. The *same* perfume that I smelled in the store the morning after you stayed. I'm sure of it. I can't believe I didn't remember it until now."

"You think it's this Sofia person," he assumes.

"I don't know what to think, but I believe someone was in the store. I believe it was someone who was with Gio those three days."

"And they didn't get what they wanted," he supplies.

"Exactly. Which is pretty disconcerting. Why are they here, looking for answers here with me, when Gio's at the heart of all of this? Where is Gio?" I slide the letter to him. "Read that, please."

He grabs my cup and sips before he glances down. He reads maybe a line at most and sets the cup aside, eyeing me. "I feel like I'm invading his privacy."

"Yeah me, too, but I still need you to read it."

He gives a quick nod and starts to read again. I have the letter memorized I've read it so many times. In my mind, I repeat Sofia's words:

When you touch me, I tremble. When I close my eyes and you're not here, I remember your touch, your hands on my body, your tongue on my skin. And when you kiss me, as silly as it might sound, I melt. I go places with you, do things with you that I never knew I could welcome in my life. But it's all about you. It's all about what you make me feel.

I know you feel that I've become your "reckless note" in the never-ending pursuit of a story you cannot leave without a proper ending. But that's just it. I'm part of this story now. I'm part of your story. And I never meant for any of this to happen. I couldn't know that we'd meet and the world would spin beneath my feet, and somehow ignite a million shades of beauty in my life. I couldn't know that I'd change how you saw, well, everything.

Please don't do this. Don't shut me out.

I don't know who I am without you anymore.

We will find the answers you need together. We will find your family "recipe." I wasn't lying. The answers you need can be found with me and at the Riptide Auction House. I promise you. Come see me. I won't keep secrets any longer. I'm done with secrets.
Love forever,
Sofia

I sip the coffee and Kace glances up at me. "That's an intense letter. I have questions."

I set the cup down. "That's how I feel, too, and I've read it about a hundred times. I thought the 'come see me' thing meant at Riptide, but that isn't the case."

"We'll talk to Mark and Crystal about her." I open my mouth to object and he holds up a hand. "We can do that without telling them who you are. And after you figure out how much you want to tell Walker. Because I think they need to be in on all of these things. Obviously, he busted her telling lies and maybe even fell in love with her."

That idea punches hard. "And I didn't even know her. He never so much as said her name to me." I press my hand to my forehead. "The divide between us these past few months was about his need to hunt our heritage. She replaced me in that hunt. And perhaps to his demise."

He rounds the island and pulls me close, stroking hair behind my ear. "Don't think like that. He's disappeared before and reappeared. "

"It feels different and maybe if I would have listened to him instead of shutting him down—"

"You didn't cause the divide. It just happened, baby. The past and family are pulling you both, and at the time, with two different perspectives in your minds. You know that, right?"

"I just want him to come home." I pick up the letter. "She's the answer. I know she is."

"Then we'll find her. One way or another, we'll find Sofia."

chapter twenty-two

Kace hangs out in the kitchen to make a few business calls while I rush through my shower and make-up, dressing for our meeting with Mark and Crystal in my go-to black slacks, heels, and a black silk blouse. Once my lips are painted pink and glossed, I grab the bag I'd collected of Gio's things and head downstairs. I'm halfway to the living room when the doorbell rings. Kace hurries down the kitchen stairwell and we meet in the center of the two stairwells in the living room.

"I'm nervous," I declare, catching his waist and leaning into him, some remote part of me aware of how easily I now touch him. I'm comfortable with Kace in ways that defy all my walls and worries. Walker Security is another story. "It's just Savage and Blake Walker we're meeting with, right?"

"Right," he confirms, folding me into the warmth of his body. "Relax, baby. Say only what you feel comfortable saying. I believe in Walker, but *you* are the one who matters here. You need to believe in them, too." He kisses my forehead and sets me away from him. "I'd better go let them in. We'll meet here in the living room." As if driving home his words, the doorbell rings again and he heads in that direction.

No less nervous than moments before, I walk further into the living room and sit down on a chair, letting the bag holding Gio's items settle by my feet. My mother's voice plays in my mind. *One reckless note can change everything.* Is this my reckless note?

I pop to my feet and step to the window, with a stunning view of the Hudson River before me. The entire apartment floats on water, delivering the kind of view any normal person savors, and yet this morning I've managed to remain oblivious.

Male voices sound, growing rapidly closer and I whirl around to find myself the single female in a room of combustible testosterone. All three men stand on the opposite side of the couch, lined up for my personal inspection. Kace is, of course, gorgeously male, while Savage is physically imposing. Blake Walker is no slouch either, though. He's tall, dark, and rather deadly looking, but good looking for sure, his dark hair tied at his nape. "Aria," he greets. "I'm Blake Walker. I'd like to talk to you alone."

He's managed to set my wheels spinning on an axle in about thirty seconds. My gaze jerks to Kace's in question. "You need to know if you trust him, baby," he says, "because *you* trust him, not because I do."

He's right. I give a quick nod. Kace closes the space between me and him, his back to the other two men, his hand on my hip, voice low. "I'll be in the kitchen. If you need me—"

"I know." It's a statement of trust. Our near break-up might have rattled us and our personal baggage created our own version of cages, but it also left me solidly planted in his life, perhaps more so than in my own.

"Good," he says softly, a small smile on his face as he backs away.

He rejoins Savage and Blake on the other side of the couch. "If he pisses you off," Savage says, "just kick him in the balls. It's his weak spot."

"Last I looked, you were my weak spot, Savage," Blake snipes back.

"Love is a weakness, man, but it's also a strength," Savage replies. "It's okay that you love me. Don't fear the love."

He and Kace fade back into the room and Blake shakes his head. "He's a piece of work but he's a damn good piece of work. Believe me, you want him on your team."

"He's grown on me," I admit. "I like how stupid and intimidating he is."

"You definitely got a taste of Savage," he says, rounding the couch to sit down in the center.

I know he sits to give me the power, but I don't care about power. I care about trust. I take his cue and claim the chair to his left. "Why are we talking alone?" I ask. "You clearly have a reason. What is it?"

"I won't talk in circles," Blake says frankly. "You're right. I have a reason but before I share that reason, I need you to understand my level of skill that has nothing to do with ego. It has everything to do with what I have to say to you."

"I'd rather just get to the reason, but I'm listening."

"I'm a highly sought-after hacker. Governments, private clients, and leaders across the world hire me for those skills. I can find things out easily that others cannot, but I always remind people that if I can find out, there is someone else who can, too."

My throat goes dry. "You know who I am."

"Yes. I know who you are." He leans forward, elbows on his knees, body angled toward mine. "Aria Stradivari."

I launch myself to my feet, my fingers curling in my palms. He stands as well, but without my urgency. "How?'

"Skill. I am not a danger to you, Aria. I could care two flips about the creation of the Stradivarius instruments. *I do*, however, care about people. You need help. I want to help."

"How do I know that I can trust you?"

"For starters, logic. I already know who you are. I'm telling you that upfront. To do otherwise felt like manipulation and dishonesty despite the fact that I knew it would set you on edge before you got to know me."

"Even if you don't want my family secrets, who says someone close to you won't?"

"That's a fair and valid question. I trust my men, but I still keep a tight team in situations of this caliber and I have had situations of this caliber. The reason I asked to speak to you alone is that I didn't know if Kace knows."

"He knows."

"That certainly makes things less complicated. Do you want me to bring him back in here now to join us?"

I think of the danger to Kace. I think of the ways he'll protect me, without giving me the chance to protect him. "No," I say. "No, not yet. Do you know where my brother is?"

"No."

"Do you know who Sofia is?"

"I hacked some communications between her and Gio, none of which were traceable."

"That's not good, right?"

"It represents skill and intent, but we don't know what the intent is. We also don't know if Sofia is an enemy or friend. That's unclear in the communications."

"Do you think Gio is in danger?"

"I think, to some degree, you're both always in danger, though I think some of that can be alleviated.

The how of that, we can talk about. Right now, we're living in the moment. We need to find your brother."

"And protect Kace. I'm worried about Kace."

"Which means you care about him. I get that. First things first, we need to establish trust. He reaches for his phone and hits a button. "References in your messages now." My phone buzzes in my pocket and he adds, "That's me. I linked you to a private server with extensive data, and references, on me and my team, for your review."

I grab my phone and confirm before I glance at him. "Did Kace give you my number?"

"He didn't have to. I can find anything I need on my own. If anyone can find your brother, I can." He motions in the direction Kace and Savage disappeared. "I'm going to go grab some coffee and let you think. If you want to continue this conversation, I'll be with Kace and Savage, waiting." He does just that. He rounds the couch and walks away.

I stare after him and then turn back to the window, but I don't see the Hudson River. Instead, I'm thrown back in time, thrust into a memory I'd shared with my mother. I'd been thirteen, only two years in the States when my school invited us all to join the orchestra. Mom had been home when Gio, then eighteen and in college, but living at home, had brought me home. *I burst into the door in excitement. "I want to play the violin, Mom! They invited me to play the violin at school."*

Mom turns from the stove to gape at me, her dark hair pulled back, the horror in her face exposed. She eyes Gio. "Did you know about this?"

"She's a kid, Mom," he argues for me as he'd promised he would on the way home. "Let her play."

Fire lights her eyes and her voice quakes with anger. "Are you serious, Gio? You know how dangerous any connection to our past is." She kneels in front of me and grabs my arm. "No violin. Ever."

"But I—"

"You will die, Aria. We will all die. People are hunting us. Don't you understand?"

"Jesus, Mom," Gio snaps. "Are you really telling her she's going to die? She's a kid."

"Who I love and want to live. This isn't just about you, me, or her. Which brings me to that girl I saw you with last night at the ice cream shop. This isn't just about you, me, or your sister. It's about the people we let close to us that could get caught in the crossfire. Don't be selfish, Gio. Don't get someone hurt because you were selfish."

I slip back into the present, but the memory of them fighting and me crying remains with me.

Kace is in the crossfire, and it's too late to change that. Perhaps the moment I fell into his arms, I created a reckless note, but it's done. I could leave, but to what end? I could insist I stay away from Kace, while Walker helps until I know he's safe. Or I could do what Kace would want, and just assume he's safe. Or even assume that it's too late to save Kace if I don't save myself and Gio, so I might as well stay by his side.

It's a critical decision, perhaps the biggest of my life. I know what my mother would do. I know what my brother would do, which is what he believes my father would do.

But this time, this is on me, all on me. I have to step forward in my own shoes.

162

chapter twenty-three

I've been conditioned to run.

I recognize this about myself. And I took enough psychology to be quite clear on how much humans are creatures of habit, even if that habit is self-destructive. There is a point, though, where we dare to walk in another direction, to face our fear of walking in another direction. And it's that time for me.

I walk up the stairs to the kitchen to face the unknown, but I'll do so with Kace by my side. That's the thing about two damaged souls who connect. Sometimes they destroy each other. But when the stars align, when the souls align with them, you heal each other. You make each other stronger. In my heart of hearts, I believe he makes me stronger. I dare to believe that I just might do the same for him.

Once I've completed the short climb, I find Kace standing behind the island, with Savage and Blake standing on the opposite side with their backs to me. As if he senses my presence, Kace's gaze lifts and finds mine, that connection between us punching me in the chest, and I know, *I know* in that moment, that I really am where I belong: *with him*.

Blake and Savage glance over their shoulders at me, and I quickly round the island to join Kace. He pulls me to him and rotates his body, placing himself between me and the island, me and the other two men.

"I wanted to come down after you, but I was trying to respect your space to make a decision."

I fall in love with him in that moment. Or maybe I fall *more* in love with him, is the better assessment. Because that's the thing about Kace. He can be alpha, protective, and even dominant, but chooses the times wisely. He gets me. He reads when not to push. He knows when to give me room to breathe.

My hand goes to his face. "I'm here. Where I belong, right?"

His eyes flash with surprise and approval, a lick of heat between us. "Yes, baby. Yes, you are."

"And so are they. We need them." I step around him to face the other two men. "I'm grateful for the help, Blake," I say, feeling remarkably solid in my decision, but then, I've felt myself shifting from flight to fight. "I choose to trust you."

"I'm glad to hear it," he says. "We won't let you down." In that moment, I understand Kace's trust in this man. There is something about Blake Walker, that screams of loyalty and honor that makes you believe any vow he speaks. "Let's dig in and find your brother. Let's start with facts."

"But first," Savage says, downing the contents of his cup, "coffee. Who needs more? I need more." He stands up, and walks to the counter, where the pot sits.

The interruption is oddly timed. I'm not sure if Savage is seeking a lighter mood he feels Blake failed to deliver, or what. Or he's just Savage, who wants more coffee and could give a damn about timing.

"Obviously," Kace murmurs in my direction, "he's been here a few times."

"Before a few of his concerts," Savage explains, appearing at the endcap with the pot in hand. "I keep telling him to stock up on some damn Doritos, but he never listens."

"Could it be that he doesn't want you to hang around?" Blake asks, his mood all jest. He's not upset at all. Maybe he, too, thinks we need to soften the mood. I am, admittedly, a bit intense. Or maybe he just really wants coffee, because he slides his cup in Savage's direction.

"Why the hell wouldn't he want me to hang around?" Savage demands. "I'm protecting his violin-playing ass."

Lighter mood achieved. I laugh and Kace also slides his cup in Savage's direction.

Once cups are filled Savage returns to his spot next to Blake and swigs his coffee. "The next best thing to tequila. After my wife, of course." He frowns. "And bacon." He goes to sip again. "And tacos. I do like my tacos."

"You left out pasta," I say. "I'm Italian. It's not respectable to ignore pasta."

"You cooking?" Savage asks.

"I'm eating," I say, and everyone laughs, but there is this group shift of mood, a seriousness taking over. "What I need from you, Aria," Blake says, setting down his mug, "is anything you think will help me find your brother and time to pick your brain, time I know you don't have today."

That leads to a back and forth conversation, in which he has me tell him a bit about Gio. I tell him about the way Gio bed hops, the cash deal that happened a few months before Gio disappeared, and Sofia, including showing him and Savage the letter I've stuffed into my pocket. Through all of it, Blake and even Savage, are unreadable. They listen. They ask questions. They are completely focused on what I have to offer.

I end my summary with the story of the perfume. "I told them about that and the calls."

"We pulled the security feed around your building," Blake says. "We didn't find anything worth seeing which tells me whoever was there, knew we'd be looking for them on those feeds."

"And the bastard knew how to hide," Savage adds.

"I need the time and date stamp on the calls," Blake says, and when I hand him my phone, he snaps a screenshot of the calls. "You already have my number in that earlier text but I'm adding Savage's." He slides my phone back in front of me.

"There was also a big giant man watching me at the pharmacy," I say. "It was probably the press chasing Kace, but I thought I'd mention it."

"As you should," Blake says. "Which pharmacy and when? We'll pull the security feed."

I give him the details and when I'm done, Kace jumps in. "Back to Sofia. We know she called the store several times."

"We've already pulled all the records from the store," Blake says. "We pinpointed a few scrambled calls. Same goes for Gio's cell which is no longer pinging."

"Which means what?" I ask.

"He could have dumped it," Blake replies. "I damn sure have mine on occasion."

"Or?" I prod.

"Don't go down that rabbit hole," Blake warns. "Let us do our jobs."

"What about that file from Nancy?" Kace asks.

"Oh right," I say. "I need to check my email. She was researching violins for Gio in an effort to find Sofia a violin. I think. I'm not really sure what Gio was up to, obviously." The email pulls up and I eye Blake. "I have it."

He slides a card in front of me. "Send it there."

I quickly do as he asks while Blake moves on to another topic. "Let's talk big picture. Aria, you and I touched on this in the living room. I want to brush over it just a bit more now. As long as you're running from your identity, you're in some degree of danger."

"Are you saying that claiming my identity is better?"

"I get why your mother hid, Aria," Blake replies, "but I wouldn't have let you do that had I been involved. Hiding says you have something to hide for."

I glance at Kace and we share a look of understanding. This is exactly what we just talked about. "We agree," Kace confirms, "but she had no resources. And right now, Aria's half in the shadow and half out. Where does that leave her?"

"In the future, I might suggest you come forward as yourself and do so safely," Blake replies, "and *there are* ways to do that safely, but not now. For now, stay the path you're on. Live life with caution and let us do our job. Until we can better assess the situation, use an abundance of caution. If you're going out, text Savage a head's up, but don't wait for a reply. Our team will be close and you'll be safe."

"And will your men know who Aria is?" Kace asks before I can.

"A few trusted men, yes," Blake confirms. "But we will keep it tight. I'll update you in the next few days." He looks at me. "If you think of anything else, call me or text me." He picks up the letter now sitting on the island. "Can I keep this?"

"Yes. There's a bag downstairs in the living room I want to give you as well."

We all stand up and head downstairs. I hand Blake the bag. "We'll go through everything inside and return it to you." He glances between us. "I know you two have a lunch with Mark and Crystal. Savage will escort you, but I'll drag the beast downstairs with me to give you time to talk trash about him. Not me, of course."

"Here's some trash," Savage says. "He likes the word fuck and his wife is all over him to stop saying it in front of clients. His wifey will be so proud of him today."

"Jesus fuck, Savage," Blake grunts.

Savage grins. "I made a hundred dollar bet with his wife that I could blow his perfect record."

"We're leaving," Blake says. "More soon."

They're in a half-turn when I say. "Wait," with a sudden realization.

They rotate back to us, and I shake my head. "I don't know why this didn't hit me until now. Denial, I think. Gio knows I didn't approve of him chasing the past. And he knows that if he disappears, I'd check his desk. I'd look for him. The letter blatantly told me that he's looking for a violin, he's chasing the past. He *wouldn't* leave that letter out for me to find."

"And this leads you to what conclusion?" Blake asks.

"He didn't intend to leave. Whatever happened was sudden and unexpected. He's in trouble. I *know* he's in trouble."

"Or opportunity knocked, and he seized it like a cowboy at a rodeo, he grabbed that bull by the horns," Savage quips.

"In other words," Blake adds, "sometimes one thing looks like another."

chapter twenty-four

When you need to take your mind off a problem, just hitch a ride with Savage and his fellow Walker Security buddy, Adrian.

Kace and I are in the back of an SUV with Savage and Adrian, who are sniping at each other in the front seat. Currently, they're jibing over who's more Texan. "You know, you might be a Texan, Adrian," Savage concedes after an Aggie and Longhorn football joke contest that Adrian won, "but you're a redneck Texan. One of those guys that stands on his roof with his water hose to get a better angle on his yard and falls off."

"Better spot to take my shot," Adrian says. "And you know, *everyone* hates a redneck until the zombie apocalypse."

Some might not think their arguing is professional, but to me, I approve. They feel human. They feel real. They feel like people who see people.

Their banter continues right up until we arrive at our destination, which is the same restaurant where I'd charged up to Mark's table, and first met Kace. "I'll follow you in and sit at the bar," Savage tells us just before we enter the restaurant, which only serves to set me on edge.

The minute Kace and I are past the door, I pull him to the side in front of an empty bench. "What don't I know?"

"What are you talking about, baby?"

"Why do we need Savage so close that he's in the restaurant during our lunch?"

"Until we get Gio back home safely, Walker is operating on high alert."

Until we get Gio home safely.

Never has anyone appreciated optimism the way I do in this man. "You're sure?"

"Positive."

"Okay."

"You sure?"

I smile. "Yes. I'm sure."

"Okay then. Then let's go lunch with the master himself."

I blink. "The master? Please tell me he doesn't make people call him that. Please tell me he doesn't make *Crystal* call him that."

"That's a story for later, but let's just say, he lives to be master of all. You get used to it."

He steps to the hostess stand, and I'm hanging back a few steps, but not so far that I miss the way the pretty blonde hostess does a double-take over Kace and then gives him bedroom eyes. Unbidden, there's a sharp pinch in my chest. Kace seems to sense my reaction, and he immediately reaches for me, wraps his arm around me, and scoops me nice and close. Somehow the woman manages to speak without biting her tongue. "Mr. and Mrs. Compton are already at their table."

"Where?" Kace asks.

"Rear booth, by the bar. I can take you."

"We'll find our own way," Kace says, turning us toward the dining room and leaning in close to whisper. "Brunettes have more fun. As in us."

My smile is instant and it's lingering as we approach Mark and Crystal. Giving me yet another reason to hold onto that smile, the minute Crystal spies us, she pops to her feet. The next thing I know, she's hugging me.

"So glad we're doing this," she says. "I'm excited to talk to you about some ideas."

She's in a pink dress and smells like amber and vanilla and new friendship. My life is filled with new and good, but I don't want any of this without my brother.

I shove aside the pinch in my chest and focus on the here and now. We all claim our seats and Kace immediately settles his hand on my leg, a dart of heat sliding up my thigh. Mark, of course, chooses that moment, to greet me with, "Ms. Alard," in his precise, judgmental way.

"Aria, Mark," Crystal scolds. "She's Aria."

Kace laughs and leans in my direction to say, "They really are the beauty and the beast, don't you think?"

I laugh now, too, and do so despite Mark's cutting gray stare. "I do actually," I dare.

Crystal grins and tilts her chin up to look at Mark. "You're the beast."

"I would agree," he replies, and his tone is dry but as he glances down at her for just a moment, I spy the tenderness in his eyes. He loves her. The beast has a heart, I decide right then. And of course, he must. He supports the charity work Kace and Chris do.

A waiter appears and with little debate, a wine is chosen and glasses are filled. Mark and Kace then begin talking about the earnings for the last charity auction. Crystal leans in closer to me and wiggles a brow, her gaze flicking to Kace and back. "How's it going?"

"Why, what do you mean?" I tease coyly.

Satisfaction etches her lovely face. "I knew it," she says as if I've just told her I was marrying Kace, which is a crazy thought that comes out of nowhere. And his hand on my leg, I think. His touch is like a drug.

"Oh," Crystal says, straightening. "I want to give you this before I forget." She reaches into her purse and slides a piece of paper across to me. "Those are the wines I have to offer right now and a few I could get if you have a buyer. I've listed the prices we'd like to get to keep them off the auction block."

I scan the list, excited about the offers. Even if Ed won't agree to a retainer, there's enough money here to help with Walker Security fees and carry me for a few months. Well, depending on the fee agreement with Riptide. I'm about to ask when Mark interjects. "Will we be seeing you in California, Ms. Alard?" Mark asks.

"Aria," I correct, feeling Kace's eye on me because I haven't actually confirmed my plan to go with him. "And yes," I add, squeezing Kace's hand and looking at him. "I'll be there."

"Good to know," he says, softly, a hint of a smile on his lips that melts me right there in my chair before I turn back to Mark. "I didn't know you'd be there."

"Now you do," he says.

"Fabulous that you're going," Crystal interjects. "And since Mark didn't explain, we own a gallery with Chris and Sara in San Francisco. We'll be holding one of the events there."

It's becoming quite clear that the three of them are close friends, but before I can explore that idea, the waiter is already back, urging us to order.

"The pasta is actually worthy of your visit, baby," Kace says leaning in close. "You'll approve."

Worthy of my visit. He's speaking of my heritage and it's surreal to actually claim that history. It's good. Everything with this man is damn good. "Spaghetti and meatballs for me then," I say, speaking to the waiter.

"We'll make that two," Kace chimes in, offering our menus to the waiter.

Once the waiter departs, Mark's attention lands on me. "Tell me, Aria. How do you know so much about violins?"

"Sounds like someone was wrong about a certain violin," Kace taunts.

He's right, of course. Mark was wrong about the violin and he obviously knows. Mark sips his wine and just looks at me. "The violin was a very good knock-off, Aria," Crystal says. "You actually saved our backsides. Our reputation is everything."

"How pissed was your buyer?" Kace asks.

"He took the violin, at a discount," Mark states.

Kace's lips quirk and he swirls his wine in his glass. "That's not an answer."

"He got over it," Crystal says. "And you, Aria, are the star of the moment. Mark says you have a client who spent time with the Stradivari family in Italy and he taught you to spot fakes?"

"That's correct," I say, but the bite of a lie to a new friend is a sharp one.

"Before the family went missing," Mark interjects dryly. "Which is—*lucky*."

"For you," Kace reminds him. "She saved your ass, remember?"

Mark's staring at me. "Did you know that the daughter of Alessandro Stradivari, the last living ancestor of Antonio, was named Aria?"

"I did, actually," I say, having practiced this exact reply with my mother about a thousand times. "My brother is also Gio. Alessandro's son was Gio."

"Really?" Crystal says, leaning closer. "How did that happen?"

"My mother's best friend was a violinist, who died tragically before finding any real fame. She was quite obsessed with Stradivarius. My mother named me and

Gio after the family to honor her. I admit to having a bit of an obsession myself with the Stradivari because of the names, which is how I bonded so readily with the client who taught me to validate the instruments."

"So much so that you did a better job than a woman who makes a living at being an expert," Mark comments.

He knows, I think, and the truth is, my story might have rolled off my tongue, but it isn't believable. I suddenly know why my mother said to avoid any connection to our past, which means the violin auction at Riptide. I stand out like a sore thumb.

Mark's gaze turns to Kace and then flicks toward the bar. "I see Bigfoot's following you around. Why?"

Kace must anticipate me running because he catches my hand. Never in my life have I hated being "the girl who ran" as much as I do now. That's not who I want to be. That's not who I feel like right now, either. That's not the person who honors my brother, who intended to stand and fight, not just for himself, but for me and our family heritage.

I don't know what to do about him knowing too much, but I'm not getting up. I'm not running.

chapter twenty-five

Actually, I do know what to do.

Kace bristles beside me, straightens, and I can feel him about to strike, no doubt in my mind to once again save me, but I beat him to the punch. "Savage is here for me," I say. "My brother's missing. Kace helped me make the connection with Walker, who is now helping me find Gio. Which brings me to how I came to that auction at Riptide. I found a letter sent to him by a woman that referenced the violin and the auction house. That's how I ended up taking the risk to expose myself and come to Riptide."

"Sofia," Crystal supplies.

"You know her?" I ask anxiously.

"No, sorry," she says, "but I remember you asking me about her." She glances at Mark. "Do you know a Sofia?"

"No," he says, his attention settling on me. "Did Gio do business with Riptide?"

"I don't know," I say. "The reference to the violin and Riptide gave me reason to believe they'd at least made contact, but I don't believe you had a Gio or Sofia on the guest list."

"Let me just double-check myself," Crystal says, pulling out an iPad. "I'll check the guest list right now for Sofia and Gio."

"They aren't on it," Mark replies with a certainty I don't question. If he knows, he knows. "That doesn't mean he didn't use another name. Do you have a photo of Sofia and Gio?"

"I've never met Sofia, but Gio, yes. Yes, I do." I grab my phone and key up my photos.

Crystal reports on her progress. "No luck. Sorry."

I slide an image of Gio between Mark and Crystal.

They both inspect his image and then Crystal glances up at me. "He's very handsome, Aria. I'd remember him. I've never seen him before."

Mark smirks. "Yes. He's very handsome. I'd remember him as well."

I blink at Mark and cling to sanity, which means anything besides the discouraging news they've just handed me. "Was that a joke?" I ask and glance at Kace. "Did he just tell a joke?"

"Hard to tell," Kace replies dryly. "He's a walking corpse."

Mark flicks him a look. "Says a man who hides behind a violin."

It's an interesting comment, one that doesn't just speak of a deeper friendship between these two than I'd previously recognized. Mark understands Kace. He knows the man beneath the rock star. I wonder how well. His promise that I will run if I know all there is to know about him, has me wondering if any of us fully know Kace.

"And I do it without a stick up my ass," Kace replies, his arm settling on the back of my chair. "You should try a few activities without that stick in your ass. For instance, sitting here at this table. I suspect it's painful."

My eyes go wide, but I swear Mark's lips quirk ever so slightly, as if he's amused, before he slips back into cold, hard Mark, and looks at me. "Walker runs our security as well. They have access to anything you need that might help, including the handful of approved guests that didn't show up to the event."

"I'll go down that list myself, too," Crystal offers, "and see if anyone stands out to me. My assistant, Lori Hamilton, helps out. I'll discreetly see what she has to offer."

Discreetly.

Because they know who I am.

We all know they know who I am, and so far, the floor hasn't opened up and sucked me into a hell of my own making. But Gio is missing, I remind myself. I have to be cautious. The formula would be priceless and for that kind of money, hell might open up and send its own army of demons to collect.

The food arrives. Italian spices tease my nose, and for a bit, the attention for all of us is on the food. After a taste, which Kace attends to with way too much interest, I grade the pasta as excellent. This earns me his charming smile and a kiss. A few bites in, Kace steals an opportune moment when Mark and Crystal are chatting, and leans in and whispers, "You handled him like the queen you are, baby. Well played. Well played."

I smile at the compliment, and shiver with the feel of his fingers on my nape, the touch teasing me in all kinds of ways and places. It amazes me how easily this can make me feel wildly inappropriate at my most tense of moments. I like this about him. I like this about me with him.

We both twirl pasta around our forks and with his voice still low, for my ears only, he glances over at me. "Based on my present thoughts, you should be blushing right now."

I grin and meet his stare, daring to reply with, "You should, too."

He laughs, a low, rough, sexy rumble that is almost as perfect as his music. Oh yes. I am feeling so very inappropriate right now. Which of course is exactly when Crystal decides to glance our direction, a knowing smile breaks on her lovely face. She then delicately clears her throat and straightens. "We should talk business before we run out of time." She checks her watch. "Oh yes. We definitely need to do this now. I have a meeting in twenty minutes."

"I'm all ears," I say, sliding my plate aside.

She picks right up where we left off. "Forty percent of our commission on the wine," she says. "If that works for you, I'll email you the structure, but it varies per negotiated terms with the clients."

"I need a negotiating tool with a particular client, so even without looking at the structure," I say, "I can make it work."

"I think you'll be pleased," she says, "and if this goes well for all parties, Mark and I have a proposition for you. We have clients that need us to move items well before auctions are held. We start mini private auctions by just calling known bidders or even hunting down new bidders. I do that. You do that, too, in your business, which makes us a perfect match. I'd like you to consider doing it for us. As a contractor to start, but we might have a more official, larger idea to discuss as well."

"*If* you do well," Mark adds. "I'm not convinced anyone can step into Crystal's shoes. Crystal seems to believe you can."

"Perhaps," Kace says, "because she saved your ass with that violin."

"She did," Mark replies, looking at me. "A feat that should have required years of training, not a crash course with a client."

"You know what I love about you, husband?" Crystal asks, glancing up at Mark. "Your extreme arrogance. It's so powerful. It really turns me on."

His lips quirk ever so slightly. "I don't believe that's an appropriate topic for the table, but if we must go there."

She smirks and looks at me. "What do you say? I could send you a list of items to give this a try."

Mark is a jerk. Crystal's wonderful. Gio's gone. I have to pay the bills. Opportunity is a blessing. And so I say, "Yes, please. I'll get started right away."

"Speaking of the violin," Mark comments. "Why did it have your brother's attention?"

"It had Sofia's attention," I say. "She had my brother's attention."

"That seems too simple," Mark comments.

But it's not simple, I think. Sex and women were always Gio's weaknesses. I'm about to reply when the waiter offers us dessert and we all decline. Mark reaches for the check and Kace doesn't fight him. Crystal's phone buzzes with a text and she gives it a glance and me a grim nod. "Our doorman, Harold, doesn't remember Gio or anyone named Sofia."

Unbidden, another dead-end stabs me with disappointment, but I manage a tight, heartfelt, "Thank you for trying." I set my napkin on the table. "I'm going to run to the ladies' room before we leave. I'll just be a moment." I don't look at Kace. If I do, I might get outwardly emotional when a quick freshening up will pull me back into check. I stand and catch a waiter. "Bathroom?"

He points to the back end of the bar, which requires me to walk past Savage. He rotates his stool around in my direction as I approach. "Bathroom," I tell him but I don't stop walking, half expecting him to follow. I hurry on my way, cutting past the bar, down the hallway, when Kace is suddenly there.

He catches my arm and turns me to him, pressing me against the wall, his fingers tangling into my hair. His masculine scent teases my nostrils and his mouth crashes over mine, his tongue doing this deep, seductive lick against mine that melts me in my shoes. The taste of him is passionate, hungry, *possessive*. I moan with the delicious assault, and when his lips lift from mine, he says, "You okay?"

"Yes," I say, and I mean it. I am okay. The danger was always present, but owning it and who I am feels good. *He* feels good, too. "I just need a minute to freshen   up."
He studies me a moment and seems to read that need as real. "Then I'll see you back at the table."

He releases me and then he's gone, and like his music, he's left me with the simplistic beauty that is Kace August. He hasn't told me what to feel, but he made darn sure I felt his presence.

I head into the bathroom, lock the single-stall room, and stare at myself, guilt stabbing at me. I'm living my life, expanding my horizons, being kissed by a rock star in a hallway, and opening business doors while my brother is missing. Maybe he's even dead. My phone buzzes with a text message. I pull it from my purse and find a strange number with too many digits. It looks like spam, but I click on it anyway. It reads: *Look for the daisy in the wind. Be careful or you'll end up dead.*

My heart starts to race and my gaze jerks to my daisy ring, a memory piercing my mind. I click on the number, but it's not a real number at all. I rush to the bathroom door, jerk it open and hurry into the restaurant. Kace and Savage are standing at the bar, and Mark and Crystal appear to have left.

One look at me and Kace heads in my direction and in a matter of seconds his hands are on my arms. "What is it?"

"This. Read this." I shove my phone at him.

He reads the message and I say, "It's not a real phone number. And the words, *a daisy in the wind,* that is something my father—"

"—used to say," he supplies, looking up at me, his eyes shadowed. "I know."

There is something in his voice, and beneath the shadows of his eyes. Something that radiates and overflows into me, and that I can only describe as tormented.

"What is it?"

"I'm the daisy in the wind."

chapter twenty-six

He's the daisy in the wind? I blink, confused. "Kace, I don't understand. *You're* the daisy in the wind?"

His jaw sets hard, the handsome lines of his face drawn tight. "It's something your father said to me."

"Right. It was his saying. We just said that."

The muscle in his jaw tenses. "He told me that I am the daisy in the wind. The only true daisy in the wind. He told me never to forget those words."

I search his handsome face, now all hard lines and shadows, looking for the answers he's not giving me. "And you think that's related to this message?"

"Yes."

"And it means what to you?"

"I don't know what it means," he says. "Not in this moment. Not in this context. I need to think." He motions Savage forward and I can feel the wall that's slammed down between us. He's shut down and I'm more than a little rattled.

"I need more than 'I need to think,' Kace," I say, rejecting his silence with a hard push. "What do you know that I don't know?"

His steps into me, his touch gentle but firm, palm resting on my hip, his voice low, for my ears only. "Let me process, baby. We'll talk when *we're alone*. When we get home."

I don't miss the fact that he's said *when we get home*, not when we get to *his apartment*.

I know enough about Kace August to know that everything he does has a purpose and he does nothing by accident. He's reminding me that I belong with him and the fact that he feels that need to do this is as unsettling as his silence. I'm back to, *what the heck does he know that I don't know*?

Urgency bubbles inside me, and I *want* to push him, but Savage steps to our side, and while I appreciate his protection, right now he's just plain, big, and intrusive. Kace places a step between us and hands Savage my phone with the text message on the screen. Savage glances down at it and then glances between us. "What does it mean?"

"It's something my father used to say," I offer. "And it means something to Kace. I just don't know what."

Savage's gaze flicks to Kace and whatever he reads there, he decides not to push him. He returns his attention to my phone, screenshots the message, and sends it to I don't know who. He then dials his own phone and says, "Adrian, we're coming out." That's it. He disconnects.

A few minutes later, we load up in the SUV, us in the back, Savage in the front with Adrian. Kace pulls me close, his hand possessively on my leg, but he's not looking at me or speaking to anyone. I'm not sure what to with that. Clearly picking up on Kace's mood, Savage operates outside his normal boisterous style. He doesn't say a word.

By the time we're in traffic, Savage is on the phone and I figure out that he's talking to Blake fairly easily. From there though, I try as I might to pick up details. The conversation feels coded, impossible to understand. Before the call is even over, Kace leans his head back against the seat and shuts his eyes. As much as I want to push him to talk, I know this is not the time or place. With forced restraint, I lower my head and shut my eyes and drift into the past.

I'm eleven, and it's a few months before my father disappeared before my life was turned upside down. I've just finished a violin lesson with him in which I failed horribly and ended up in tears. He'd called me heavy-handed and no matter how hard I tried, I'd failed. It's just me and him now, alone in a field of daisies, my white lace dress blowing in the wind. He'd placed a bow in my hands and knelt in front of me, and spoke to me in Italian.

"What do you see?"

"The bow. The daisies."

"We are the bow and the daisies."

"I don't understand, Daddy."

He turns me and has me face the daisies. "Watch the daisies blow in the wind. They are delicate and fierce like our instruments, like our family. They bend but they do not break." He rotates me again. "Listen, my little angel, and remember this always. When you feel defeated, do not break. Listen to the music in your heart."

The vehicle halts and my eyes pop open, my head turning toward Kace, only to find him staring at me. His blue eyes are flecked with amber from the afternoon sun but without a clue to where his mind lies. I reach over and press my palm to his face. He leans into the touch, his lashes lowering until he rolls into my palm and presses his lips to the center. The doorman opens his side of the vehicle and while the moment is lost, it's left me hopeful and eager, for our time alone. We exit the SUV and it's all I can do to endure the normally enjoyable greetings with the staff.

Savage is right there with us and once the three of us are inside the building elevator, he breaks the silence. "Blake will be here to discuss the situation in half an hour."

Kace inclines his chin. I, in turn, want to scream my objection at a meeting that delays my chance to have a real one-on-one with Kace. I do not, however, do so, as memories of my father whisper in my ear—a daisy, a *Stradivari,* is delicate but fierce. We do not scream. I glance down at my ring, a gift from my mother to represent my bond with my father and do so with the realization that she never fully understood its meaning.

We do not hide.

Hiding is not fierce.

Once we're at the front door of Kace's apartment, he stuns me by pulling me in front of him to indicate the security panel. Obviously, he wants me to open the door. He's continuing to drive home a point that *I belong here.* That I belong with *him.* Any other time, I'd revel in this message. Right now, I just want in the door and to get him alone.

I punch in the code, open the door, and hurry inside, shrugging out of my coat to hang it on the coatrack. Kace and Savage don't immediately follow, but I can hear Kace's indiscernible murmurs to Savage before both men enter the apartment. Savage shuts the door and locks up. Kace shrugs out of his coat and hangs it up. It all feels robotic and excruciatingly slow.

That is until Kace's big hand closes around mine, and he starts walking, taking me with him. My heart is racing, our energy like a bouncy ball, volleying back and forth between us. Wordlessly, he leads me up the stairs and we don't stop until we're in his office, where the vault is set-up.

"I'll be right back," he says, opening the vault door and entering on his own.

I stand there a moment or two, waiting, my heart still racing. I begin to pace and I can't take it. I enter the vault to find him standing next to a giant drawer that's open and built into a wall. He's facing away from me, leaning on the wall, chin to his chest, tension in his broad shoulders.

"Kace?"

He straightens and shuts the drawer before he rotates to face me. He crosses to halt just in front of me, the tension still in his shoulders also rippling along his jawline. "When I visited your father, I was with him for two full weeks."

"You were? I don't remember that."

"I do. Every day of my life, in some way, be it conscious or not, I know he's there. I connected in a way that I never connected to my own father. He was a man of honor. A man to admire. A man to aspire to please."

"I know. He was. I—miss him often." I touch his arm. "Tell me about the daisy in the wind."

"After only a few days together, he told me that I was the true daisy in the wind, the only true daisy in the wind and that I must not ever forget that. We wrote a song together. It was the first song I ever wrote and I promised him I'd never use it for profit." He hands me a sheet of music. "It's called 'The Daisy in the Wind.'"

I glance down at the song, my chest tightens. I read over the musical notes and glance up at him. "This is special. And it's going to make me cry because it's a part of you and him together, but I don't understand why you're as upset as you are right now."

He repeats the text message. "*Look for the daisy in the wind. Be careful or you'll end up dead.* Someone knows about the song. Someone knows I'm the daisy in the wind. Not 'a' daisy in the wind Aria. The message says, *the* daisy in the wind. Someone is trying to scare you away from me."

"He told me the daisies represent our family." I show him my ring. "That's why I wear the ring. I didn't know he called you the daisy in the wind. I wouldn't know this meant you and why wouldn't they just say beware of Kace?"

"I don't know. What I do know is that someone is playing a game with us. And our paths crossing again doesn't feel like such a coincidence any longer."

"What are you thinking?"

"You said your brother would never have left that letter for you to find. You also think someone has the security code to your building."

"Which I didn't change, I just realized, but where are you going with this?"

"I was always going to be at that auction," he says. "And once you believed your brother might be there, so were you."

My mind races with this possibility. "But why bring us together? To try to scare me away?"

"Maybe the same person who brought us together didn't send you that text."

"Who would want us together?" I ask.

"And who would want us apart?" he counters.

chapter twenty-seven

Who would want us together?

Who would want us apart?

Kace and I are still in his vault with those questions hanging in the air when the doorbell rings.

"I don't want that song given to Walker Security. I trust them, but I gave your father my word that I would show it to no one. I don't know why that mattered to him the way it did, but it did. You are the only person I have ever shown it to."

I offer it back to him and close my hands over his. "I believe you were supposed to show it to me just as much as I believe I'm supposed to give it back to you."

He studies me for a long few beats, an emotion I cannot name in his stare. "The drawer is unlocked and the song is labeled as 'daisy.'"

It's an obvious invitation for me to go into the files and pull that song out anytime I wish, but he doesn't wait for my reply. He walks to the drawer, offering me his back in the process, his spine remaining stiff, his shoulders as knotted as they were when I'd found him in here.

The doorbell rings again.

Kace rotates, and in an out of character outward sign of frustration, scrubs his jaw. "I guess Savage isn't answering the door. Let's talk to Walker and get them out of here." He heads for the door, but not without catching my hand and taking me with him.

I'm becoming accustomed to just how together we are, and it's both wonderful and scary at the same time.

Sometimes two people come together, but they are really only boats passing in a sea of possibilities, and they become nothing but a whispered wind, soon forgotten. I'm way beyond Kace ever being a whispered wind. If we part ways, I already know that my sails, and my heart, will be shredded.

Somehow he snuck inside me, settled in, and made me fall in love with him.

Once we're downstairs, we find Blake, and only Blake, waiting on us. "I sent Savage and Adrian downstairs," he says. "Sometimes too many voices drown out the ones I need to hear, which is yours. And I know you, Kace. You are not a 'many is better' kind of guy."

It's a statement that tells me that he and Blake have communicated one-on-one, and not just in passing. Blake seems to read my mind and he glances over at me. "I hitched a ride to Europe with him a few years back when I needed a cover story his events provided and learned a lot about him in the process."

"And clearly you really did," Kace says. "You alone is a good call today."

Fifteen minutes later, we're in the living room, with Blake and I perched on chairs with a coffee table between us. Kace is standing in front of the window with the Hudson River at his back and so far, we've told Blake everything about the note, the song, my father calling Kace the one true daisy.

"Let me get this straight," Blake says, leaning forward, elbows on his jean-clad knees. "You think Sofia's letter was a setup by her or someone else to bring Aria to you?"

Kace's hands settle on his waist. "I do. That's what my gut is telling me."

Blake glances at me. "What do you think?"

"Gio would know I'd check his office. He'd know I'd find that letter and if he wanted me to know about Sofia, he would have told me about Sofia. Therefore, there are only two options, at least in my mind. As I've said in the past, at least to Kace if not you, it reads to me like he left suddenly, without expecting to leave. Or now with this new information, perhaps the letter was planted. The question is why? Why would anyone push me into Kace's path?"

Blake eyes Kace and arches a brow in a silent question.

"I don't know," Kace replies, "but that text she got reads more like someone trying to get her away from me."

"So someone pushed her to you, and someone wants to pull her away," Blake says, seeming to think out loud. His lips press together. "Hmmm. Unless it's the same person with an agenda we don't understand, but I don't think so. I buy into the two different someones more than I do the latter." He looks between us. "Let's backtrack. Let's start with what we know."

Kace sits down next to me on the chair. "Obviously, it's someone who knows I spent that time with her father."

"And someone who knows he called you the one true daisy," I add.

"No one knows that," Kace argues. "Just me and your father."

"What about Gio?" Blake suggests. "Wasn't he there, too?"

"He was," Kace agrees, "but he was never present when I was with her father."

"Maybe her father told him about his time with you," Blake offers.

"Gio doesn't even play an instrument," I say. "He didn't ever *want* to play. He wanted to learn the business side of violin-making. Which to point out: Kace's training wouldn't have been a topic my father and Gio would have discussed."

"You can't know that," Blake says. "You are assuming and we can't afford to assume. That said, anyone close to your father, or even Kace, who had handlers and security, might have picked up on something between them. And as we all know, the formula is a priceless commodity."

"We wrote a song," Kace says. "*Just* a song."

"You know that," Blake counters. "Only you. And her father, who is missing."

"Who is *dead*," I say, my throat tight with those words despite the years that have passed.

Blake doesn't comment. He's focused on Kace. "What if Gio thinks you have the formula? His father did call you the one real daisy. Maybe that's some sort of code for the keeper of the formula."

Kace grimaces. "He, or anyone else for that matter, can't possibly believe his father gave a sixteen-year-old stranger a formula."

"Sometimes a stranger is safer than those close to you," Blake replies. "And you were never a normal kid or teenager. Think about it. This gives us a reason that Gio would want Aria to get close to you. That allows him to get close to you and the formula."

"He's not even here," I say. "He's missing. And my brother knows I'd kill him for pulling such a stunt."

"Exactly why he might not ask for the help," Blake suggests. "He'd set you up to give it to him."

"And yet I get a text message that's warning me away from Kace?" I challenge.

"*Is it* a warning?" he counters. "Digest the words of that text: *Look for the daisy in the wind. Be careful or you'll end up dead.* That could be instructions, perhaps from Gio himself."

I shake my head. "No. No, this is not Gio. I don't believe that. This is not how he'd communicate with me."

"Let's cut to the chase," Kace says, frustration roughening up his tone. "Where does this leave us? Can the text be traced?"

"It cannot," Blake replies. "Unfortunately, there's a wild array of ways to send an untraceable text. Which is why, no doubt, this came to Aria as a text. As for where this leaves us? It leaves me doing my job. There's an operation called The Underground. They treasure hunt and play a role in keeping the modern-day mob in check, which I won't get into. They're worldwide, but the leader of the European operation, Kayden Wilkens, is a close friend. If someone wanted to hire someone to find it, they'd eventually end up with The Underground. And since this originates in Europe, in Italy where he's based, they'd end up with him."

"You think my brother had gone, or will go, to him?" I ask.

"I think your brother wouldn't have a reason to go to him if he thinks Kace has the formula."

"We don't know that he thinks any such thing," I remind him.

"Fair enough," Blake concedes, "but I also don't think your brother had the funds to hire The Underground. They aren't cheap."

"He handed me a wad of cash," I rebut. "He could have cash I don't know about."

"Or," Blake replies, "maybe we'll find out that someone else, with or without Gio's involvement, funded the money to hire The Underground."

"Like Sofia," Kace suggests.

"Like Sofia," Blake agrees. His phone buzzes with a text and he yanks it from his pocket, glances at the message, and then back at us. "I need to run unless you can think of something else?" He stands up and sticks his phone back into his pocket.

Kace and I are already on our feet as well. "What's your take on Aria being in danger?" Kace asks.

"And Kace being in danger?" I ask, glancing up at him. "You're the one true daisy, remember?"

"Quite well," he says tightly, his lips pressed together.

"Nothing has changed," Blake says. "And if this is Gio we're dealing with, the risk is even less. He's not going to hurt Aria or risk hurting Aria."

"It's not Gio," I insist.

"I'm looking at all options or I wouldn't be calling Kayden Wilkens," Blake assures me before he eyes Kace. "Can I get a copy of that song you wrote with Aria's father?"

"No," Kace says, his tone absolute. "I promised Aria's father no one would see it. That man impacted my life. I'm not dishonoring his."

Blake's lips quirk. "And you wonder why he would trust a sixteen-year-old with the formula. You won't even give me a song." He heads for the door.

Kace and I watch him leave and when the door shuts, Kace turns to me. "You know I wasn't hiding the song from you, right?"

"Kace, you told me the minute you saw the text. I've only known you know who I am for two days. You didn't have the chance. And you didn't have to tell me

194

at all." I wrap my arms around him. "I know you would have told me."

He folds me close. "I would have. Aria, I promise you. I knew it would be emotional for you. I was waiting for the right moment."

"It's special, Kace. It's like having a piece of my father through you."

His expression darkens, his change of mood palpable. "What is it, Kace?"

He cups my face, studying me with such intensity it's as if he means to memorize every arch and plane. "I don't know how we came together, Aria," he says, a stark quality to his voice, "or why, but right or wrong, we're here now."

My hand goes to his hand. "What is this Kace? What are you saying?"

"Facts. I'm just speaking the truth."

Tensions curls inside me. "I don't understand."

"I know. Aria, there are parts of me you aren't going to like, parts that I don't want you to even know about."

"Why are you saying this now?" "

"Because I need you to know, that none of them have to do with your family or that formula."

"I believe you."

Tension ripples down his jawline. "You *won't* like those parts of me."

"Are you telling me or inviting me to find out for myself and make that decision?"

"Against my better judgment and because I can't walk away from you, I'm asking you to stay."

"Gio is not going to come back and convince me to leave, if that's what you think."

"I'm not worried about Gio, Aria. I'm just telling you that sooner or later you will have to decide to stay or go. I'm asking you to *stay.*"

I study him and I can see the torment splintering in the haze of his blue eyes. Something about that song, about his past with my father, has triggered him and I'm reminded of the cage he lives inside. Alone. He lives there alone. And even with me here, he's still alone, until I find a key.

And so I press my hand to his face and say what I feel, and what I hope he wants to hear. "I don't have to be told twice."

His mouth crashes down on mine and there is fire and torment in his kiss. There is hunger. There is so much hunger. Hunger that stirs hunger. I reach for his T-shirt, finding hot, taut skin over rippling muscle. He tugs it over his head and reaches for my blouse and soon his mouth and hands are all over my naked breasts and nipples. It's a frenzy of touching, kissing. Needing. One minute we're dressed. The next we're both naked, no taking turns this time.

In a blur of passion, we are on the couch. He is sitting against the cushion and I am on top of him, straddling him, sliding down the hard length of him, the Hudson River at my back, the man I know I'm falling in love with in front of me. I roll forward, resting my good hand on his shoulder, while his hand is on my head, dragging my mouth to his, dragging me into the heady rush of his kiss.

He caresses a path up my spine, fingers splaying between my shoulders, molding me close, the sway of our hips soft and sultry, sensations rocking my body. This is not just sex. This is everything. This is about this bond I share with this man that changes the way two people feel when they are naked. I know this now. I didn't know before I met Kace.

Somewhere amid the passion, the hunger shifts and becomes more demanding. I lean back, I ride him, and he watches me, his hot stare all over my body, my breasts. The taut, intense, aroused look on his face empowers me, but while I would rock and ride, he folds me into him, against him, and rolls us to our sides, molding my hips to his hips, and we end in pants and shivers. For long moments, we lay there until I feel the sticky dampness between my legs.

My lashes pop open. "Kace, I've only been on the pill a few days. We didn't use a condom."

He grabs a tissue from the table behind me and slides it between my legs, replacing himself with it, but he stays right here with me. He settles me on my back and him half on top of me. "It's been days."

"One day, Kace."

"You're not pregnant, baby." He strokes the hair from my eyes. "Do you *want* kids?"

"I cannot, I *will not* bring a child into this world only to tell him or her to hide and look over their shoulder. I can't do that. I saw how it tormented my mother."

"Any child of ours wouldn't have to hide. I wouldn't allow that."

Our child.

The words do funny things to my belly.

"They'd be my ancestry, Kace. We can't change the risk that comes with that."

"But we can. And we will." He doesn't give me time to debate. He sits up and takes me with him. "I want to play something for you." A few minutes later, we're back to sharing his clothes. He's in his pants. I'm in his shirt, sitting on the piano bench and he's holding his violin. "The song your father and I wrote together that I have never played for anyone."

His bow begins to move and the magic of his skill and his instrument fills the air. My hand balls at my

197

chest where emotions well. I swear I am instantly back in that field of daisies with my father, the bow in my own hand. I shut my eyes and listen to the song that is a mix of delicacy and fierceness, the same mix of delicacy and fierceness my father called our family. It's magical and unbidden, tears leak from my eyes and water my cheeks. I can feel my father in the music. I can feel Kace. I can feel my family, my history, my loves and losses, my laughter, and joy.

When the song is over, I'm standing in front of Kace when he lowers his instrument and his bow. I step to him and wrap my arms around him, tilting my chin up to look at him. "No one plays a Stradivarius the way you play a Stradivarius. I understand what my father meant. You are one with the instrument, a part of it, a part of us. You are the one true daisy in the wind."

chapter twenty-eight

The next morning, I wake to Kace's violin, and with a smile on my face, slippers on my feet, and a pink silk robe to my knees, I head downstairs. Kace is shirtless in sweatpants and for a few minutes, I just stand on the stairs, leaning over the banister, drinking in the sight of his tattooed muscular body, his gorgeous everything, really, while luxuriating in his music. He never looks up, but I know he knows I'm here.

A few minutes later, I head to the kitchen and make coffee. When the pot is done, he joins me and it feels like the making of a routine. Of course, I won't be here forever, but for now, it's wonderful.

"Some women would have a problem with me playing in the mornings," he says accepting the cup of steaming brew I offer him.

"Smart women would kill to watch you half-naked playing that violin. And I consider myself quite smart right about now. I love it."

His eyes burn. "You love it?"

"I do," I say freely, sipping my coffee. "Very much, Kace."

"I'm glad you do."

We sit at the island and review the pictures of the Fetzer violin on my MacBook, both of us studying them in great detail. "It looks good, Kace. It really does."

"I'll talk to Nix." He grabs his phone and makes the call. A few minutes later, he says, "The lead came to him from a friend of a friend because they knew I was his client. He can't vouch for our seller, but he'll help

Walker look into him. I'm shooting Blake a text." He keys in the message and sets his phone down. "We couldn't even think about going for a few weeks. Not with the California events coming up. Can you buy us time?"

"He wants this violin to go to you, Kace. He wants the perfect buyer which I'm trying not to think of as convenient. Or too good to be true. You are Kace August. And bottom line: we just need to tell him when we'll be there."

"We're getting Walker involved. In the meantime, ask when in November or December he can see us."

"Okay." I type a message to the attorney who sent me the photos. "Done." I close my computer and sip my coffee.

"Do you have a passport?"

"Believe it or not I do. My mother believed we needed an escape route out of the country. I know it's not a logical move for a woman who wouldn't even get a driver's license, but it was nevertheless just what she did."

"Then we're set for Italy and Paris."

"I can't believe I might really do this."

"But you are," he says.

"Maybe," I say, and I don't miss the wistful quality in my voice. "It would be crazy to see my home again but painful. Good and bad memories. You know?"

"I do know. You know I know. I was in Greece when I found out about my sister. I've never been back."

"Never?"

"Never."

"The charity work you do must be hard at times. It must drudge up painful memories of her."

"Yeah, but I didn't save her. I owe her this and more."

I rotate more in his direction. "You were a kid. You couldn't have saved her. You know that, right?"

"I'm past most of the blame but I knew she was a troubled soul. A good soul, too. Really sweet to the core. She wanted to tattoo because she wanted to express herself artistically like I do. Sadly, Chris could have helped her get a real start, but she was gone when I met him."

"You two have a crazy amount in common."

"More than you know. His ex-girlfriend, who took her own life, was a tattoo artist."

I shiver and run my hands over my arms. "Okay. I just got a chill."

"I know. It's insane. You can see how Chris and I connected."

"I can and Sara is pretty wonderful."

"Is that right? I didn't realize you got to know her."

"She dove right into the friendship thing. She gave me advice about you, about being with men like you and Chris."

He arches a brow. "Like—me and Chris? Meaning what?"

"Larger than life, Kace. I know you know that's who you are."

"I'm just a man, baby."

"That's what Sara said."

"I think I need you to spend more time with Sara. What else did she say?"

"She said not to question, 'why me?' Because there was only one answer. The answer Chris gives her."

"Because you're you, Aria."

"Yes," I say softly. "But you know it's because you're you, too."

He catches my hands and kisses it, his expression softening, his knuckles brushing my cheek. "Aria, I—"

His cellphone rings where it sits on the counter next to him and he inhales. "Bad timing," he says, glancing at the number. "And it's Jenny, who always means well."

"Who loves you," I say, sipping my coffee, but I burn to know what he was about to say.

"Morning, Jenny," he greets, answering the call. He listens a minute and glances in my direction as he says, "Yes. She's here."

And now she knows I stayed the night, I think, but I'm pretty sure she knew anyway, so I just go with it. "Morning, Jenny," I call out.

Kace winks at me. "Tomorrow night? Hold on." He covers the phone. "Tomorrow's Halloween, which I'd forgotten. She wants to know if we'll come help hand out cookies to the kids, and then we'll go next door to her favorite diner and eat instead of doing brunch Sunday. They're headed to the Hamptons."

"It sounds like fun," I say. "I'd love that." He returns to the call. "We'll be there. Yes. Yes. I'll keep her. If she lets me." He hangs up. "She's very excited that you're coming."

"I'm excited, too, but that means more cookies. If I keep eating like we've been eating, I'm going to need a new wardrobe. I need to workout."

"I workout before I play in the morning. Why don't you get up with me in the morning?"

"I'd like that," I say.

He stands and helps me off my stool. "Let's go shower and I want to show you something on the way."

That something is a rectangle-shaped den-style office upstairs. A modern stainless steel and gray half-moon-shaped desk sits center stage as you enter and to the left is an extended room with rows and rows of books framing two cozy-looking gray chairs to the left.

He leans on the desk. "You think you can make this work for an office? I know you have business to attend to and that you're eager to dive into that Riptide offer Mark and Crystal made you. I saw it in your face."

"Kace, Mark, and Crystal know who I am."

"I know that, which is why I want you to see this." He snags his phone from his pocket punching keys before he hands it to me.

I glance at the screen to find a contract. My brows dip and my eyes jerk to his. "This is your power of attorney. Why am I looking at your power of attorney? You are not allowed to die."

He laughs. "I don't intend to. Look at who it's assigned to."

Reluctantly, I eye the document, and then once again my gaze jerks to his. "Mark has your power of attorney?"

"I trust him and I travel too much not to have someone in place. He knows how to manage financial assets, and he won't kill me off for my money. He has his own. And if I were to die, he knows who to take care of and how. My point is, I trust him quite literally with my life."

"As much as you are worth, some believe I possess a priceless jewel in that formula."

"He won't burn you and neither will Crystal." He snags my hip and walks me to him, fitting my legs to his. "I know it's hard to get used to, but you now have a circle of trust filled with friends."

"It's hard to think of that as a real possibility."

"It'll take time and trust is earned."

"Trust is earned," I repeat, and my mind goes to that exchange with Alexander.

And it's still on my mind when we head to the master bathroom. Kace reaches for my robe. I press my hand to his, flatten it on my hip.

"Kace, I need to bring up something awkward."

"There's no such thing as awkward between us. Tell me."

"Did you hear what Alexander said to me that day at the shop?"

There's a slight hardening of his jaw. "I heard enough."

"I told him not to tell me anything."

"I know that."

"But he did blurt something out. I feel like I should tell you what he said."

"What's between us is between us, not us and Alexander. I don't want to know." He turns me, and drags the silk of my robe down my shoulders, tossing it away, and leaving me naked. I am always so naked with this man.

The next thing I know, I'm in the shower, pressed against the wall, with him buried inside me, and this is not making love. It's fucking, wild, wicked, wonderful fucking, but it's fucking. And this is about his secrets. The ones he says will make me run. The ones he says he knows he has to tell me but he's clearly just not ready.

But I'm going to have to be. That is clear.

chapter twenty-nine

It's almost ten when I settle in behind the desk in my new office space, my hair smelling like flowers from a perfumed shampoo and conditioner I found in the bags of things Kace bought me. Instead of work attire, I'm in clothes Kace bought for me: a comfy, but figure-hugging pair of black jeans and a teal sweater that I've paired with ridiculously expensive but amazing knee-high boots. The outfit feels like fall and fall is here based on the chilly temperatures outside. I love the fall. I used to love the holidays and if Gio wasn't missing, I think I'd look forward to this season.

I've just keyed my MacBook to life when Kace appears in the doorway. He's freshly shaven in a brown snug T-shirt, with snug faded jeans and biker boots, his dark hair a bit messed up. He looks way better than fall. He looks like everything I ever wanted in a man and didn't know I wanted until I met him.

"Mark called," he says. "He wants to talk. He wants to meet for coffee, just me and him."

"About me," I assume.

"He didn't say as much, but I assume so, of course."

"Are you going to tell him who I am?"

"He knows, baby. You know he knows."

"He *thinks* he knows. Are you going to tell him?"

"What do you want me to do?"

I hesitate, but only a moment. "Whatever feels right. You have my blessing."

He pushes off the doorjamb and rounds the desk, leaning over to kiss me. "I'll play it by ear. How's your hand?"

"Good. Really good." I rotate my chair toward him and indicate my bandages. "I think I can move to a large Band-Aid now."

"I'll grab you some. I need to run to the bank, too. I'll call you on my way back and bring lunch." He kisses me again and heads for the door.

"A salad," I call after him. "I can't keep eating pasta and cookies."

He pauses at the door and winks. "A salad or I can help you work off some pasta." He doesn't give me time to reply. He heads out of the door.

"You and salad!" I call out. "We're having cookies tomorrow."

"A salad!" he calls back. "I promise."

I'm smiling when I dive into my work and start scouring the data Crystal has sent me. She was right when she said that I'd be pleased. There are a lot of items beyond wine to sell and a lot of money to be made. If Ed buys all the wine, it will be lucrative. Enough to pay my bills and pay for part of Walker, if not all. Okay, probably part of Walker. My mortgage was technically due a week ago. I'd really feel more secure if I paid for it and I suspect they are quite expensive.

For now, that wine makes my first order of business Ed. I dial his number and he answers on the first ring.

"Aria," he greets. "Your follow-up to our last meeting is surprisingly slow."

I glance at my bandaged hand and use it for what it's worth. "I tried to slice the top of my hand off. Fortunately, I failed. And fortunately, I'm coming back strong. I managed to gain access to a healthy list of collectible wines."

"Am I bidding against Alexander Voss?"

"No, you are not, but this is a contract through an auction house. I have to bring in a price that makes skipping the auction process worthwhile."

He doesn't mince words. "Okay then. When can we meet?"

"When do you want to meet?"

"Now. I'm in my office at my apartment."

"I'm actually around the corner, but I'm not dressed in work attire. If you can live with that, I can head over."

"Bring the wine list," he says. "And I don't give two cents about business attire." We disconnect and I dial Savage.

"Aria," he greets.

"I have to run to a client's offices around the corner. I'm new to this bodyguard thing. I know you said to text you, but I just text and go? It's okay?"

"Do your thing. We'll do ours. Just text us a heads-up on your way out of the door. We have a team watching you."

I blink. "A team?"

"Yes, a team."

"I was right," I murmur. "You're expensive."

"But we rock your world in all the right ways. Text us the address where we're headed, then when the price is right, come on down." He says it like I'm on a game show.

"You have a strange sense of humor, Savage."

"Thank you, Aria. Come on down." He hangs up.

I text Kace: *Going by that client's place right around the corner to try to sell the wine list Crystal gave me. Savage knows.*

Good luck, baby, he replies. *Text me your news.*

I stare down at his message and then type: *I appreciate so much right now that you didn't tell me to be careful.*

He calls me. "I wanted to," he says when I answer.

"You wanted to?"

"Hell yes. It took all I had not to say it. I know Walker says you're safe, but I'm worried. In case you didn't notice, you *matter* to me."

My chest does this fluttery thing. "You matter to me, too, Kace." I sound breathless.

"Good. Call me after your meeting and maybe we can just meet for lunch."

"I will. Are you with Mark?"

"Not yet. We're meeting close to Riptide. I just got off the subway a few blocks down."

"You took the subway?"

"When I'm not trying to impress you, it's faster."

I laugh. "You already impressed me a long time ago, Kace August."

"Scratch the lunch," he says. "I'll meet you at home and you can show me."

I laugh yet again and he adds, "And the trend toward colder than normal this year remains. It's in the thirties. Bundle up in a coat until you can snuggle up to me."

We say a short goodbye but that word home still lingers when I head to the door to do as Kace said and bundle up. He keeps calling his place home like I live here, too. It affects me. Deeply. I think—I think I've just never really felt at home my entire life here in the States.

I'm still thinking about that conversation when I head through the lobby and then step outside to greet

Steven. "Good day, Aria," he greets, standing tall in his blue jacket. "How are you?"

"So much better. Thank you, Steven."

"Excellent. Excellent. Kace told me to take good care of you. I've ordered the wife to get to baking."

"You are too kind," I say, when I hear, "Aria."

Steven's expression tightens at the sound of Alexander's voice, a reaction that tells me he knows he's problematic. I whirl around to find Alexander standing a bit too close, and of course, he's in one of his perfect, expensive suits. This one is gray. "What are you doing here, Alexander?"

"I live here. What are *you* doing here?" His lips thin. "You were with Kace."

I bristle. "Do you really want to continue a conversation that will only take us back to my fury?"

His lips quirk. "Fury? Really? It's that intense, is it?"

"Yes. *It is.* I told you not to tell me—"

"Did you ask him?"

"Stop, Alexander."

Savage steps to my side, an unexpected action on his part, but a welcome one. "Ready to go, buttercup?" he asks.

Alexander smirks at Savage and then eyes me. "I wonder why Kace has Savage guarding you so closely and from me of all people. He's a man with something to hide, Aria. Ask the question." He turns and enters the building.

I rotate to face Savage, who just plain towers over me. "I don't know why you did that, but thank you."

He motions me forward. "Let's walk."

I nod and wave to Steven as Savage and I head toward my meeting. A few steps in, Savage says, "It wasn't because Kace has me guarding you from Alexander or some secret."

"I know that. I believe Kace trusts me enough to know that I won't let Alexander manipulate me or him that way."

"Then you know that Alexander wants to play tic-tac-toe in your pants to hurt Kace."

I laugh. "You are such a man of words Savage, but yes, I know but it's more than that. He and this client I'm going to meet have something between them. He wants me to sell him any wine Ed wants to buy. It's like a childish vendetta."

"With your recent interactions with Ed and Alexander," Savage says, "we looked into both men."

I stop walking and face him. "And?"

"Ed mentored Alexander."

"I knew he worked for him."

"And Ed got very close to Alexander and his then-fiancée. Suddenly, Ed and the fiancée dumped him. Feels connected."

"Like Ed and the fiancée got together?" I ask.

"Could be," Savage says. "Which makes this personal for Alexander. You don't want in the middle of that kind of personal. I've seen how Alexander burns people close to him."

"You mean Kace." I hold up my hand. "And no, I wasn't asking you to tell me. That's Kace's story to tell."

"I wouldn't have told you anyway. You're right. That's Kace's story to tell."

A story Kace says he will never be ready to tell me, and more and more that feels like a problem. Not for me but for him.

chapter thirty

Savage and I end our walk in front of Ed's building. "Text me when you're ready to leave," he says.

"Thank you, Savage."

"For what?"

"Giving me another reason to trust you," I say. "I can tell you're a loyal person and that you truly want to protect Kace."

"And you, Aria. I'm protecting you. You can trust me."

"I know," I say, and the statement feels right and good to a girl who has trusted no one.

I turn and hurry inside the fancy high-rise building. It's not long until the doorman has approved my entry and I'm upstairs. Ed answers the door and he is, as always, professional and rather regal in his carriage. He's in dress pants, and a dress shirt, his sleeves rolled up to display a surprising amount of colorful ink. There's a skeleton of all things, and I believe an ace card. His tie is blue to match a few bits of the ink. The tats are a side of Ed I did not expect.

He's a complicated, powerful man. I'm not sure he's someone Alexander really wants to go to war with, but that's none of my business.

Ed leads me back to his preferred meeting spot of his library, rows of books, and heavy mahogany furnishings as our backdrop. We sit in two high back chairs with a table between us. I reach into my Gucci purse and hand him the list of wines.

He glances at the list and his lips do an odd quirk. "It's a fine list, an enviable list." He glances up at me. "Have you offered it to Alexander?"

This is a question he's asked, and I've answered. But I answer again. "No. To be frank, Ed, he offered me a large retainer to ensure you get nothing you want. I'm not comfortable being part of that and you were my customer before he ever tried to become my customer."

"Honor is a hard trait to come by, Aria." He hands it back to me. "I'm going to pass."

I blink, surprised, accepting the paper. "Do you mind me asking why?"

"Because if you give me this wine instead of Alexander, he'll see that as an act of war. It would put him on alert in a way I don't want him on alert. Step away from this and sell the wine to someone else that isn't he or I."

Disappointment stabs at me. I want this payday. I wanted to impress Riptide. I *need* this payday.

"I do have a proposition for you," he surprises me by saying, removing a checkbook from his pocket, and then proceeding to write a check before handing it to me. "Sometimes old school paper makes an impact. I believe this is one of those times."

I accept said old school paper and my lips part at the sixty-thousand-dollar figure. "What is this for?"

"I'd like a unique piece of jewelry for a client. She's a collector. Something one of a kind." He glances at my hand. "Something one of kind, like your daisy, Aria."

I go cold inside, my throat drier than a desert. One of a kind? Like my ring? The room spins a moment but I manage to remain composed? "What does she like? Flowers? Butterflies? Classic jewels?"

"She likes one of a kind. Find her something to blow her away. I have a lot of money riding on this." It's hard to think right now, but I manage to remember a jewel on the Riptide list. "I might have something." I hold up a finger. "Give me a moment." I tap my phone and it takes a few moments but I produce photos of a stunning emerald bracelet. Presenting him the images, I add, "It belonged to a member of a royal family." I continue and read him the details of the family.

He slides through the photos and then offers me my phone back. "How much?"

I glance at my listing which reads: *The client wants seventy thousand but will settle for sixty.* The commission is twenty percent, of which I get forty percent. Six thousand dollars. It's not much, but it will help with my mortgage. "Seventy-five," I tell Ed. "It's been validated by Riptide Auction House and comes with paperwork."

He whistles. "Steep, but I'll take it. Arrange delivery and I'll pay the remaining balance on possession and inspection."

He stands and walks me to the door. "We should do that dinner, Aria. I do believe you and I could work magic together. But it's going to require some quality conversations."

"We'll see if you approve of your purchase first," I say, sidestepping the invitation.

"I know I will."

I depart and by the time I'm in the elevator, I'm already texting Savage. Once I'm outside, I dial Kace. "Are you with Mark?"

"I am and why do you sound excited?"

"Tell him I sold the royal stone for seventy-five thousand. I have sixty thousand of it in my hand."

"Did you now?"

"Yes." There's a smile and lots of pride in that one word. A little win feels really big. "Tell him, Kace," I urge.

He murmurs the news to Mark and then says, "He wants you to meet us at Riptide. He wants to see the check himself."

"That man, I swear, Kace. He's just—"

"Should I supply a word?" he offers.

"No. You're with him."

"Exactly."

"You're bad," I scold.

"Don't you like that about me?"

I smile. "Sometimes."

"I know when."

"Stop," I order. "The check is made out to me. I need to go deposit it, so it's going to take a few days to clear my bank."

"It won't with mine," he says. "Meet me at Riptide. I'll handle it for you."

"Kace—"

"Aria," he says softly. "I got this. You got this. *Congratulations.*"

We disconnect and I smile all over again. I did this. He's right. And I'm proud. I head toward the subway when an SUV pulls up and the window rolls down as Savage motions me forward.

I hurry forward and climb inside. "Where to, my dear?" Savage asks grandly.

"I need to go to Riptide."

"Adrian," Savage says. "to Riptide, where Mark Compton thinks he rules, but Crystal is queen and has him by his balls."

I facepalm and sink back into the soft leather of my seat, laughing, until my gaze catches on my ring. Ed called it a one of a kind. It is. It's one of a kind and special, but he couldn't have known that. *The one true daisy in the wind.* That's what my father had called Kace, and those words just feel too close to *one of a kind.*

That coincidence is still bothering me when we arrive at Riptide. Kace is at my door waiting on me when it opens, lifting me out of the backseat. My feet settle on the ground and I catch Kace's lapels. He catches my waist. Suddenly, we're at eye level, and a blast of awareness shakes me to the core. It's sexual. It's red-hot chemistry. It's emotional. It's so many things. I am lost in the power of this man, but that is also why I read the edge to him, the simmer of something dark, beneath his surface.

"What is it? What's wrong?"

"Alexander is what's wrong."

My pulse leaps. "He didn't tell me anything."

"You didn't tell me either."

"Savage walked me to my meeting. I didn't think it was that big of a deal." The wind gusts and my teeth chatter. "It's freezing."

He reacts, linking our arms and we hurry toward the entrance of Riptide, all the while my mind races, not sure where this is going. The doorman opens the double glass doors for us, and warm heat welcomes us as we enter the glitzy lobby. The doorman offers to take out coats, but Kace waves him off. "We're leaving again," he says, without a pause. On a mission for privacy, we keep walking, and clearly, Kace is well-vetted here because no one stops our progress.

Once we're inside an office, Kace shuts us inside, and then I'm against the door, and his hands planted on either side of me. "Alexander—"

"—is trouble. I know."

"He's dangerous, Aria. I need you to understand that this isn't some cockfight between two men."

His jaw tics. His energy ping pongs in the room. He's not touching me so I touch him. I press my hand to his chest. "I don't know what this is—"

"Dangerous," he repeats, his hand covering mine. "This isn't jealousy. This isn't a game."

"What do you think I did?"

His lashes lower and then lift. "I don't think you did anything."

"You're angry."

"Not at you. I'm pissed at myself. I didn't warn you. I didn't say the word 'dangerous' because I don't want to talk about this but that means that I didn't protect you. I brought you to his doorstep."

"Wait." I search his face. "Do you regret me being there?"

He snags my hips and walks me to him. "No. Hell no. I regret *him* being here."

My fingers curl on his chest. "You're confusing me."

"I know."

"That's all? *I know*?"

He releases me and leans back on the chair behind him, hands on the leather, withdrawing even before he says, "For now."

I know he has secrets. I know he knows we can't hide from them forever. And so I repeat, "For now," making sure he's clear that for now, is not forever. "I have another situation."

"With Alexander?"

"No. With Ed, my client. He looked at my ring and said he wanted something one of a kind like it. Am I being paranoid? How would he know it's one of a kind? And he's never mentioned it before. I mean, the timing just feels odd."

"I agree," he says, "but he did buy a piece of jewelry. Referencing another piece of jewelry is logical. It's probably nothing to worry about, but we'll talk to Blake and Savage. And then," he adds, twining his fingers with mine and walking me to him. "We'll go celebrate your success, you and me, and a bottle of wine."

His voice is soft now, his mood with it and I press my palm to his face. "After I do some more work. Gio was a major source of income for me. I need to turn this sale into more."

He covers my hand with his and brings my fingers to his lips. "You know you're not alone anymore, right?"

"I know that. I do, but I still have responsibilities."

"Let me help."

"No."

"Please."

"Don't say please. Please no."

"Yes." He stands up, and still holding my hand, steps toward the door. "Let's go."

"Where?"

"To the bank. We're going to make sure you're taken care of."

"No." I shove on his chest. "No. No. *No.*" I place myself between him and the door again. "I swear I will go back to my place, Kace if you try to do this. *Don't* do this. I do not want to feel like I'm your charity case. I can't be that."

He cups my head and presses my forehead to his. "Baby, you matter to me. I care about you." His eyes find mine. "I need you to let me help and there's more I'd say about that if we weren't here at Riptide right now."

"You *are* helping. You're paying for Walker."

"That's not what I mean."

"I don't need other help—"

"Aria—"

"*Yet*, Kace. Not yet. Maybe I won't now that I have Riptide."

"And how will I know when you do? I need you to promise me you'll tell me."

"I will."

"You promise?"

"Yes." I concede. "I promise. Thank you. Thank you so much."

"I don't want your thanks. You know that."

"You have it anyway and just to be clear," my voice softens, "you matter to me, too. I care about you, too."

His hand slides under my hair to my neck and he lowers his mouth to mine. "Aria Stradivari, you need to know that I'm too damn selfish to let you go. I've decided you don't get to run."

"Does this mean you're going to stop telling me I should?"

"Yes. It does."

"Thank *God*."

His lips curve and he leans in, his lips a whisper from mine, when there's a knock on the door. "Ms. Alard. I'm waiting."

At the sound of Mark's arrogant, demanding voice, we laugh, and Kace kisses me hard and fast. "I'll kiss you properly at home."

chapter thirty-one

Crystal hugs me when she hears the news of my sale and gloats mercilessly on my behalf to Mark. While I do not think Mark Compton is a man most would dare cross, it becomes clear that Crystal has him wrapped around her finger. And him her. They are in love and I remotely wonder about her being sick before the Riptide event. She was a little secretive about it which is probably just me looking for secrets, because I have so many secrets. It was probably a flu bug.

But could she be pregnant? God, could I? We didn't use a condom way too soon. We're still not using condoms. It's a thought I'm forced to set aside as Crystal has me coordinate the delivery of the bracelet with Ed. Afterward, there is also the visit to the bank in which the staff treats Kace like the rock god that he is, but I'm pretty sure it's because of the size of his bank account, not his impressive violin. It's hours later when we head to the apartment where, as promised, Kace most definitely kisses the whole of me and quite properly. Once we've pulled on a few items of limited clothing, we decide to do something I haven't done in a long time. We set aside everything going on around us. We order pizza and watch a movie. We just relax.

Together.

Kace and I wake up on Halloween and work out in his gym. We take turns on the treadmill and weights and I'm stunned by how fast that man runs and how hard he lifts weights, but then, it shouldn't surprise me at all. It requires extreme discipline to play a violin the way he plays, to be the only real daisy in the wind. And he is. I know why my father called him that. His skill, his devotion to his craft, his way of speaking through his music is without reproach, and yet he'd tell you it is. He isn't arrogant. He respects his gift and his instrument.

When we're done with the workout, he proves my point. He dives into his daily practice, which he seems to prefer to do shirtless, which suits me just fine, especially after he's been pumping weights. While he plays, seducing the morning with his version of Beethoven's 5th, I start the coffee. I've had time to down a full cup, set up my MacBook, and email a few customers about some of the items from the Riptide list, when he sets his violin down. I pour him a cup and we meet at the island where I hand him his coffee, and we claim stools we rotate to face each other.

"I like having you here with me like this," he says.

I'm charmed by the sincerity in his voice. "I like being here."

"Good. Keep liking it," he says, sipping his coffee. "We're supposed to head over to the bakery about four. They're giving out free cookies from five to seven and trust me, it's a madhouse."

"They do this every year?"

"They did it last year and I wasn't here, but they sent me photos of the line-up. And this year, we'll both find out firsthand."

"I finally get to meet Jerry."

"Yes, you do. You'll like him. He's a good match for Jenny."

We spend the next two hours just talking about everything under the sun, including that text message, which I still do not believe came from Gio. "I remember exactly who was with me during that trip. I sent the names to Blake yesterday on my way to see Mark."

"That was a long time ago."

"And I remember everything about that trip. Gio was actually on a school trip for most of my visit. I think I saw him once. And yes, I told Blake when I gave him the names. Could Gio want me away from you for fear I'm after the formula? Yes. If he came home and found us together, I could see that. Did he push us together? Doubtful."

Eventually, the conversation moves to other topics, and we eat Rice Krispies while laughing about our childhoods. We end on the topic of the holidays. "Mine were on the road," he says, "usually performing."

"That's horrible."

"It was my life and I enjoyed the audiences. Plus, I didn't know anything different. I want to now."

"And yet you're performing in Paris this year?"

"Not on the actual holiday and if you go with me, we can make it special. I can show you Paris."

"I want to. You know I want to."

"But?" he prods.

"But we'll see. I need more time to find Gio."

"Staying here won't make him materialize. It will torture you."

"I know. And I keep feeling like he's not coming back. Perhaps that's one of the reasons I know that text wasn't from him. I'd feel him if he were alive. I know I would."

"That could be nothing but fear. Let's get back on topic. Tell me about your holidays."

"Mine were always traditional until my mother died. Church on Christmas Eve. Gifts on Christmas morning. Since she left us, not so much. Gio spent the last two Christmases in bed with a different woman each year."

"And you did what?"

"Went to the movies by myself. I haven't put up a tree in years."

"I've never put up a tree. I'm never home to do it, but this year is different. Starting with Halloween."

His phone buzzes and he glances down at a message. "We have a delivery on the way up."

"We?"

"That's what Steven said."

"His wife was baking for us. I'm going to need another workout."

He stands and leans in close, his lips close to mine. "I'll step up and offer myself up as your next workout." The security buzzer goes off. "More on your workout soon." He kisses me and heads to the door.

Smiling, I stand up and load our bowls and cups into the dishwasher, remarkably comfortable in Kace's home. I believe that's because I'm remarkably comfortable with him. Kace returns with a bag in hand that reads Jerry and Jenny's Cookies. "Please tell me they didn't send us cookies to eat before the cookies this afternoon."

We convene at the island and he pulls out what appears to be shirts, one pink and one blue. "I do believe we have a uniform for tonight," he says, holding his up to his chest, for me to read. "Cookies, ghosts, and goblins, oh my!" And there are ghosts and goblins eating cookies.

"That's cute." I laugh. "It might not fit your tattooed, leather, and biker boots image, though."

"But you do, baby, and that's all that matters."

"I'm the opposite of leather and tattoos."

He sets the shirt down and steps into me, his hand branding my hip. "And yet here you are with me. Care to rethink that?"

I offer him a defiant tilt of my chin. "Not at all. If the leather and tattoos are on you, I'm a leather and tattoo girl all the way."

His eyes light with mischief. "Is that right?"

"Yes. It is."

"Show me," he dares.

I've never been bold sexually. Or at least, I've never explored myself sexually, but then there is Kace, and now I'm a different me. I step back from him and pull my T-shirt over my head, tossing it away. I immediately reach for my leggings. Kace steps into me, his hands sliding under the cotton to cup my backside. "I like how you show me."

The next thing I know, I'm on top of the island and he's inside me.

By the time we're in the shower together, I've decided Halloween is my favorite holiday ever.

Kace and I spend the afternoon in my new office. He settles in a cozy chair by the bookshelves to write music, while I claim the desk to get some work done. It's a unique experience for me to share every moment with Kace, but I like it. I like it probably too much. If we fizzle out, I will hurt. I hurt just thinking about it, which is why I remind myself to live in the moment.

I focus on my work. I pay Nancy and the bills, and while I survived this month, that six thousand I have coming from Riptide will be welcomed. I also text and email with a couple of customers about a few Riptide items. It's later afternoon, and close to the time to head out to help Jerry and Jenny, I've lined up a viewing of a painting at Riptide Monday morning. If the sales happen, I'll be set for the month of November.

About three-thirty, we change into our shirts and I can't stop smiling at him in his. And how does he make ghosts and goblins hot? I don't know but he does.

On our way out of the apartment, Kace pulls on his coat and helps me with mine. "You need a casual coat."

"This coat is warm. I love it." I turn to face him. "Don't go flexing your wallet. I am closing a big sale on Monday."

He catches the lapels of my coat and pulls me to him. He smells good, all spice and maybe cinnamon? "You eventually have to get used to my money," he says.

"How about I just focus on you, Kace?"

"It's a part of me, Aria. You have to know that."

"There are many things to love about you that are not your money, Kace." It's out before I can stop it.

His eyes narrow and soften. "Is that right?"

I don't back down. I'm all in with this man. "Yes. Starting with you wearing that shirt and handing out cookies. Take me to the cookies. We didn't eat lunch."

"Because you wanted to wait on cookies," he reminds me.

"I can't be rude."

A deep rumble of delicious laughter escapes his perfect chest. A chest made this night for ghosts, goblins, and my hands and mouth. "That's a good excuse," he says. "I'll let you use it."

We're still smiling and laughing about random things as we make our short walk. In the back of my mind, Gio is always there, or rather not here, but the laughter is the medicine I need; sanity in fact. We arrive at the cookie shop to find a crazy long line of ghosts and goblins, oh my! Kace catches my hand and we zigzag through the crowd for him to knock on the door.

Soon we are inside and Jenny, who is wearing a good witch costume, is hugging me. "You made it. How is your hand?"

There is a pinch in my chest with her mothering that is bittersweet, considering the loss of my own mother. "Much better. I forgot about it most of the day. And you look amazing. We're underdressed."

"Nonsense. You rock that shirt."

I swear, she's funny and hip and younger than her years.

"'Bout damn time you make it for a holiday," a bellowing male voice blasts, and I turn to find a tall man with thick gray hair, fit, too, in a way that screams willpower considering the sweet smell of cookies teasing my nostrils right now. He's also rocking his ghosts and goblins T-shirt.

Kace points to his shirt. "If I would have known there was a T-shirt in it for me I would have come sooner."

"You do look pretty, boy," Jerry says his attention turning to me. "And who might this be?"

"Hi Jerry," I say. "I love your cookies."

"Hello, Aria," he replies, glancing at Kace. "She's a pretty one, Kace. Prettier than your ugly ass deserves."

I laugh, which gains me Jerry's attention again. "Thank you for getting him here."

I hold up my hands. "He invited me," I say. "I take no credit."

"You don't get enough credit, but we do. You give him a reason to stay home, a feat no one else has achieved." The alarm on his watch goes off. "Doors open! Let's do this."

For the next few hours Kace and I hand out endless cookies, and it's a complete blast. When the event is over, Jerry and Jenny leave the staff to clean up with a generous bonus for doing so that has them grinning from ear-to-ear, and we head next door to a cozy restaurant. It's not long before we're sitting at a high table across from them, with dim lights, orange cushioned seats, and a fun mix of the eighties, nineties, and two-thousands music. Soon we have wine and fried mozzarella, all of us enjoying tonight's stories involving the kids enjoying their cookies tonight.

We order food, and I behave quite nicely, showing restraint by ignoring all forms of pasta which is rough considering they have mac n' cheese. I choose a salad, while Kace orders a chicken sandwich that makes me feel a little better about my choice. The comfortable chatter continues and I decide Jerry and Jenny love this man like a son. And he loves them. And I kind of love them all right now. We eat and I'm into another glass of wine that I shouldn't drink because I'm feeling tipsy when the inevitable happens. "Aria," Jerry says. "Tell us about yourself."

The dreaded question that breeds lies I don't want to tell.

Kace's hand catches mine under the table, his touch remarkably steadying even with wine on the brain. "My brother and I own a collectibles business," I say. "That's how I met Kace. I was trying to buy a violin for a client."

"She saved my ass," Kace says. "It was a knock-off. She told me not to bid. And it turned out she was right."

"Are you a fan of Kace's, Aria?" Jenny asks.

"I'm a huge fan of the man now, of course," I say, "but when I met him I was a fan of his music. Skill doesn't mean the man is likable. In fact, sometimes it means he's unbearable."

"She speaks the truth," Jerry agrees, speaking to Jenny and then to me, "You speak the truth, Aria. We told him we'd beat his ass if he became a pompous arrogant ass."

"*You* told him that," Jenny says. "*I* promised to protect him."

"I protect him," Jerry assures us all. "From everyone but me."

Kace laughs and sips his wine. "See what I put up with."

"Seems pretty perfect, Kace, especially considering—you know, I ah—" I grab my wine before I start talking about his parents. "You shouldn't have given me this," I add, indicating the glass.

"Interesting," Jenny says, eyeing me. "You know about his parents."

"I do," I say, and I glance up at Kace. "Sorry."

"Don't be sorry, baby. They know you wouldn't be here if you weren't important to me."

I'm stunned that he says this in front of them, but before I can really recover, Jenny asks, "Where are your parents, Aria?"

I'm so worried about Kace, that the question takes me off guard. My lashes lower with the emotional hit, no doubt, punching harder as I see this little family together while drinking wine on top of it. Kace wraps his arm around me and comes to the rescue. "Her mother was killed in a mugging."

I open my eyes. "Ten years ago. My father disappeared when I was eleven."

"She was in Italy," Kace adds. "She moved here shortly after with her American mother."

Jenny reaches over the table and squeezes my hand. "Sounds like you need to inherit a pair of godparents to me."

Tears threaten but somehow I manage to joke. "Do I get cookies?"

Jerry laughs. "Yes, you get cookies."

At this point, the dance floor is packed and Kace stands up and rounds the table to offer me his hand. "Let's go dance."

My eyes go wide. "You dance?"

"Don't look so shocked. Music is my life."

"We shall see," I tease, thankful for the escape, he's offered me. I place my hand in his, the tingling up my arm shockingly profound, his eyes laden with nothing but me.

He folds our elbows, pulling our bodies tight together as we walk through the crowd and to the other side of the dance floor. The music shifts and the song "Can I Be Him" by James Arthur begins to play. Kace folds me into his arms, leans in, his breath warm on my neck as he sings the first two lines to me.

You walked into the room and now my heart has been stolen

You took me back in time to when I was unbroken

He pulls back, his eyes meeting mine and I can barely breathe for what I find in those baby blues. He means these words. He nuzzles my neck and we sway to the music. And when the song is over, he leads me toward a back room. We cross under a doorway and I have no idea where we are but he turns me and presses me against the wall, out of sight of the dining area. "I don't want you to go back to your apartment. Ever. Move in with me."

I blanch, stunned. "You want—"

"Yes. I want. You're already living with me and I don't want you to leave. I know it's fast. You don't have to tell me now. I know there is Gio and—"

"Gio makes decisions for Gio. He does." My hand flattens on his chest. "Yes. Yes, I will."

"You will?"

"Yes. I just I have to figure out my place and—"

"I'll pay it off and when Gio gets back—"

"No, Kace. You are not—"

He lifts me off the wall and molds me close, body to body, his chest to my chest. He makes me stronger. "I *am* paying it off," he says. "Then you always know you're not captive to my money like my mother was to my father's. You will always feel you have a place to go, but home is with me now. Say it."

These words about his mother is another peek into his past that he's allowed me. He's inviting me to live in his world. And I'm inviting him into mine when I thought I'd never open that door to anyone. "I already feel like you're the only home I've had in a long time, Kace."

"As you are for me. The only home."

My fingers find the rough stubble of his jaw. "The one true daisy in the wind."

There is something warm and yet dark in his eyes with those words that I cannot name and I don't even try. He kisses me then, deep, crazy kisses, and then we go back to the table to share the news, but in the back of my mind, I feel like I'm forgetting Gio. I'm giving up on my brother. And I silently vow that is not true. I will never give up on Gio.

chapter thirty-two

I wake Monday morning to Kace wrapped around me and the sound of his cellphone vibrating on the nightstand. Somehow I'm on his side of the bed, and with a groan, he reaches over me and glances at the number. With another groan, he rolls to his back and answers the call.

"It's six AM, Mark. Why are you calling me?" Whatever Mark says has him sitting up. "You've got to be kidding me. Holly hell. Now what?"

Nerves erupt in my belly and I scoot up against the headboard, knees to my chest, waiting for him to hang up. When he finally does, I pounce. "What is it?"

"The L.A. event center for our performance burned down last night. We're moving the San Francisco event to a museum that can accommodate tickets for both events."

"It burned down." My throat goes dry. "Kace, that feels funny to me. Is that—could that be—"

"No. It was electrical." He pulls me down and under him. "Stop worrying."

"It feels off."

He pulls me down on the mattress and slides between my legs. "I'll have Blake check into it."

"Yes, but—"

He slides down my body and about the time his lips touch my belly button, I stop talking. When his tongue follows, I have no idea what we were talking about. I now share a home with Kace. My bed is no longer cold or lonely.

By Monday evening, he's managed to get movers to my apartment. I don't even want to know how much a rush service cost him.

By Tuesday, he's paid off the building Gio and I own and I've left the documents on Gio's desk. By Wednesday, I've made three sales for Riptide and involved Nancy in the process with great success. Kace has also filled my closet with clothes and shoes and my head is spinning. I try to slow down his spending, but he declares, "I've decided you'll get used to my money with exposure. So here we go, baby."

I fight, but not hard. For some reason, Kace needs to do these things for me, but I also know he needs to know I'm here for him, not for a luxurious lifestyle. I don't know how to do that but I'm determined to figure it out.

A declaration that proves it's not done easily or quickly.

Thursday morning, we're having our morning coffee at the kitchen island, when he slides a credit card onto the counter. That's where I draw the line. "No." I slide it back to him. "No. And no."

"So you can pick things you want rather than settling for what some personal shopper buys for you."

"I'm making money. You paid off my building. I have a load off financially. I can buy what I need, Kace."

"Aria, I'm worth an ungodly amount of money. I don't want to spend it alone. Just take it. Then we both know if you need it you have it."

There is such an earnestness to this request that I pick up the card. Apparently, this is not where I draw the line, but I look for that balance. "For emergencies."

"It's a start," he approves. "I can live with that."

My cellphone buzzes with a message and I slide it close to read the message. "Donelle says he'll wait to sell the violin until you can get to Italy, as long as it's this year."

"Well there you go," he says. "It might just work out."

I sip my coffee, trying to bury the sense for foreboding in my belly. It's just too good to be true. Going after that violin is dangerous and yet I know we're going to do it.

On Friday, Blake joins us for our morning coffee and offers us a full update on his investigations. With him across from us at the kitchen island, I pray for good news. He starts with the man in the pharmacy who turns out to be just what we thought: press. No lead there to help find Gio. "Let's talk about Kayden Wilkens," he says, moving on, "the head of The Underground in Europe, I mentioned when I was here last. Kayden's confirmed that there are, in fact, rumblings of someone trying to find the formula, but they didn't come to his people."

I frown. "That's unexpected, right? You thought that anyone looking for the formula would end up with him?"

"Eventually, they'll end up finding him if they really want that prize. Everyone who wants the impossible ends up with Kayden. Whoever this is clearly isn't willing, or ready, to risk trusting them."

"It could be Gio," I say. "Or not. I don't know. I thought he was dead, but Gio wouldn't trust an outsider. He'd try to hunt on his own. But he also doesn't have the skills to disappear on his own. Or I didn't think he did."

"Maybe this Sofia person does," Blake offers, "though I doubt that's her real name."

All and all, it's a discouraging conversation that ends with the promise of another update.

Scarily, considering Gio's prolonged silence, I blink and another week has passed and it's time for Kace's charity event. Mark and Crystal leave days before us. That leaves Kace and I, along with Savage and Adrian, on a private jet to San Francisco the eve of the event. The rest of the Walker security team for the event will be local. The flight is long, and using a practice violin, Kace runs through his performance pieces. It's surreal, flying thirty thousand feet in the air while this man plays a violin. The music that has always been in my heart and blood seems to blossom with every passing moment, into a new tree of life through this man.

Once we arrive in San Francisco, I have my moments of awe over the Golden Gate Bridge, the water, and the mountains. We check into the Ritz and before long, it's us, Chris and Sara, Mark and Crystal, all in our living area, with wine ready to pour, but for Chris and Kace, opt for beer. A surprising choice from Kace, who loves his wine, but I say what the heck and drink beer, too.

"You know, Aria," Sara says. "I do pretty much what you're doing now, only with art. I can start sending you a list of the pieces I have to sell, if you like. I'll meet Riptide's forty percent."

"Do I get any Chris Merit originals?" I ask hopefully.

"I'll paint you one for you," Chris offers. "But if you sell it, one of my two charities get the funds."

"If you paint me a painting, I will never sell it."

"I've been trying to get him to paint me something for the living room," Kace says. "Now he offers to paint for you? What the hell?"

"Ms. Merit," Mark begins, displeasure in his voice. "Are you trying to bribe Aria away from us?"

"Mrs.," Chris corrects.

"Sara," Sara corrects.

I laugh and everyone looks at me. "I just didn't know he talked like that to anyone but me."

Now, everyone laughs and for the first time in my life, since age eleven, I'm in a room of friends. Kace did that for me. I glance over at him and I see it in his eyes. He knows what I'm feeling. He's the only person who's ever been close enough to me to know what I'm feeling.

The morning of the show, which is Saturday, we wake and order room service. The amazing thing about San Francisco is that the weather is mild year-round. We're able to enjoy our coffee on the patio, with an incredible view of the Golden Gate Bridge. I lean on the railing and Kace steps behind me. "What are you thinking?"

"I never thought I'd leave my neighborhood in New York City. Thank you for bringing me." I turn to face him. "You've changed my life."

"The feeling is mutual, baby. You have to know that."

"Yes, but you—"

A knock sounds on the door. "Hold that thought. I have a surprise for you." He winks and heads inside. I step back into the living area to find him rolling a rack of dresses back into the room. "What have you done?"

"You need a dress that does you justice tonight. I knew you wouldn't go buy it, and you didn't, despite my prodding all week."

"I have a dress."

235

"It's not one of these dresses. This event is going to be over the top glitz. And if you don't like any of these, we'll go hunting for one you do like." He pulls a dress from the rack. "I asked for this one."

It's a gorgeous dress, floor length with a beaded V-neck in a flesh-tone, but the bottom is a stunning chiffon sunshine-hued skirt with a slit down the leg. "It's beautiful. Like a daisy."

"Exactly." He carries it to me. "It matches your ring."

My fingers catch on the chiffon of the skirt. It's a Cinderella dress.

"Want to try it on?" he asks.

"I do," I say. "Very much."

His eyes light. "Good. Then go try it on."

I take the dress and start to leave, but pause to push to my toes and kiss him. "Thank you."

His hand settles on my lower back and he molds me close. "Anything for you, Aria. That's what I want you to understand. I'm not the man I was before I met you. I would do anything for you. Don't forget that." His voice is low, rough, affected.

I don't know what he's talking about. I don't ask. He doesn't want me to ask. Because as he knows me, I've come to know him. He has secrets. He has pain. He has damage. And I don't care. I'm the one affected by him and on the deepest of levels. I need him and that has nothing to do with a dress. He could hurt me and maybe he will, but I cannot turn back now, damn the consequences, and at times, I know there will consequences.

Once I'm in the bathroom, I slip out of the robe and into the dress and I'm in love with it and Kace. I glance at my ring and then at myself in the mirror. It's perfect. Everything about this dress is perfect. A rush of nostalgia has me grabbing my phone from my robe pocket and dialing Gio for the first time in a week. It goes straight to voicemail.

I text the message sender that sent me that strange message: *Please contact me, Gio.*

The message bounces back. And I don't know why I even sent that message. Gio didn't send me that text. I know he didn't.

A knock sounds on the door. "You going to let me see the dress?" Kace calls out.

"Not until tonight." I slip out of it and pull on the robe, opening the door.

He's right there, waiting on me. "Then you're keeping the dress?"

"Yes. I love it so much."

"You have others to try on."

"No need." My fingers curl in his T-shirt. "You picked this one and you know, I really love—" I stop myself before I tell him I love him. God, what am I doing?

His cellphone rings. He ignores it. "You really love—" he prods, his hands on my waist as he steps into me. "You love what, Aria?"

"The dress," I say.

"And I love," he pauses, "the dress, too." His lips, his really sexy lips, quirk at the edges.

He loves the dress? No. No that's not what we're talking about right now. My God, have we just confessed our love to each other?

"Aria," he says and there's a knock on the door.

He curses under his breath and presses his forehead to mine before he cups my head and kisses me. "I *really* love that damn dress," he says and heads toward the door.

Leaving me breathless.

I don't know what just happened, but I want to pull him back to me right away and finish this conversation but that soon proves impossible. Our visitor is Savage.

"Ho ho ho," he greets, taking over the room, as he does every room he enters. "Christmas comes early. I'm here. I bring cookies and plans for tonight's event."

We spend a good hour with him and our moment of confessions have passed. With the day passing quickly, we shower and head out to explore the city, which includes the pier, a light lunch, and a bakery with what he claims to have "the best chocolate cake on planet Earth." He's right. It is.

"You know," he says as we sit in the cute little bakery at a wooden table, "in Paris, I can show you a lot of things you've never experienced. Chris and Sara live there half the year. Maybe we could do the same with Italy."

"I can't go back to Italy. What about Germany? And I can't even believe I'm talking about living anywhere but New York City. But you love Germany and you said I'd love the spaetzle."

"Which I still haven't gotten you." He stands and takes me with him. "I'm going to give you back Italy. I promise and I don't make promises I can't keep. You wait and see."

If anyone else said that to me I wouldn't believe him. But this is Kace. And he seems to make all things possible. What he didn't say, though, is that he's promising to bring Gio back to me. But then, he doesn't make promises he can't keep.

After a fabulous afternoon, Kace and I arrive back to the room around five to shower and dress. Once

Kace is done shaving, I kick him out of the bathroom to finish dressing. I don't want him to see the dress until I'm perfect. And so, I fret over just that—the perfect make-up in muted browns. My hair is loving the new product Kace bought me and it flat irons long and a silky dark brown around my shoulders. My final step before pulling on the dress is a pair of diamond-studded strappy high heels that I absolutely adore. The dress is last and I slip it into place over a perfect glittery gold bra that gives me just the right amount of cleavage. After a quick inspection of my image in the mirror, I'm feeling like Cinderella all over again. It's a dress for a princess and I'm ready for my prince. I inhale and open the door.

Kace isn't in the bedroom, so I walk through the door to the living room. He's standing by the window on the phone and the minute he sees me, he says, "I know. We'll be ready," and hangs up.

His eyes sweep over me, his expression filled with masculine appreciation. "You look beautiful, baby. So damn beautiful." He steps closer and I do the same, meeting him in the middle of the room, just outside the line of the living area.

He's dressed for his rock star image, in all black, denim and boots, tattoos dancing along his arms the way music will dance off his bow to a wondrous crowd a short while from now.

"So do you," I say.

His lips curve. "I look beautiful, huh?" He closes the very small space left between us, his fingers splaying at my hips. Heat radiates off his palm and seeps through my dress to scorch my skin. My hand goes to his hand, as if I can stop the assault on my senses his touch and the look in his eyes creates. "You are," I say.

"Show me later." It's one of his favorite statements. One I always make sure I answer. *Later.*

"I have something for you," he says and he reaches into his pocket and pulls out a black box. "I wasn't sure what neckline you'd choose, and I wanted something you could look down and see anytime you wanted." He opens the lid and I gasp at the gorgeous bracelet that is made up of yellow daisies with diamonds glistening in the center of each flower. "Oh my God, Kace. It's gorgeous and it's," I look up at him, "so very special."

"I wanted it to match your ring. Try it on." He removes it from the velvet and sets the box on the back of the couch before slipping it around my wrist. "I had it sized. You have tiny wrists and fingers."

"Which isn't good for playing the violin," I say.

His brows furrow. "Who told you that?"

I think back to a day with my father, years before. "My father."

"You can tell me that story later, but that's the first thing I don't agree with him on." He seals the clasp and I stare down at the beauty twinkling back at him, memories of the moment my mother gave me my ring in my mind.

Kace's fingers brush my cheek. "What are you thinking?"

"It was my sixteenth birthday when my mother gave me my ring. She said it was her way of bringing my father to the day. And now, she's here with me, with us, because of you." I wrap my arms around him and tilt my chin up. "Kace, I—I really—"

There's a knock on the door and both of us suck in air. "It's Savage," Kace says. "*Again.*"

"He has really bad timing," I say.

"Yes, he does." He cups my face. "And I really—*too.*"

chapter thirty-three

"Rock and roll, people," Savage orders, snapping his fingers. "Pronto."

"Sometimes you're a pain in the ass, Savage," Kace says.

"My wife agrees." He opens the door and says nothing more.

Kace settles a velvet cape around me that I've never seen before. "You had to have something to match the dress."

"I do," I say, lifting my arm and the bracelet.

"You do," he says with a smile, and the man really does have a devastating smile.

Once we're loaded up in an SUV and on our way to the event, Savage pumps up Kace's pre-event music, quite literally with the old-school "Pump Up the Jam," followed by Prince's "Purple Rain." We're all singing and laughing when we pull up to the event and it's a madhouse, the front entrance to the museum is literally packed with people, including press, cameras, and a few obvious movie stars. "This is much bigger than the Riptide event," I say, nerves assailing me. "I'm so glad you talked me into this dress. Not that you had to try hard, but you know what I mean."

"It's Chris's home city," he says, "and we both called in some favors from some big names. We want the last US event to be huge."

"It's like a red-carpet event."

"Don't be nervous," he says, kissing my hand. "You're going to steal the show in that dress." He leans in and kisses my neck. The door beside him opens and he starts to get out. I catch his arm. "We're going to be photographed."

"Own it, baby. I talked to Blake about this. Act like you have nothing to hide. Whoever knows who you are, already knows. And I promise you every Hollywood star here has something to hide. *Or* we can go around back and sneak in."

Sneak in, I repeat in my mind.

Hide.

No.

"No," I say. "Let's go."

He smiles his approval before he exits the vehicle and helps me out. Flashes go off immediately and Kace's hand settles at my hip, fitting me snuggly to his side. We start walking and Savage and Adrian are right beside us, leaving the SUV for someone else to deal with. Microphones are shoved at Kace and questions asked about me, but he doesn't respond to anyone.

Once we're inside the building, calmness ensues. We check our coats, and Kace is left in his T-shirt and tattoos. We start walking a grand hall with arched ceilings, and walls covered in historic paintings, and I tease him about his rock star image. He slides an arm around me. "I'm wearing a tuxedo in Paris."

"Really? Now I *have* to go."

"That's what I want to hear."

"Let's find the food, baby," Kace says. "I know I said I wasn't hungry earlier, but I changed my mind."

"Me, too," I say, "but I don't think real humans eat food around movie stars."

"It's the movie stars that don't eat, at least not if they plan to keep it down."

I crinkle my nose. "That was a bad joke."

"Bad jokes are good jokes," he says with a wink as we step into a room with a domed ceiling etched in ancient images. Fancy dresses and tuxedos dot our path as do waiters with food trays. Kace grabs an egg salad sandwich for both of us and I wave him off. I just can't eat here, but he sure can. He inhales both. "You were smart to pass," he says after he swallows the last bite. "They sucked, they were tiny, and I need energy. Look for the chocolate and you'll find Chris and Sara. Well Sara, but where Sara is, Chris is."

We both start scanning the room and sure enough, I find a chocolate fountain and Sara is there. "And there she is," I say, pointing.

"And there's Chris, right by her side."

And just like Kace, he's in jeans and a T-shirt with boots. Two rebels in a crowd of tuxedos. I kind of love it.

"Come," Kace says, attaching my hand to his elbow as we start maneuvering through the more densely populated areas of the room to make our way to Chris and Sara. Every time Kace reaches for another snack, which is often, someone is in front of him, trying to talk to him. People love him and I can't help but feel pride. We are finally just this close to Chris and Sara when a distinguished elderly man with solid gray hair intercepts us and he is just gushing over Kace. Ten minutes later, he continues gushing and Kace is graciously interacting with him.

Chris appears beside us and pats the man's shoulder. "Charlie, if you don't let me feed him, he might pass out while he performs."

"Oh my," Charlie says. "I didn't mean to delay your preparation for your performance. Energy matters. You go, son. I can't wait to watch you perform." Charlie hurries away and now Kace slaps Chris on the back. "I owe you again."

"If we hit our goal tonight," Chris says, "you owe me nothing."

"I need food if that's going to happen."

"I figured," Chris says, "You were eyeing the waiters like you could eat an arm." He greets me and motions us toward Sara, who is still guarding the chocolate fountain.

Kace's arm slides around me and we join Sara as she finishes off a cake pop. "I couldn't help myself," she says. "You should try one of all of them. They're so good and," she gives me a once over, "you, Aria, look lovely." She sets her plate down on a table.

She herself is in a red dress that hugs her figure to her knees. "And you look stunning."

"Thank you," she says and her eyes catch on my bracelet. "Oh wow. *That's* stunning." She captures my hand and flattens it on hers to view my wrist. "I love it."

"Kace gave it to me."

"He did good." She eyes Kace. "You did good." She glances at Chris. "It reminds me of the daisies in some of the regions of Italy." Her attention returns to me. "I loved the daisies there. Have you seen them?"

Reflexively, I pull my hand back and hug myself. Kace's hand splays on my back and he leans in and whispers, "Easy, baby. We have a small circle. They're in it."

In other words, he trusts them and the truth is that I'm already regretting my reaction. I like Sara and I feel nothing negative with Chris.

Concern etches Sara's brow. "Did I say something wrong? If so, please accept my apology."

"No," I say quickly, my arms uncurling, body language relaxing. "I'm the one who is sorry. It was a knee-jerk reaction to something from my past."

"I certainly have a few hotspots myself," Sara assures me, reaching over and giving my hand a tiny squeeze.

It's a warm moment, a bonding moment, one that new friends, who are becoming real friends, experience. Or so I've seen on TV. This is new to me. All of it is new to me.

A waiter appears and Kace grabs two more finger sandwiches, all the waiter has left. "Damn," he mumbles, "I'm never getting properly fed."

"I'll handle it," Sara says, flagging down a waiter, and in about two minutes she's back. "They're bringing the two stars of the night special plates, pronto."

"You're the rock star," I say, already feeling myself easing back into the evening and out of the past.

"I'm the supporting cast and I like it that way." She pushes to her toes and kisses Chris's cheek before she moves toward me. "Let's give them a minute."

She means she wants a minute with me, but I'm remarkably okay with that. I don't believe Sara will pressure me for information. As if she's read my mind, once we're at a small standing table, that's exactly what she says, "No pressure. No questions. I just want you to know that if you need to talk, I'm a safe zone. Completely safe."

"I believe you." And also, remarkably, I do. Maybe it's Kace's trust. Maybe it's a feeling. But I do believe they're safe. I do believe my reaction was knee-jerk.

"Good," she says. "So just know that if you need to talk, even in circles, I'm here."

I don't know what happens, but my mouth opens, and then words just spew out. "I'm Aria Stradivari, perhaps now the last living Stradivari. My ancestor created the Stradivarius instruments Kace favors. My brother is missing. People, there are always these unknown people, who are hunting the secret to the instruments' creation. Kace has Walker protecting me and someone named Kayden Wilkens helping us from some underground organization."

She grabs my hand. "Okay, breathe. Thank you for trusting me and wow. Just wow, but how amazing you and Kace would end up finding each other. You are obviously where you belong."

"I'm hunted. He'll be hunted because of me."

"He can handle it. It takes powerful people to fight powerful people. He's powerful. I know. I've lived that and I've seen it as truth. As for Kayden, his wife, Ella, is my best friend. They saved our lives and honestly, she saved me from being raped. They're badasses, honorable, and dangerous to the wrong people, which means the bad guys."

"Raped?"

"Yes, well, that was me trusting you. That's between us. It's a long story that I'll tell you sometime over chocolate, but the bottom line is that Ella is always being hunted. As her only family, and we are sisters in our hearts, I am family, and I am always a potential target."

"How do you live like that?"

"You're asking me that?"

"I did it alone. You have Chris. You're always in the open and high profile."

"And guarded. We keep security. Chris worries. I choose not to. I don't function well that way and neither does he. He just needs that control. And just for the record, Crystal and Mark have been through some similar stuff, too. They're in your city. I swear to you that you can trust them."

"I feel that. I like Crystal."

"And Mark?" she asks.

"He's," I hesitate, and settle on, "hard."

"He is," she agrees, "but Mark's guarded because of his past. He takes time to get to know and appreciate. Oh and I hear you're living with Kace."

I smile. "Yes. I am. It's pretty wonderful."

"I'd have known if Kace hadn't told Chris. I could see the love blossoming between you."

My brows shoot up. "He told Chris?"

"Yes. They talk. Before Kace, Chris only talked to me. Now they talk. I'm thankful they found each other."

"I'm actually really not surprised," I say, this knowledge giving new depth to Kace's reference to them being a part of our circle. "They have a lot of weird coincidences in their pasts," I add.

"They do and for that reason, I'm going to give you some last words of advice because we might not see each other until Paris. Because of Chris and Kace talking, I know you know a lot about Kace and I know you know there are things you don't yet know."

"He's afraid to tell me."

"But he's told you that, and that matters. Because, like Chris, some things in their background make them hate themselves. You have to love him when he can't love himself."

"I haven't told him I love him. We haven't said those words. Almost, I think."

"You will," she says confidently. "You absolutely will, but no matter how much you love each other when his past comes out, and it will, expect him to push you away. That's survival. That's fear of rejection. You have to pull him back. You have to fight for him. At some point, this conversation is going to feel like foreshadowing. Fate has brought you to us. You are where you belong. Don't let him forget that."

Kace steps behind me, his body warm, his hands possessively on my waist, his lips to my ear. "See?" he murmurs softly. "Everyone knows you're where you belong."

I reach back and touch his face, and while I agree that I'm where I belong, fate isn't all that's at play. Kace doesn't believe that any more than I do and right now, I really wish we could make all the other stuff just go away. Sara and I share a look of friendship and then I twist around in Kace's arms to face him. "Mark and Crystal want us in the back in fifteen minutes," he says, his hand laying on my lower back, a warm, even possessive, touch. "Let's work the crowd on our way there" he adds, lowering his voice. "How did that go with Sara?"

"I kind of love her already. I told her, Kace."

Surprise flits across his face. "And?"

"And a lot of things we can talk about later, but she's friends with Kayden and his wife, Ella. I do think they can help."

"Sounds like I owe Sara a thank you. You seem more relaxed."

"I am," I say, only now realizing that it's true. I flatten my hand on his chest. "And you, sir, have a show to perform and crowd to work." I slide my arm around his and we begin the mingling and Kace is an easy, sought after target but it's all pretty wonderful. We slip into a good time chatting with people and I don't miss how Kace introduces me to everyone and is always touching me. He has a way of making me feel like that princess for sure, even with a few gorgeous movie stars that have me just a tiny bit starstruck.

We're almost to the door that leads to the ultimate performance room when to my shock, Alexander, decked out in a tuxedo, steps in front of us. "I thought I was going to miss the start of the night," he says.

Kace's fingers flex on my back and I can I feel the undercurrent of his anger. "What are you doing here, Alexander?" he asks, his voice low, even, but there is a whip beneath the surface that I do not miss.

"I bought tickets to all of your events," Alexander says. "Important people seem to find you. It's a good place to be." He eyes me. "Like Aria. She's important enough to claim your arm." His gaze flicks back to Kace. "Did you tell her about Maggie?"

"Stop," Kace warns.

"That's a no." He looks at me. "He ruined her."

"Stop, Alexander," Kace warns again. "*Now.*" That one word is low but no less lethal.

Alexander does not stop. "He's the reason she's dead," he continues. "He *wanted* her dead. He wouldn't stop until she was dead. She killed herself. That's how humiliated she was after he was through with her."

Kace does what I never believed he'd do. He steps toward Alexander and instinctively, I place myself between them, my back to Alexander, my hands pressed to Kace's chest. "He's not worth it," I say softly, for his ears only. "The charity matters. He does not."

But he's not looking at me. His stare is locked on Alexander and I can feel the moment his anger recoils, replaced swiftly by something quieter, darker, and far more dangerous. "There's a price to pay, Alexander," Kace says, his voice a blade that promises to draw blood. "One you've escaped far too long."

A guard appears by our sides. "Is there a problem, Mr. August?"

Kace eyes the guard. "Remove this man. *Now*." He says nothing more. He rotates and starts walking away, and he does so without me.

I whirl on Alexander. "How dare you do this on a night he performs."

"You needed to know. This organization needs to know the hypocrisy that is Kace August."

I eye the guard. "Get him out of here. Kace just told you he wants him out of here." I rotate back to Alexander and I don't think. I slap him hard on the face. His head jerks with the force, but he just laughs. I give him my back and run toward the door to the performance room, just as Kace disappears to the other side.

I'm there just after him, my hand on the knob, when Sara catches my arm. "What's going on?"

"Get Chris. Kace needs him. Your foreshadowing is tonight. Alexander, I don't know if you know who is—"

"I do. He's here?"

"He is and he just told me a lot of things in front of Kace. Bad things. Things that had no business here in this room tonight."

She pales. "Oh God. Yes. I'll get Chris." She rushes away.

I enter the performance room and the stage and seating area are empty. Kace is missing. I run toward a door by the stage and exit to find a huge hall on the other side, and a guard by the door. "Where did Kace go?"

He bristles with the demand. "Who are you?"

I try to explain, but he refuses to let me go after Kace without a certain kind of security pass. I end up arguing with him until finally, Sara saves me.

"They gave you the wrong card," she says, handing me a different pass and when I hold it up, the guard finally, begrudgingly concedes and says, "He's in his dressing room. North Hall."

Sara points me in the right direction and we start walking. "Chris is with a big donor," she explains. "He can't shut him down right now, but they perform in fifteen minutes. You need to get to Kace before he goes on stage."

"I don't know how he's going to perform," I say. "You don't know how upset he was."

"He won't let the charity or Chris down. He'll perform." She opens another door that is like a giant room with dressing room doors. She points to a door that has Kace's name on it. "Good luck." She disappears back into the main hall.

I hurry to Kace's door and I don't knock. I just enter. I find him standing in the center of the room doing nothing. Just standing there, his handsome face all hard lines, his eyes wrought with shadows. I shut the door behind me and lean against it.

"Kace—"

"I told you to run," he says. "You didn't listen."

The door I just shut opens behind me and one of Kace's band members, Marvin, pokes his head in. "We need you on stage, Kace." He must sense my presence because he peeks around the door and eyes me. "Oh hey, Aria."

"Hi," I say. "He'll be right there."

"Yes, but Mark—"

"We need a minute, Marvin" I insist and my voice is as fierce as I have ever heard it. "Okay?"

Marvin grimaces. "Right. Yeah. Okay." He mumbles a, "Woman," comment and then disappears. The door shuts and Kace walks toward me or maybe the door. I step in front of it again. He leans on it, hands on either side of me, but he doesn't touch me.

"I need a violin in my hands right now, Aria." His voice is low, taut, vibrating. "I need you to understand that."

"Yes, I—" My hand presses to his chest. "Kace, I—"

"Aria, listen to what I am saying to you. I *need* a violin in my hands right now if I'm going to be able to perform."

"Yes. Yes, okay." It hurts, it hurts so much, but I step aside and without any hesitation, he leaves.

I follow him out of the door and Sara's waiting on me in the hallway. "Well?"

I give a grim shake of my head. "He won't talk to me."

"You have to make him."

"He has to perform."

"He needs to go on that stage knowing you aren't leaving." She snags my hand and leads me to another long hallway like the one behind the stage at Riptide. "He'll come back here before he performs."

"Thank you. Can Chris talk to him?"

"He's still working on that massive donation. He's trying to get free." She leaves and I'm left alone in the hallway.

And so, I pace and pace and wait. When finally, the band returns to the hallway, Kace isn't there. "Where is he?" I ask Marvin.

"He said he needed a few minutes alone."

My heart sinks. He must think I'm back in his dressing room and when I'm not there, he'll think I left. I run down the hallway and burst into the larger hall, to run to the dressing room area. Once I'm in Kace's room, he's not there. I text him: *Where are you?*

I don't wait for an answer. I exit the room and a guard swears he's in yet another room with water and refreshments. I go there. He's not there and I'm losing my mind. I give up the hunt and head back to the hallway behind the stage. Thank God, he's there with his band and crew, but no one is near him. They seem to know he needs to be left alone. He's facing the wall, his hands on the hard surface, head low. "Five minutes," someone says over an intercom. "Kace and Chris, you have seven."

I can't spot Chris anywhere near, but the rest of the band and crew exit to the performance room. Kace doesn't move, but I know he knows I'm here. I slide under Kace's arm, between him and the wall. "Kace." My hand is back on his chest, his thundering heart beneath my palm.

His stare is heavy-lidded, expression as taut as his tone. "What are you doing, Aria?"

"Getting ready to watch you perform." And then I dare to confess, "I just want you to know that I love you, Kace. I *love* you."

His reaction is instant, visceral. He cups my head, tilts my face to his. "Do not say that to me when you don't even know who I am." His voice vibrates, his teeth clenched.

"I do know. I know you."

"No," he says. "You don't. So don't say that to me now. It's not real."

In thirty seconds, his words have ripped at the very fabric of our relationship and did all they could to shred it. They cut. They cut deep, and suddenly Chris is at our sides, his hand on Kace's back. "We have to go on, man. I'm sorry I wasn't here sooner, but Alexander is gone."

Kace releases me and turns to him. "I'm going to need to change the lineup tonight. We're going dark."

"Throw it at me, man. I'll go there with you."

There's a knock on the door. "That means lights out," Chris says. "We have to go."

Chris opens the door and exits and Kace follows. He's gone. And I'm alone. So very alone.

chapter thirty-four

I stare at the door and then at the bracelet Kace gave me and all of Sara's words tumble through my mind, play in my head. She told me he'd push me away. She told me I'd have to fight for him. And she was right. As if I've willed her presence, she opens the door and catches my hand. "We need to take our seats. You need to be there for him. He'll know. It will matter. Come."

I nod and hurry forward and out into the dark room where an usher with a flashlight helps us to our seats in the front row. Dramatic lights start flickering and my heart starts to race. The audience's excitement expands in the room. The sound of a violin touches everyone's ears, teasing us all, before the lights come on. Kace is center stage. He commands that stage. He begins to play dark, heavy music, Black Sabbath at one point, AC/DC's "Back in Black." The more classical but sinister "Dark Waltz." But it's all *beautifully* dark. All of his anger, his passion, his pain come through that instrument and flows to Chris's paintbrush. Chris paints a storyboard of a hurricane-brushed night in San Francisco with haunting images of people rushing through the streets, fighting the force of wind. I watch and listen in wonder as does everyone else. I now know how Kace performed the night his parents died. *I need a violin in my hands right now. I need you to understand that.* The violin is how he grieved and survived. When the performance is over he and Chris claim their seats with me and Sara. Kace sits next to me but he doesn't touch me. I touch him though. I take his hand and it's not until the bid on the violin goes ridiculously high that his hand closes around mine. The three paintings Chris created are next and the bids go nuts, once again. As soon as Chris's auctions are over, Kace stands and takes me with him, heading for the door.

We enter the hallway and Savage is there waiting on us. "Let's go," Kace says, pulling me down the hallway. Chris is suddenly here with us, too, and the hallway is just wide enough for him to step to Kace's side and grab his arm. "Wait. Man, I know this isn't how you wanted this to go down, but it did. It's here. It's now. Tell her everything. Just tell her. Tell her and face it together."

"Let go of me, Chris," Kace orders.

"Not yet."

Kace shocks me by shoving him against the wall. "I said *let* go of me."

"You want to fight," Chris challenges. "You want us both to screw up our hands? Maybe you do. You're on a mission to punish yourself, but you're punishing her, too. I've been here, man. You know I have. It goes no place good."

Seconds tick by and Kace steps back from him and scrubs his jaw, cursing under his breath. He grabs my hand again, and starts walking, charging toward the exit and I have to double-step to keep up. He all but blasts through the exit and thankfully the SUV is waiting on us. Adrian is leaning on the door and quickly straightens.

"Behind you," Savage says, as Adrian opens the door for us.

Kace pulls me in front of him and I climb into the backseat. He follows but he's back to not touching me. I'm insanely aware of him not touching me, too. Savage and Adrian climb inside the front of the vehicle and

Adrian sets us in motion. "Someone needs to pack up our room," Kace says. "We're going to the airport. I need the plane ready now."

I rotate to face him. "No. No, we are not going home tonight, Kace."

"We're going home, Aria. Decision made."

"Because it's your life, not our life?"

"Because it's the right decision."

"For who? Alexander? He wanted to get to you. He did. He wanted to destroy us, you're trying to let him. Do not do this."

"We both need out of this city."

"What we need is to talk."

"No," he says. "No, we really do not need to talk."

"Damn it, Kace. I love you."

He grabs me and pulls me around and half in his lap. "I told you not to say that."

"I love you, but right now you're letting all the wrong things control you."

"You don't know what this is, Aria."

"Because you won't tell me. And because you didn't, you gave him the chance to burn us. Don't let him win."

He sets me back down in the seat. "Airport. Turn up the radio."

Savage flicks us a look and turns up the radio. Kace's rejection twists and turns inside me, cutting me every which way. *Screw it*, I think. I maneuver my skirts and I climb right on top of Kace's lap, straddling him. The music is now blasting and I lean into Kace, my lips at his ear. "Sara told me to fight for you but she assumed you cared about me. She was wrong. Obviously, you were looking for an out." I move to get off of him and he catches my waist.

"I'm doing what's best for you."

"Liar. You're the one running." I try to move again. He holds onto me. "Let me go. Why are you bothering to hold me now, Kace?"

His jaw tics and then he releases me. The minute I climb off of him, he calls forward to Savage. "Go to the hotel."

Relief washes over me. He's not completely checked out. The man I know is still present, beneath all of that anger.

Not anger, I amend. Self-hate. He hates himself. And as Sara so rightfully said. I have to love him when he cannot love himself.

The ride is short, but it feels eternal. We sit there, not touching. It's excruciating.

We arrive at the hotel and Savage opens my side of the vehicle. I slide out and Kace doesn't follow. He gets out on the other side. He might as well cut me with a knife. I'm suddenly not sure he brought me here to work through this or just break up with me. I don't know what I'm doing. We are not Chris and Sara. We're new, and obviously not as close as I'd believed.

My eyes meet Savage's and he says, "Don't give up."

"He already did," I breathe out.

"No he hasn't. Don't give up."

My lashes lower and I nod, but I can't look at him again. I'm spiraling inside and trying to hold it together. I step away from the door, shivering as I realize now that my coat is still at the museum. Thankfully this is San Francisco, not New York and it's only in the fifties or so, but the wind is cold. Kace is waiting on me, and he, too, is coatless but he's not shivering. Hugging myself I start walking toward the door. Kace falls into step beside me and we enter the hotel just like that. Side-by-side, not touching, not looking at each other. We don't stop once we're in the lobby. We keep walking toward the elevator and Kace punches the button. The door opens and I step inside the car. Kace follows and swipes his card to punch in our floor. He leans on the wall to face me. I lean on the wall, too, but only a shoulder as I face the door. I can feel him watching me but can't look at him right now. I'm now officially angry.

The doors open and I exit, walking ahead of him toward our room. I can feel Kace at my back, watching my every step, but he doesn't try to catch up to me. Of course, I've achieved nothing but charging ahead. I'm at the door and forced to wait on him. This is all on his terms. He's in control. And that's how he likes it. He decides when we live or die. Emotions are pounding on me and I'm an explosion waiting to happen.

He claims the space beside me and I can feel his presence. He's like a glass of whiskey—it burns and then warms you all over before it sizzles your nerve endings. And I drank the whole bottle. He slides the card and I notice his hands, his talented hands that play that violin like no other human being. Hands that touched me in ways I've never been touched. Hands that can melt me in a single caress. I'm suffocating in too much everything and I couldn't even explain what that means to anyone who asked.

The minute the security light turns green, I open the door and step inside the room. I take only a few steps and whirl on him. He's already inside, the door shutting behind him.

"Already can't look at me, I see," he says. "Or touch me."

"Are you serious? I'm looking at you now. I was afraid I'd start yelling at you if I looked at you in the elevator."

"Is that right?"

"You're baiting me. Stop it. You are the one doing all this Kace. You. I'm angry and hurt because of how you're acting, not because of what Alexander said. I could give a damn what Alexander has to say."

"We both know that's not true."

"You were just waiting for the moment you could do this. You were never in this all the way."

"I told you I had a side you wouldn't like."

"If this is it, you're right. I don't like it. We *should* go home. You go to your apartment and I'll go to mine. Of course, I don't have one because you own it now."

"You own it. It's deeded in your name."

"I don't want your hand-me-downs, Kace. I'll sign it over to you and find a new place."

In a blink he's in front of me, catching my arm and pulling me to him. "I told you you'd run."

"I'm not running. You shoved me out the door. You didn't even give me a chance to know the truth. I trusted you with my life and you can't even trust me with something bad that happened in yours? I love you, Kace, but that isn't enough for you and it's not enough for me. Let me go."

"You want to know the truth, Aria?"

"I want you to trust me. I want to know all of you, not just the parts you think I can handle."

"You can't handle this."

"Then why were we playing this game together? Let me go and I don't mean my arm. Let. Me. Go."

His mouth closes down over mine, hot and hard, a lick of demand on his tongue before he says, "You want to know all of me? Take the dress off." He sets me away from him.

I stumble back and grab the back of the couch behind me. He stands there, waiting, watching and this doesn't feel like any time I've undressed for him before.

But he needs control right now. I feel that. I knew that in the hallway. Alexander took it. Now, I'm taking it by demanding answers. He needs to balance that, to control me in other ways. And I know him enough to understand that comes from some deep, damaged place he buries all the pain in his life. And that pain runs deep.

He needs to know that I still trust him enough to be vulnerable with him.

I reach for my side zipper and then slide my dress down, stepping out of it. I'm wearing a gorgeous gold studded bra and panty set and when I set the dress on the couch, his hot gaze sweeps over my body, and then lifts. "All of it. Except the heels."

There's a coldness to him that I don't like, and yet, I am helpless to control my desire for this man. I am wet and wanting. I am also certain that he's trying to intimidate me and it won't work. He's still him and I'm still me. I unhook the bra and toss it aside, my nipples puckering with the cool hotel air in contrast to his hot stare. My fingers catch the small strings at my hips and I slide them down. Kace's stare traces their path, with such intensity he might as well be touching me. I step out of the panties and straighten.

"Now what, Kace?" I ask.

He tears his shirt over his head and stalks toward me. "Don't push me, Aria," he says, his hands on my sides, over my ribcage and I'm hyperaware of his long, talented fingers just beneath my breath. "You won't like the results."

"Still trying to get me to run?"

"Baby, we both know you're going to run."

"I'm here, Kace, I'm naked in every way with you. It's your turn."

"You want to know how dark I can get?" His hand is on my breast, his touch rough but erotic, fingers pinching my nipple.

"Yes," I breathe out.

"You think you can handle that? You *really* think you can handle that?" He doesn't wait for an answer. He turns me to face the couch, forcing me to catch my hands on the cushion. He presses into me, and his hand is on my backside. He smacks my cheek and I yelp. It's not hard, but it shocks me, which is his intent.

I suck in a breath preparing for more, and he leans in and cups my breasts, his lips at my ear and he says, "That's only the beginning. Still think you can handle it?"

I suddenly don't.

This is not a gateway for him to have control and give it away, by talking to me. This is him just plain pushing me further out the door.

"Stop," I hiss and his grip eases. "Stop, Kace." I turn in his arms and stare up at him. "I won't ever be able to love you enough, will I?"

He must sense the shift in me, the defeat, because he softens instantly. "Aria."

"I can't give you all of me, and I have, and feel like you've got one foot out the door, Kace. I've lost too many people. I'd rather just be alone. So just let me off the couch. I'll go home. I'll take a flight and—"

"No," he says, his fingers twining in my hair and dragging my gaze to his. "You go home with me. *You go home with me.*" His mouth closes down on mine, and his kiss is different now, gentler, but desperate, demanding, but not controlling. A deep, soul-searing kiss, that melts me oh so easily. He scoops me up and carries me to the bedroom, lays me on the mattress, and comes down on top of me. "I'm sorry."

My fingers tangle in his dark hair. "Don't push me away."

"I'll try."

"Kace—"

"I need to feel you next to me right now." His mouth closes down on mine, and I don't fight him for answers. I sink into the kiss and his touch, and what follows is us making love the first time after our confession of love. He undresses, and I get rid of the only thing I'm still wearing—my high heels. And then he's kissing me, so many delicious places, that I can say, I'm owned. I'm so very owned by this man and I like it. I don't fear it. I don't fight it. I fall into it and him. I feel our bond again, and God, I needed to feel it. I feel our love. With him inside me, kissing me, our bodies swaying together, I am complete, my world is right again. When it's over, he stands up and walks to the bathroom. My heart is racing with where this goes next, but he returns and brings me a towel, sliding it between my legs, and we roll into each other, side-by-side, facing each other. He strokes my hair from my face. "I do love you, Aria. Like I didn't think I could love anyone."

"I love you, too."

"You are not alone."

"Neither are you, Kace. You know that, right?"

His lashes lower and he rolls to his back and stares at the ceiling. "I met her at a Riptide event. She was a producer out of L.A. I hired her and she went on the road with me." He looks over at me. "I never loved her. I never pretended to love her. I have never told anyone but you that I love them." He looks back at the ceiling, as if the rest he can't speak while looking at me. "Easy sex. Companionship." He sits up. "We were together for a year. She told me she loved me. I knew I'd been selfish. I knew I had to end it. And so I did."

"And?" I grab a throw blanket and wrap it around me. He stands up and pulls on his pants.

"She lashed out. She did interviews and said I'd cheated and abused her, none of which was true. I think it was meant to distract me and it worked. She hopped in Alexander's bed and used insider information to cut me. One of my songbooks I'd long-wanted back from a studio finally had a contract expiring. She and Alexander bought it out from underneath me. He now owns some of my best, most profitable music."

"I'm—speechless. I'm—I really am."

"I wasn't. I was furious. I became my father's son. An eye for an eye. I went to war, Aria. I went at her first. I made sure she didn't work in the industry again. I went at her hard. I ruined her. Alexander was next but he threatened to lock down my music. It didn't matter. I didn't care about the money. I have plenty of money but that was my life's work. It was personal. I was coming for him."

My throat goes dry because I know she's dead. "And something happened?"

"Yes. To give you history, she'd met Chris. She knew his story. She knew about my sister—" He looks down.

"And she knew how this would affect you."

"She did. It was like a final 'fuck you,' an 'I won. I threw the last punch. I beat you, you bastard.'" His eyes meet mine. "Now you see the monster I can be. The mind my father made."

"No." I scramble off the bed and rush to him. I let the throw fall away, and wrap my arms around him. "No. You are not a monster. You did what anyone under attack would do. What did you do to Alexander?"

"Before tonight, I decided revenge was my mistake. I needed to just stop. After tonight, I'm coming for him."

"He had to know you would. Why did he even come here tonight? I don't understand."

"I think he loved her. He always seemed to have a thing for her, even when we were together. There is no other logical reason."

"I don't know Kace." I grab the blanket again and wrap it around me. "How much did he make off your music?"

"An ungodly amount."

"Can you take him to court over your music?"

"I could and I'd win but he'd splatter this suicide stuff all over the news. It would hurt the charity. It would attach to Chris and Mark, and I can't do that to them. Or you. That's not the answer."

"Her dying worked in his favor. I don't mean to be a conspiracy theorist, but what if he killed her to save himself?

"Meaning what?"

"Her supposed suicide is what made you back off. You're afraid it will hurt people you care about. He knows that."

"No," he says quickly. "I believe he loved her. And I don't believe he would have shown up here tonight to bait me."

"Maybe he wasn't baiting you. Maybe he was using me to seal up the deal. To give you just another reason not to go public by taking him to court."

"He reminded me why I will go after him and crush him."

"How?"

"Harshly. And it won't be in a way that he can hurt those I love." He catches my arms and molds me to him. "Don't run."

"I'm not running. I'm naked, always completely naked with you. I always have been with you, Kace. About time you joined me."

He throws away my blanket and takes me back to bed.

chapter thirty-five

The next morning, Kace and I have breakfast with Chris, Sara, Mark, and Crystal, at Chris and Sara's lovely apartment. Mark and Crystal are staying a few days and Kace and I just want to go home, our home together.

After a smooth private flight home, with only Savage and Adrian along for the ride, we land in New York City. Once we're in a Walker-driven SUV, Gio's silence is back on my mind. "I know Walker has looked over the shop, but I just—can we go and just see if there is any sign of Gio? And again, I know that's illogical. I know Walker would know but—"

Kace leans in and kisses me. "Of course." He gives Adrian the instruction and it's not long before we're at the shop, the chilly now-November wind gushing around us.

I punch in the code, eager to get into the warm storefront, and Kace pushes it open for me. I step inside with him on my heels and gasp.

Gio is standing there, and his gaze goes to Kace. "What the fuck are you doing with my sister, Kace?"

THE END...FOR NOW

Readers,
Yes, I know that was a doozy of a cliffhanger and a lot of emotions to go through toward the end of the

book, but you have only a month to find out how all this ends for Kace and Aria and now, Gio! I hope you loved A WICKED SONG, if you're so inclined, you'll consider leaving a review, if you're able to. Thank you for choosing to spend your time with my books.

Love,
Lisa

The third and final book, A SINFUL ENCORE, is out on September 22nd, and available for pre-order everywhere now!

https://www.lisareneejones.com/brilliance-trilogy.html

Did you enjoy Mark and Crystal & Chris and Sara? You can read both couples' story in my INSIDE OUT series which is in development for TV/movies! All of the books are available now, so no need to wait it out.

HERE'S A SEXY MINI EXCERPT FROM BOOK ONE OF THE INSIDE OUT SERIES, IF I WERE YOU

"Hands over your head," he orders, pressing my palms to the glass above me, his body shadowing mine. "Stay like that."

My pulse jumps wildly and adrenaline surges. I've been ordered around during sex, but in a clinical, bend over and give me what I want kind of way I tried to convince myself was hot. It wasn't. I hated every second, every instance, and I'd endured it. This is different though, erotic in a way I've never experienced, enticingly full of promise. My body is sensitized, pulsing with arousal. I am hot where Chris is touching me and cold where he isn't.

When he seems satisfied I'll comply with his orders, Chris slowly caresses a path down my arms, and then up and down my sides, brushing the curves of my breasts. He's in no hurry, but I am. I am literally quivering by the time his hands cover my breasts, welcoming the way he squeezes them roughly, before tugging on my nipples. I gasp with the pinching sensation he repeats over and over, creating waves of pleasure verging on pain, and the music is fading away, and so is the past. *There is pleasure in pain.* The words come back to me, and this time they resonate.

His hands are suddenly gone, and I pant in desperation, trying to pull them back.

Chris captures my hands and forces them back to the glass above me, his breath warm by my ear, his hard body framing mine. "Move them again and I'll stop what I'm doing, no matter how good it might feel."

I quiver inside at the erotic command, surprised again by how enticed I am by this game we are playing. "Just remember," I warn, still panting, still burning for his touch. "Payback is Hell."

His teeth scrape my shoulder. "Looking forward to it, baby," he rasps. *"More than you can possibly know."*

lisa renee jones

https://www.lisareneejones.com/the-inside-out-series.html

Don't forget, if you want to be the first to know about upcoming books, giveaways, sales and any other exciting news I have to share please be sure you're signed up for my newsletter! As an added bonus everyone receives a free ebook when they sign-up!

http://lisareneejones.com/newsletter-sign-up/

walker security returns!

ADRIAN'S TRILOGY IS COMING THIS WINTER

As a member of Walker Security, Adrian Ramos has found redemption for a walk on the dark side. For six years the former FBI agent was undercover in the notorious Texas Kings biker club. For six years he changed, he became one of them and when the bust happened, he didn't know who he was anymore. On a hitlist with a price on his head, he disappeared and joined Walk Security, but now, the trial is set to start and witnesses are dropping like flies.

Assistant District Attorney, Priscilla Miller is tasked with the conviction of The King himself, and she's passionate about taking him down, but her case is falling apart. She's also in trouble, and while she resists Adrian, the sexy ex-FBI agent with a killer reputation, and his team at Walker Security are her answer, in more ways than one.

He touches her, she melts.

He shields her, she survives.

But everything is not as it seems. Friends are enemies. Secrets are really lies. And the one time in his life Adrian lets his heart do the thinking, passion might just be deadly.

FIND OUT MORE ABOUT ADRIAN'S TRILOGY HERE:

https://www.lisareneejones.com/walker-security-adrians-trilogy.html

excerpt from
the savage trilogy

He's here.

Rick is standing right in front of me, bigger than life, and so damn him, in that him kind of way that I couldn't explain if I tried. He steps closer and I drop my bag on the counter. He will hurt me again, I remind myself, but like that first night, I don't seem to care.

I step toward him, but he's already there, already here, right here with me. I can't even believe it's true. He folds me close, his big, hard body absorbing mine. His fingers tangle in my hair, his lips slanting over my lips. And then he's kissing me, kissing me with the intensity of a man who can't breathe without me. And I can't breathe without him. I haven't drawn a real breath since he sent me that letter.

My arms slide under his tuxedo jacket, wrapping his body, muscles flexing under my touch. The heat of his body burning into mine, sunshine warming the ice in my heart he created when he left. And that's what scares me. Just this quickly, I'm consumed by him, the princess and the warrior, as he used to call us. My man. My hero. And those are dangerous things for me to feel, so very dangerous. Because they're not real. He showed me that they aren't real.

"This means nothing," I say, tearing my mouth from his, my hand planting on the hard wall of his chest. "This is sex. Just sex. This changes nothing."

"Baby, we were never just sex."

"We are not the us of the past," I say, grabbing his lapel. "I just need—you owe me this. You owe me a proper—"

"Everything," he says. "In ways you don't understand, but, baby, you will. I promise you, you will."

I don't try to understand that statement and I really don't get the chance. His mouth is back on my mouth.

The very idea of forever with this man is one part perfect, another part absolute pain. Because there is no forever with this man. But he doesn't give me time to object to a fantasy I'll never own, that I'm not sure I want to try and own again. I don't need forever. I need right now. I need him. I sink back into the kiss and he's ravenous. Claiming me. Taking me. Kissing the hell out of me and God, I love it. God, I need it. I need *him*.

FIND OUT MORE ABOUT THE SAVAGE TRILOGY HERE:

https://www.lisareneejones.com/savage-trilogy.html

also by lisa renee jones

THE INSIDE OUT SERIES

If I Were You
Being Me
Revealing Us
His Secrets*
Rebecca's Lost Journals
The Master Undone*
My Hunger*
No In Between
My Control*
I Belong to You
All of Me*

THE SECRET LIFE OF AMY BENSEN

Escaping Reality
Infinite Possibilities
Forsaken
Unbroken*

CARELESS WHISPERS

Denial
Demand
Surrender

WHITE LIES

Provocative
Shameless

THE NAKED TRILOGY

One Man
One Woman
Two Together

THE SAVAGE TRILOGY

Savage Hunger
Savage Burn
Savage Love

THE BRILLIANCE TRILOGY

A Reckless Note
A Wicked Song
A Sinful Encore (Sept. 2020)

ADRIAN'S TRILOGY

When He's Dirty (October 2020)
When He's Bad (December 2020)
When He's Wild (March 2021)

*eBook only

about the author

New York Times and USA Today bestselling author Lisa Renee Jones is the author of the highly acclaimed INSIDE OUT series.

In addition to the success of Lisa's INSIDE OUT series, she has published many successful titles. The TALL, DARK AND DEADLY series and THE SECRET LIFE OF AMY BENSEN series, both spent several months on a combination of the New York Times and USA Today bestselling lists. Lisa is also the author of the bestselling the bestselling DIRTY MONEY and WHITE LIES series. And will be publishing the first book in her Lilah Love suspense series with Amazon Publishing in March 2018.

Prior to publishing Lisa owned multi-state staffing agency that was recognized many times by The Austin Business Journal and also praised by the Dallas Women's Magazine. In 1998 Lisa was listed as the #7 growing women owned business in Entrepreneur Magazine.

Lisa loves to hear from her readers. You can reach her at www.lisareneejones.com and she is active on Twitter and Facebook daily.